MASON'S DAUGHTER

Cynthia J. Stone

TREATY OAK PUBLISHERS

★★★★★

"A powerful debut novel . . . Stone skillfully propels you through the truth of a family tragedy that reverberates from one generation to the next, as she unravels a complicated mess, trying to right the wrong with memorable characters you feel you know from somewhere. Possibly your own family."

Ann Leifeste, producer, PBS

★★★★★

"*Mason's Daughter* was a captivating read. I couldn't put it down. First-time novelist Cynthia J. Stone is a great storyteller. She captures the flavor of family secrets and small town Texas class warfare in a tale that both delights and surprises. I can't wait to read her next book because this rich story left me anxious to learn more about the past and future of this cast of lively characters. The surprise ending would make O. Henry proud, so don't read it before the beginning, or you will spoil your reading pleasure!"

Gloria Gene Moore, 3rd generation native Texan
entrepreneur and voracious reader of fine fiction

PUBLISHER'S NOTE

This is a work of fiction. None of the characters, business establishments, or events is based on actual people, living or dead, or their lives or circumstances. All material is a product of the author's imagination. If you think you recognize someone or some place and want to make something of it, go and write your own damn book. Seriously, any resemblance to actual people, businesses, or places is just a coincidence and purely unintentional.

Printed and published in the United States of America

TREATY OAK PUBLISHERS

ISBN-13: 978-1-938749-02-5

ISBN-10: 1938749022

Also Available In E-Book Format on Amazon.Com

ISBN-13: 978-1-938749-00-1

ISBN-10: 1938749006

For Gerald and for Jordan

MASON'S DAUGHTER

CHAPTER ONE

It took the county sheriff less than two days to investigate my husband's death, and when the ruling came back suicide, I didn't believe it, not for a moment. If it hadn't been for the angry note we found later, we all might have been persuaded Jack simply wasn't paying attention. It still pains me to think it, but lack of focus described him better than despondent or vengeful. Besides, Jack was too cheerful to kill anything, especially himself.

All of which makes me wish I had been kinder to Jack while he was alive. If I'd shown a little more enthusiasm in our relationship, maybe I wouldn't spend so many sleepless nights now. Guilt has proved a miserable companion in the wee hours.

He never complained, but I can try to make it up to him, starting today.

Just after sunrise I plop on a long redwood bench against the back wall of my greenhouse, always the most peaceful place I can find. Maybe because geraniums don't make any noise.

With Jack's appointment book in my lap, I take a sip of coffee from Grandmother Mason's heirloom Limoges cup and settle it in its delicate saucer. This morning, I finally feel bold, recovered enough to take a peek at what occupied him during his last year. I open the book to March 1975, the month Jack died, and try to concentrate.

His loopy handwriting makes me smile. All his random notes look like he had jotted them down while racing out the door. Typical Jack. Nothing in his mood or his outlook ever hinted of despair.

Today, on the first anniversary of his death, I am determined to search for anything to prove Jack hadn't taken his own life. Despite the official version, my husband is worthy of a peaceful ending. And more important, our young son Colton needs to feel better about his dad.

Nothing like a family suicide to make you hang your head in public. Especially in a small town like Mason's Crossing.

And shame is just the tip of the community iceberg. It won't be long before I go broke paying for Colton's recent mishaps and pranks. A wrecked bicycle and wanton application of spray paint have already made a dent in my checking account.

I am not very good at recognizing emotions or judging what's behind them. But his destructive behavior is a cry for help too loud to ignore, which tells me I have to try to change our past. Finding a different truth between the covers of Jack's appointment book would be powerful alchemy.

Leaning forward, I flip the pages ahead to the week of his death. The exact date burns my eyes until mist covers the page like a spider web and it turns blurry.

Jack loved me much more than I deserved. He had no clue I married him for reasons other than love and passion, hoping those feelings would eventually develop. In our fifteen years together, Jack never fussed that the best I could manage was friendly affection. Well, at least it was better than what either of us saw in our parents' marriages.

At the sight of Colton's name written over several evenings and the weekend, I sit upright and my eyes fill with moisture. Jack had intended to show up for Colton's pony league tryouts. They missed more than baseball that week.

"Your thumb turned anything brown yet?"

With a quiet laugh, I look toward the greenhouse entrance. "Breakfast will be ready in a few minutes."

When had Colton grown so tall? Blond like me, but with Jack's dark eyes, his sturdy thirteen-year-old frame fills the doorway. He turns to leave.

I wipe my cheeks with the heels of my hands. "Hey, come take a look at this." Maybe it would reassure Colton to see his father's entry about his basketball game the Friday night before they moved on to baseball the next day.

He saunters down the aisle in my direction, a man-child who ducks his head to avoid the hanging baskets of angel wing begonias, and stops in front of me. "What'cha got there?"

I pat the seat next to me and wait for him to sit down. "How's your ankle?"

He tilts his face toward the ceiling, but can't hide the rolling of his eyes. "I have to leave for school soon."

Pursing my lips, I look up at him and tap the bench with my fingernail.

He whirls around and sits down in a huff. "You're always springing stuff on me at the last minute."

I hand Colton the appointment book and point to the pages

with his name and sports activities. "I thought you might like to see how much Dad enjoyed being part of your life. He was always so proud of you."

Colton spreads the book open on his lap and studies each entry. He runs his fingertips over the ink as if he can feel ridges on the letters. I watch his expression for any trace of sorrow, but he shows not the slightest hint.

He turns the pages and reads more, flips back, and starts over. After a moment, he asks, "What did Dad have to do with your father?"

"What do you mean?" I grab the book. He might as well have spritzed me with my garden hose.

"Here's Nate Wallace's name and phone number in his book." He jerks his thumb toward the Monday after Jack's funeral. "Am I ever going to meet my other grandfather?"

We hadn't spoken to my father since our wedding day. Jack and I agreed never to contact him, even after Nate became a grandfather, and I had kept my end of the bargain.

Jack had deceived me. The bastard.

While my face grows red hot, I scan the pages for clues that will make sense. "I have no idea–"

Colton snorts and crosses his arms. "What are you hiding? Aren't you ever going to talk about him?"

"Not if you badger me." My empty stomach churns acid. "I'm sure Jack didn't . . . make that call." What will I say if Colton asks me why Nate has never been introduced to him? Or even allowed in our house. I hold my breath. "This is too strange, well, even for Jack."

"Dad must have been working on something." Colton shuffles the pages forward. "Look what he wrote."

I stumble through the words 'submit proposal/spreadsheet,' grateful for the change of topic. Jack might have written them in Turkish for all the logic they conjure. How in the world could someone who had trouble sitting still for more than five minutes come up with a business plan? Is that why he tried to contact my father, who uses his millions to manipulate people? Jack should have known better.

Taking a deep breath, I try to stay calm. "Dad evidently had some ideas he was floating. You know how optimistic he was." I cannot tell Colton his father hatched one half-baked plan after another. If I hadn't stepped in two years ago, Jack would have blown all our hard-earned savings on a fish scheme. How anyone can make money by feeding fish instead of catching them, he could never explain.

"Looks like he tried to get everybody he knew involved, even your cousin Charlie."

"You're kidding." I grimace at the thought of Jack exposing his lack of business sense to strangers. Each daytime and evening time slot reveals outside appointments with people whose names I don't recognize, except for Charlie Cromwell, our banker. "Who are all these people?"

As a popular salesman in his father's sporting goods store, Jack had always worked at play and played at work, never more so than his last two weeks. He loved the store and counted on its long family history and local appeal as part of his identity. "How could he take so much time off to meet with all those customers at their places of business?"

The coffee has turned cold by now and my hand trembles, so I set the cup and saucer back on the potting table. My gaze wanders to the rafters while I struggle to remember my last conversation with Jack. I sit up straight and catch the book just before it slides off my lap. "You know what this means?"

Colton shakes his head.

I snap my fingers. "It means Dad made plans for the future."

"So?"

"Guys who look forward to events and getting together with people for future projects don't usually do away with themselves."

"How do you know?"

"It just makes sense. Now everything will fall into place." I stand up and turn to face him. "Jack didn't intentionally take his own life. It had to be an accident." I hand him the book.

Colton shuffles to his feet, lays the book on the table, and walks toward the entrance. "I have to get to school."

Balancing the china cup and saucer with care, I follow him out of the greenhouse, around the garage, and through the back door into the kitchen. He doesn't want to discuss his father's death, and no one could blame him. But surely the possibility of changing the coroner's ruling will be worth the pain of opening old wounds. How much trouble could I get into by asking a few questions? And perhaps I can wriggle enough answers out of people without telephoning Nate Wallace.

"All I have to do is call those numbers Jack scribbled in the margin." I fill a plate with cheesy scrambled eggs and pass it to Colton. "Maybe you can help decipher his handwriting, so I get the names right."

"Don't ask me to do that." He sits hunkered at the breakfast table, gulping down the eggs, drowning them in a river of milk, barely swallowing. When his plate and his glass are empty, he announces, "Get Charlie to help you, because I won't."

"Why not?"

"This is your crazy idea. I don't want to go through all that again. You can't make me."

I sigh and realize it's time to call retreat. Again. It does no good to stir up Colton's anger and grief. Except I also have to find a way around it. "All right. But I'm making the calls, just the same."

Silence.

"I'm going upstairs to brush my teeth." I rinse out my coffee cup and set it upside down on the drain board. "Meet you back down here in five minutes."

"Stop digging all this up. It won't do any good."

"But it will. Don't you see?" I raise my voice to his level.

"All I see is you wanting to change what happened," he yells. "You can't change it, so just drop it." He grabs a piece of dry toast and tears off a corner. Without another word, he stalks across the kitchen and halts near the back door.

"Five minutes." I don't wait for his answer or his argument. "After you take your dishes to the sink."

When I return to the kitchen, Colton is still standing in the same spot. The back door gapes open, letting in the cool morning air, but he doesn't move.

What gut-wrenching memories he must have. Is he remembering a year ago when he walked through the same door out to the garage and discovered Jack's body slumped over in his truck?

Colton lowers his head and his shoulders shiver, but no

sound comes out. When the shaking subsides, he turns sideways and whispers, "Mom, don't make me–"

"I realize you feel very sad, and I'm sorry this has upset you." No one can say I'm not trying to understand. I step toward him. "My eagerness, or let's say, my hope, has carried me away. We should have talked about it later. Do you want to go wash your face before I drive you to school?"

"I'm fine." Little puffs of morning mist curl around his head as he crosses the patio. Before I can suggest he needs a jacket, he opens the side door to the garage and presses the garage door opener. Once it rattles up all the way, he walks around the back of my car and climbs into the front seat.

He didn't limp, but he is broken all the same. When bones don't heal properly, as a last resort, someone has to break them once more to reset them right. Otherwise, he'll never be able to stand up straight and walk normally again. Same with emotions.

I pick up my purse, follow him, and settle into the driver's seat. Before starting the engine, I turn toward him. "Colton, you know what a happy-go-never-mind kind of guy Dad was. He wouldn't ever have . . . well, if I can prove Dad's death was an accident, we'll both feel better."

He stares at me with his huge brown eyes, murky pools, bottomless and impenetrable. "I wish you were the one who died."

CHAPTER TWO

After dropping Colton at school, I cruise through downtown Mason's Crossing. It will do me good to stop and chat with folks I've known all my life, because arguing with Colton leaves me feeling like a failure. I sigh and wonder how long it will be until we take pleasure in each other's company again. Surely he didn't mean he wants me dead, but he might as well have poked a straw in me and sucked the life out.

Sheriff Avery's shiny blue Mercury Marauder pulls up behind me, triggering an automatic flash of electricity from my guts to my fingertips. Brake lights will only draw his attention. My speed dwindles to a crawl past the Hot Crossed Buns Diner, and I spot a silver Chevy pickup parked in the side lot.

Who better to ask about the names and numbers in the appointment book than my father-in-law? Big Jack Edwards keeps a detailed chart on each customer and supplier, enough info to make an FBI agent proud.

Get him to help. But I had left the book at home.

Because he likes to linger over the baked goods, he'll probably stay put until I return. Maybe I can talk him out of ordering anything made of sugar and white flour. His arteries already look like a sackful of pastries.

The traffic light changes to green. I press on the accelerator, glance in the rear view mirror, and immediately let up. Officer Avery waves and points at the back of my car.

I jerk the turn signal to the off position. A ticket for absent-minded driving is another expense I can ill afford.

Officer Avery turns left at the next corner. I speed up. Is it too soon to feel cautiously optimistic? What if I discover something that improves the past for all of us? For months, I prayed Jack's death was some bizarre accident instead of a deliberate choice. Even a fatal illness wouldn't have clawed my thoughts to shreds this past year. I can picture Colton bleeding inside from grief.

Damn the so-called facts, my husband didn't kill himself! Right after his funeral, everyone in town said it wasn't like him.

Driving a little faster, I plot my strategy. Once Big Jack agrees with my logic, he'll help me persuade Colton. The county coroner will fall into line as well.

The car vents crank out too much warmth, and I roll down the window to let the cool morning air bathe my flushed face. Ahead a banged-up VW Beetle covered with leftover peace symbol stickers sits idling. I swerve around it just in time to stop at the train tracks. Resting my forehead on the steering wheel, I wish with all my heart I could turn back the calendar.

Someone behind the Volkswagen honks. The weekly freight train from East Texas has already passed and the guardrails lift. The driver of the Beetle flashes the 'V' at me.

Peace. If only.

I dash across the tracks.

No way can I see peace on the horizon except by proving Jack's death was accidental. My optimism vanishes like vapor. This could turn out to be a wild goose chase, and all I will accomplish is to open fresh wounds. Left alone, scars might serve us just as well.

Three minutes later, I pull into my driveway. Good heavens, I left the side door open. Tense scenes with Colton make me twice as forgetful. Today, at least, I remember what I came home to do.

In the kitchen, Grandmother's china cup and saucer catch my eye, right next to the coffee pot. Nothing except Colton's dirty dishes in the sink. I head toward the back door. One drawer sticks out and I bump it with my hip as I pass. Something flat and brown lies inside.

How on earth did Jack's appointment book wind up in the kitchen drawer?

I stare at the leather cover and fan the pages to be sure it is the same book. My fingers stroke the ones at the middle of March and stop. I look closer.

Water spots? The paper is crinkled where a few droplets have fallen. They still feel damp.

I flop into the kitchen chair and mentally retrace my steps from the time Colton appeared in the greenhouse. Nothing convinces me I didn't carry Jack's book to the kitchen, unless . . .

When I was a young girl, a family friend comforted me by promising my mother would become my guardian angel after she died. For years I awaited an epiphany. Maybe she finally chose today. Either that, or Colton was trying to hide it when I came downstairs.

No, the water droplets must be tears. Mine? I don't remember crying. No matter. I grasp the book and run out the kitchen door.

The car door stands open, as if waiting for my return. Had I forgotten to close it or . . .? Now is not the time to get carried away. I climb into the front seat and turn the key in the ignition. Jack's book with its troublesome contents lies on the passenger seat. My stomach flutters, and I rev the engine while it's still in neutral.

Do this for Colton.

I take off down the street. At the edge of downtown, my speed drops to the legal limit. By the time I reach Mason Boulevard, Big Jack's truck hasn't moved. I pull into the adjacent lot and park three spaces over.

While I rely on him to recognize every name and number in Jack's book, I worry I might start a fire I can't put out. At home in private, Jack often accused his father of acting overbearing to the extreme. But because Big Jack owns the corner gas station, the feed store, and the sporting goods outlet, he occupies a unique position to gather all the gossip and unofficial news. Everyone, from locals and rurals to folks merely passing through town, becomes acquainted with Big Jack and vice versa.

My late mother-in-law would have given me even more help. No one in Mason's Crossing knew more about folks than Trixie Edwards, past chair of the school board and in the choir at the First Methodist Church.

From the entrance, I catch sight of Big Jack in his usual booth. His attention is buried in *The Central Texas Journal*. As I slide into the seat opposite, I nod at Lois, our favorite waitress, to bring more coffee.

"Good morning."

"Whaaat?" Big Jack lowers his newspaper and glares at me for a split second before his face softens into a friendly smile. "Oh, hi, Sally-Girl."

I like it when he uses his affectionate nickname for me. "What's up with the world today?" Flinging my hair over my shoulder, I try to adopt the persona of a lost tourist.

"After that idiot President Ford pardoned Nixon last September, I thought Congress should hang 'em both." His mouth stretches into a grin. "But now the Big Three have been sentenced–"

"I can see you're worried sick about them. Which three?"

"Ehrlichman, Haldeman, and Mitchell are going to jail."

"For how long?"

"Not long enough, the sorry sons of bitches."

"Still, it's nice to have some . . . resolution." I sip my coffee.

Big Jack emits a 'hmmmm' while he shuffles his paper. He doesn't cover his face, but he wants to get back to the article. It would be easier to navigate a field of landmines than capture his attention, but I have no choice except to move forward or else give up.

"Speaking of resolution, your help would be really valuable with something." I finger the appointment book tucked under my arm and out of his sight.

The newspaper crackles as he folds it and lays it to one side. "You bet, Sally-Girl." He pulls his checkbook out of his back pocket. "Is Colton causing trouble again? Just tell me how much you need."

I had made it a rule that Jack and I would never ask for

financial assistance from our parents, not even for Colton. Jack's older sisters soon regretted accepting their father's generosity after they learned it always came with strings attached.

"Colton's fine."

"What is it, then?"

"I found something, um, of Jack's that I want you to see." I smile and try to come across like a student asking her teacher for an explanation. His return smile fades when I place Jack's appointment book in front of him and open the cover. "Remember this?"

He nods.

"Please skip over to March. Start at the nineteenth. Would you mind taking a look at the lists of names and numbers and identifying them?"

He hesitates, and then flips the pages one by one until the book lies open to mid-January. Big Jack's eyes graze my face while he grunts and squints, pushing his reading glasses up the bridge of his nose. He fans the pages past February and the first half of March and stops. "What about it?"

"See all those meetings and appointments on the day Jack died? Look at the following day, and several days after. Same thing, even into the next week."

"I see them."

"He made lots of plans after the nineteenth. Doesn't that tell you anything?"

Shrugging, he closes the cover and nudges the book toward me.

I reopen it and tap my index finger on the page. "Despite what the coroner said, Jack never intended to kill himself. He had some project in the works. Look at all those names. Who *are* those people? If I get in touch with them, I bet they could at least tell me *something*."

"Sally, you've got to stop poking through all this." He removes his glasses, closes the book again, and shuffles it across the table. "You can squint your pretty blue eyes at me, but it won't do anybody any good."

"Yes, it will!" I ignore his scowl. "For Colton's sake, I've got to prove Jack's death was accidental. It'll make you feel better, too, if . . . well, can't you help me?"

"I don't know any of those folks." He wipes his hand over his mouth, as if trying to shove the words back inside.

"Sure you do."

With a quick jerk of his head, he stares at the parking lot. I follow his gaze. Outside a man in a black business suit wipes his sweaty forehead while he changes a front tire. Big Jack draws his lips together and blinks several times, as if counting the lug nuts. He exhales for so long, a smaller person would turn blue.

When he looks at me, his expression has grown frosty. "Never mention this again."

I collapse against the back of the booth. "I didn't mean to push you into a corner."

"Forget it."

Sally-Girl has blown it, and I wonder how to wriggle the truth out of him. "Okay." I try my softest young-lady voice; it has worked in the past. "Maybe you can just tell me one tiny thing, then?"

Through narrow slits, he eyes me.

I clear my throat. "Why did Jack write my father's name in his book?"

"Let me see that thing again." He grabs the book and dogpaddles through the pages to find March. "Where?"

"The twenty-second." I sit up straight. "Also his phone number."

I've never seen anyone's face turn crimson so fast. Fearing he would suddenly clutch his chest and keel over, I reach across to pat the back of his hand, a risky move since he shuns physical affection.

"Dammit to hell!" He bangs the book shut, hard enough that a few startled customers look at us. "Leave it alone, you hear me?"

Across the room, Lois springs to action with her coffee pot appendage and heads in our direction, but I hold up a hand.

Big Jack stands and stretches to his full height, so his silver belt buckle comes level with my eyes. "Nate Wallace, that lousy bastard. Your father better not set foot in Mason's Crossing now." He snatches too much cash from his wallet for the three-fifty blue plate special and drops it on the table. As he stomps out of the diner, his boots clunk against the old mesquite floorboards.

When Lois appears at the edge of the booth, I try to smile, but my mouth feels dry and prickly. She fills my coffee mug and pulls a ticket from her apron pocket, matching it with the two five-dollar bills Big Jack left.

She gazes out the window as Big Jack climbs into the cab of his truck and slams the door. Within seconds, the engine roars to life. Lois tucks the ticket and the money into her pocket. "Didn't care much for them eggs today, did he?"

"I . . . I guess not."

"That wife of his, Miss Trixie, she was a saint, I reckon."

Nodding, I reach for my purse, but Lois pushes my hand away. "Coffee's on him."

I sigh and pick up the appointment book. If both Colton and Big Jack won't change their minds, fighting them will make my misery worse. Is pain better than unanswered questions? I can't rest without finding out what really went on with Jack.

Why did Colton hide Jack's book in the kitchen drawer? It couldn't be Saint Trixie or my crazy mother, rival guardian angels maneuvering from heaven. How was my father involved in Jack's wheeler-dealing? What made Big Jack lie about knowing those names?

One significant person in Mason's Crossing has always helped me find answers. I hope Officer Avery has let her out of jail by now.

CHAPTER THREE

Sheriff Mike Avery sits at an olive green metal desk behind the counter of the police station, filling out paperwork. When I set my purse on the countertop, he doesn't raise his head.

I drop my keys. "Did you arrest all those Earth Day demonstrators yesterday?"

"Oh, hi, Sally." He stands up so fast his chair tips over. Chuckling, he bends and sets the chair upright. "Nah, our jail's too small. State troopers carted off 'most everyone to Austin." He drops his pen on the stack of papers and approaches the counter. "Can I get you some coffee?"

"No time, but thanks anyway. I'm here on business. For Angelique."

"But you're not her daughter or her lawyer."

"I'll pay her fine." Brave words, but I know she will reimburse me.

"Too late to spring her. I already sent Angelique on her way." He glances over his shoulder at the wall clock. "About an hour ago."

Since we first met in elementary school, our paths crossed

often enough for me to consider Mike a friend, but not a confidant. Yet there is something about his demeanor I find comforting. Or maybe it is his penny loafers.

"I caught the news last night. She insisted you book her and lock her up, didn't she?"

"You know how stubborn she can be. I offered to drive her home after the diner delivered her favorite supper, but she wanted to keep the faith." He shakes his head. "I'm throwing her fingerprints out."

I admire Mike Avery for his old-fashioned good manners and because he sings like Elvis with his weekend rock-and-roll band. "Is that why you have so much paperwork today?"

With a laugh, Mike sidesteps around the counter, pushes through the swinging gate, and stops about two feet from me. "How's Colton's ankle? Not still limping, is he?"

"All healed, thank goodness."

"I climbed on the same roof when I was about his age. Lucky for me, I didn't fall off."

"Let's hope Colton's luck improves."

"It already has. The owner didn't want to press charges after all."

"He was pretty angry. What changed his mind?"

Mike glances at his loafers. "Teenaged boys need to keep busy."

"Speaking from personal experience or so you've been informed?"

"Both." He smiles and ducks his head. "I take my nephews fishing on the Brazos every chance I get. Maybe Colton would like to come along sometime."

"Thanks, that's very kind of you. He likes to fish."

I have every reason to trust Mike Avery. On the morning Colton discovered Jack's body in our garage, Mike arrived first on the scene, and he labored for two days afterward to rule out any suspicion of foul play.

A comfortable silence settles between us. We might as well turn the clock back eighteen years and meet in the high school cafeteria. "I should let you get back to work. Is there anything else to handle for Angelique?"

"She was going to stop by the judge's office to pay her fine, but I've got the paperwork ready to dismiss."

I ask if he would like me to deliver the documents across Courthouse Square, and Mike agrees at first, then changes his mind. "I'll walk you to your car."

He holds the door open for me as I slide behind the wheel, a courtesy I forgot some men extended. "Take care of yourself." He pats the roof of my car. "And tell Angelique to stick to her artwork and keep off government property."

I smile. "If you find any graffiti in the Impressionist style, you'll know who painted it."

We both laugh. Acting friendly with a sweet man like Mike Avery lifts my spirits.

As I drive, I croon "Mr. Bojangles" with Jerry Jeff Walker on the radio until I reach Angelique's sprawling ranch house on twenty acres beyond the other side of town.

Angelique swings the front door open and holds up her palm. "I don't want to discuss it." She absorbs me in a huge embrace, and then pulls back. "Let me gaze at you! You've trimmed your gorgeous hair."

With a grin, I hug her tighter and nestle my cheek on her shoulder. I don't want to let go. Since I was nine years old, she has been the only older female in my life whose eyes light up whenever she sees me.

At just under six feet tall, Angelique is the most graceful person I have ever known. Like an exotic dark-eyed queen, she floats into each room, making every head turn, her jet-black hair always tucked straight back. She has racked up two wealthy ex-husbands like hunting trophies, and now at age fifty-two, has enjoyed the attention of more than one younger boyfriend. Her current beau, a restaurateur close to my age named Raúl, moved in with her six weeks ago.

"You looked good on TV last night, very sexy in that tight red sweater and dangly earrings," I say. "How does it feel to be a jailbird?"

She raises her eyebrows and then draws me by the arm into the entryway. "I got a terrific night's sleep." She spins me around. "My, aren't you pretty today. New outfit?"

"I wish. Just spent all my money on the new sprinkler system. Landscaping business expense, of course, so it's tax-deductible."

After we tour her studio and I admire her latest paintings, Angelique sets a tray on a small wrought-iron table outside. We recline on cushioned chaises, sipping hot tea and enjoying the view of the Brazos valley from her terrace. The sunlight scatters crystals on the river's gently flowing surface.

I share with her my morning discoveries. "For some reason, Big Jack is another one who despises my father. I can't blame him, but his refusal to look at Jack's appointment book doesn't make sense."

"Do you think he's hiding anything?"

I suck in my breath and hold it. Big Jack probably never did an illegal thing in his life. Bent or slightly twisted, no doubt. I shrug. "Also I don't know what to think about Jack's attempt to come up with a spreadsheet. He couldn't even balance his own checkbook."

Angelique sets her teacup on the table. "Could be he got interested in something else, something his father wouldn't approve? Maybe Jack went job-hunting after deer season."

"As unbelievable as it sounds, it does look like Jack had some kind of deal in the works." I squint at Angelique. After a moment, I blink. "A secret partnership with my father?"

"Would that have been such a catastrophe? Nate could have given Jack invaluable financial advice about a start-up situation."

My husband and my father in cahoots? One after another, possibilities click through my mind, but I can't make myself believe any of them. Except one. "If Big Jack found out his son tried to make a separate arrangement with his archenemy, he would pitch a conniption."

"Didn't you just witness one?"

"This morning I sure pushed his hot button. But perhaps most fathers and sons who work together are eventually headed for a showdown."

"In their case, it would be two short-horned bulls in the same pasture." Angelique crosses her legs at the ankles. "Still, one has to wonder what tiptoed through Jack's head that night."

"It's possible he had something in mind other than ending his miserable life, the giant shithead." I sit up and punch the cushion behind me. "Twice the legal limit. What was he thinking?"

"You've been mad at Jack since the day you married him simply to spite your father. Poor guy, he can't win for anything, not even dying."

"I don't know why you feel sorry for him. Look at what he did to me. If it *was* suicide, no explanation, no signatures on important papers, no hints at good-bye."

"Not to quash your righteous indignation, but doesn't the note he left on the front seat count for anything?"

"I've thought about it every day since, and it still doesn't make any sense. I can't believe he would threaten me about getting along without him."

"You're right, the note is a strange memento. But otherwise, why would you expect Jack to behave any differently? Correct me if I'm wrong, my dear, but I always got the impression that he knew you preferred making your decisions solo."

I set my teacup down to jab the air with my finger. "Now the whole responsibility for . . . he's left me completely alone."

"Not to mention Colton."

"Even if all his cylinders were firing right now, Colton is a handful. He needs a father." I run my fingertips around the top edge of the armrest. "My life will get more stressful, and he's not even driving yet."

"What's wrong with Colton's cylinders now?"

A cool breeze wafts across the terrace as I tell Angelique about my argument with Colton and his reaction to my new goal. Maybe she can help me understand his hostility while I get my own under control.

"All his little—what shall we call them?—accidents or incidents must give you a clue." Angelique places her hand on my arm.

"Does Colton ever tell you how he feels?"

"He shuts me out completely. Won't talk, except to argue with me, and won't listen at all."

"Ah, kids these days. How well I know."

"What do you mean? You don't have any children."

Angelique raises herself from the chaise and pours more tea into our cups. "Mind if I explore some parallels?"

"I'm all ears."

Angelique begins to pace, and the words flow with her movements. She reminds me I was fourteen the year my mother died, and I'd never spoken to Colton about my life without her. To this day, I am still furious with my father for letting her die.

She stops in front of me. "Nate had no control over your mother's insanity."

I try to nod, but my neck has stiffened.

"Perhaps he deserved it. But you've pushed your father so far out of your life, he hasn't come back to Mason's Crossing for anything, not even Jack's funeral." Angelique lights a cigarette. "Believe it or not, Nate did the best he could."

"It wasn't good enough."

She arches one eyebrow. "Now Colton's a volcanic mess, and with all these minor accidents lately, he's headed for a meltdown."

"I simply can't let that happen."

Angelique drifts to the edge of the terrace and turns to face me. "Would that be so terrible?"

"I'm going to prove Jack's death was an accident. It's the best way to help Colton." My hands shake as I set my cup down. "Besides I don't know how much longer I can stand his . . ."

"In Colton's eyes, you're really strong and tough. Possibly he blames you for not preventing his father's death." She sighs. "Sound familiar?"

I stare at her until tears sting the rims of my eyelids.

"Sally, you don't communicate with Nate. Colton doesn't speak to you. Do you really want another generation of this horrible rejection? Find a way to stop it."

"This has to do with Colton's father, not mine."

"Jack is dead. Talk to Nate."

Angelique might as well offer me chopped worms with my tea.

"Show Colton things can be different." She steps forward and pauses near the foot of my chaise. "Teach him how forgiveness and reconciliation work. Make the first move." She bends to stir her tea. "It doesn't have to be much. Send Nate a postcard."

I haven't mailed anyone a postcard for a very long while.

It isn't an easy thing to do, especially the first time.

I waited in front of the counter of the Hot Springs Hotel and Spa and stood on my tiptoes to ask the desk clerk for a stamp. He wore a dark jacket with the hotel monogram on the pocket. His pale brown hair was slicked back, making his smooth forehead look bigger than his face. He leaned over and peered down at me. "Postcard or letter?"

"Postcard, please." He reminded me of a skinnier version of Ichabod Crane from my storybook, but I didn't feel like smiling, missing two more baby teeth since last week. "I wrote a postcard to my mother." She would like the photo. The porch with columns across the front of the hotel looked like our house, only bigger. Even their geraniums bloomed in the same colors as ours.

"That'll be one cent." He passed me the stamp. "Isn't your mother with you?"

With a shake of my head, I reached in my pink satin coin purse and handed him the five-dollar bill my father's assistant, Clyde, gave me before we left home.

The clerk took it between his thumb and one fingertip, like I could pass him cooties. "Nothing smaller, I suppose," he muttered.

I licked the stamp and worked it carefully into the upper right corner. Maybe Mother wouldn't notice I got it crooked. "She had to stay home. She wasn't feeling well enough to make the trip, so Aunt Mary came instead."

As he counted out my change, he glanced around the lobby. "Where is your aunt now?"

"Upstairs in bed." I could tell this man didn't like children, so I quickly scooped the money into my purse. "Where's the dining room, please?"

"Perhaps you should go back upstairs and get her." He sniffed. "Change clothes while you're at it. We don't allow–"

"But I always eat breakfast in my robe and pajamas. Mrs. Gussmann doesn't mind."

"Is that your name? Gussmann?"

He reminded me of a mean dog the neighbors used to have. He barked all night until my father went over to talk some manners into him. "No, it's Sally Mason Wallace."

His face turned pale. "Oh, my god. Your father is Nate Wallace?"

I nodded and reached up toward the counter and laid the stamped postcard on it. With my fingertip I scooted it toward him, in case he was the one with cooties.

In a flash, he came out from behind the front desk. "I had no idea. Please, let me show you to the dining room. This way, Miss Wallace."

I followed his stinky Aqua Velva odor across the lobby, my pink bunny slippers padding over the Oriental rugs and dark wood floors, and through some thick double doors. As we entered the dining room, my mouth watered at the smell of bacon and cinnamon, and I was thirsty for orange juice to wash away the leftover glue on my tongue. The desk clerk pulled out a huge cushioned armchair for me and told the waiter to bring whatever I wanted.

"Put it on Mr. Wallace's tab," he ordered. "And hurry up. She's hungry." He smiled, bowed, and asked if there was anything else he could do for me.

"Thank you. That will be all." I'd heard my father say exactly those words when he didn't want the servants to hang around. I wondered how the man kept from tripping over an empty dessert cart as he backed out of the dining room.

Before my French toast was half eaten, Aunt Mary appeared at my side, frowning and pressing her hand against her tummy. "Here you are. I was worried about you."

"Sorry. I woke up starving and you were still asleep." I held up a piece of toast toward her mouth and felt the syrup drip down my wrist. "Want some?"

She dodged the food like it was poison and placed a hand to her forehead. As she flopped in the chair next to me, she closed her eyes and waited. Her lips moved as if she silently counted something, and then she burped.

I giggled. "Wow! Clyde would be proud of that one!" Last year he taught me to "burp with gusto," as he said, but warned me not to tell anyone, especially my aunt.

Aunt Mary squinted, and for a moment her gaze darted around the ceiling as if she didn't remember where she was. "Sally, I can't take you anywhere today. The medicine is making me sick to my stomach."

My eyes went damp in the corners and my voice shrank. "Will Daddy take me?"

"He's busy in meetings all day, but I've arranged for a babysitter. Gwen'll be here soon." She took a sip out of my water glass. "We shouldn't have come along on this trip," she mumbled from behind the napkin. "But Nate wouldn't let us stay home alone. What with Clyde gone and all."

After breakfast, I changed clothes and returned to the lobby to wait. Gwen took me to the hotel gift shop and bought me a swimsuit decorated with yellow daisies, a matching towel, flip-flops, sunglasses, and a purple dragon inner tube. She picked out some movie magazines for herself. On a shelf behind the cash register, I spied a heart-shaped crystal perfume bottle. The squeeze ball was covered in gold lace with a black tassel. I asked her to add it to our purchases.

"It'll just wash off in the pool," she said while signing the ticket.

"It's not for me." I couldn't remember Mother's favorite perfume, but the clerk said 'Summer Romance' was close enough. She'd love it anyway.

We headed for the pool and stayed there until our hands and feet turned pruney. At lunch, the babysitter ordered turkey sandwiches brought to us poolside. For two days in a row, Gwen took me to the park, the movies, and the ice cream parlor. There wasn't much else to do in the little town of Hot Springs for my father either, because at the end of the second day he announced we were leaving in the morning.

"Do you like our hotel?" he asked.

"Well enough, I guess." I shrugged.

"Good. Because I just bought it."

"I'd like it better if Mother had come with us."

He hid behind his newspaper.

By the time we returned home, Aunt Mary needed a doctor, and one waited for us at the house to whisk her upstairs. I carried my shopping bag of swim gear and the special box with the perfume into the entry hall. Mrs. Gussmann had planted herself at the bottom of the stairs, ready to help with luggage. At the console table, my father shuffled through four days' worth of mail.

"Look what I got!" I squealed. I pulled out the box to show Mrs. Gussmann my gift for Mother. I opened the lid so the crystal could catch the light from the chandelier.

"Oh, how perfectly lovely!" she said. "Did your father give you that fancy bottle for your birthday?"

Blinking, I looked at him. He stopped sorting the mail and stared first at Mrs. Gussmann, then at me.

Mrs. Gussmann picked up my suitcase. "It's too bad you didn't have a little friend along to help you celebrate yesterday." She began her lumbering climb up the stairs. "I bet you had a nice cake at the hotel. How many candles on it this year? Six or seven?"

Without a word, my father turned and went into his office and closed the door. I held my breath. Surely he disappeared for a moment to get my present, the one he forgot to bring along on the trip. After several minutes, I realized he was not coming out. He had no idea yesterday was my birthday, and I gave up expecting him to remember what day I was born.

Angelique jiggles my foot with her hand. "Will you at least think about what I've said?"

"Sorry, what was it?"

"Get in touch with Nate."

"I . . . I can't."

"When the situation with Colton gets painful enough, you will." She stretches out her hand to take hold of mine. "How about some lunch? I made turkey Waldorf salad."

She leads me into the kitchen and I plop down where she points. Our conversation turns casual, about Raúl's new restaurant on the lake and her gallery reps in Santa Fe and La Jolla. We agree Big Jack's periodic belligerence elevated my late mother-in-law Trixie to sainthood, and Angelique expresses interest in the workings of my new sprinkler system.

I explain how to set the timer. "But something odd happened this morning."

Chewing slowly, Angelique listens to my story of the appointment book. She never even asks a question.

"Unless Colton moved it, I can't imagine how . . . like magic." I sigh. "Either that, or my mind is going. But thank goodness, otherwise the book would have been ruined. It's got all the clues I'm going to follow."

"Trixie certainly would have reason to want her son's named cleared of suicide, but she was never sharp enough to manage a rescue of such magnitude. It had to be your clever mother. She's your guardian angel, you know." Angelique makes it sound easy, like checking last night's scores in today's paper.

"Now I believe those far-fetched rumors about you."

"Which ones, dear?"

"That you are descended from a gypsy who married into Polish nobility. Supernatural events strike you as perfectly normal. Not so much, the rest of us."

"Do you have another explanation?"

"Colton is trying to hide Jack's book from me."

"Why would he do that?" She laughs. "Of course, keeping it safe isn't the same as deciphering the information inside. You can rely on your mother only for so much. The rest is up to you."

I start to protest, but the doorbell rings. Angelique returns to the kitchen with her arm linked through Officer Avery's. "Look who's come to see you, Sally. Don't you just love a handsome man in uniform?" She waves him to a place at the table.

"Thanks, I've already eaten." Mike squeezes the brim of his hat and nods at me. "Hello again."

I smile up at him. "How did you know I would still be here?"

"A sudden funny feeling. I dunno . . . can't explain it."

While Angelique shoots me a knowing wink, he twirls his hat and stares at his loafers. "Big Jack's had a nasty fall in the warehouse." Mike raises his head to look me full in the face.

"How badly is he hurt?" I can't make sense of the words. Big Jack is too belligerent to let himself be injured.

"They've taken him to the emergency room. He's in pretty rough shape."

Before I have a chance to ask further, Angelique bustles us out the front door, and I follow Mike's squad car and its wailing siren to the hospital. When we arrive, the ER doctor informs us Big Jack has gone into surgery, but I lose track of whether it was for the broken hip or the head injury. "Don't expect too much, ma'am. Mr. Edwards wasn't breathing at the time his secretary found him."

I clutch Mike's hand and let him lead me to a seat in the lobby.

Some guardian angel Saint Trixie turned out to be, if she became one. She can't even keep her husband from falling off a ladder.

On the other hand, I wonder if my mother would be capable of an even more difficult assignment.

CHAPTER FOUR

I have two choices. Sit at the hospital until Big Jack gets out of surgery, which could take all day, or finish my errands and return later.

When Mike Avery leaves to resume his obligations in town, I pace in the empty hallway. Jack was right. Years ago God pitched out virtues, and patience flew right past me. After several minutes, I pick up my purse and head toward the exit, but realize it isn't lack of patience that prods me. I cannot force myself to stay in a place that reminds me of my mother's unhappy last years. Besides, I have other matters to resolve.

Detoured to the ladies room, I splash water on my face. If Saint Trixie wants to scold me for deserting her husband, her words will fall on deaf ears. No way will I trade my own sanity for camping out at the hospital, however undutiful to my father-in-law it might seem. On my way out, I hand the ER doctor my business card and drive home.

On the kitchen table, I spread out the telephone directory, a yellow legal pad, three No. 2 pencils, and Jack's appointment book. I call the first two names listed on March sixteenth last year and get some vague answers. Jack wanted to borrow money, engage a partner, plan an expansion or relocation of the business, and make a deal with someone besides his father.

Which deal? Jack's plans included a second deal, which never got airborne, perhaps because he died. If the second one had failed, too, I knew him well enough to believe he would have tried to launch a third. He was that cheerful and persistent, but also that unrealistic.

I clutch the crumb of evidence. Jack couldn't have killed himself. Anyone could see he hadn't given up. Maybe his optimism will rub off on me.

The next call gives me hope and points me toward the potential mother lode, the name of the man in the midst of each deal. For once, Jack's scribbles prove useful. A moment after I scrawl "Dr. Brett Kennedy" at the top of the page and underline it, my phone rings.

Oh, hell! It's Big Jack's secretary. The pique in her voice blames me for something besides forgetting to call her.

After she summoned the ambulance, Harlene couldn't leave the office and later the hospital staff informed her only family members can be privy to patient information. I apologize for my lack of communication and hope she blames it on anxiety.

"I've never seen Big Jack so spitting mad," Harlene begins. "When he got here after breakfast, I thought he would break something."

Already I can picture Big Jack's scowling face.

"I couldn't even get his signature on this stack of checks. He stormed out to the warehouse, and I could hear him cussing and shoving cartons around."

I detect sniveling. Her lacquered face must be streaked with black.

Harlene blows her nose. "I didn't go hunting for him until he didn't answer my page, maybe twenty minutes later. Customers had started to come in, so I never heard the crash when he fell off the ladder."

"It's not your fault, Harlene."

"What happened this time to set him off like that?" She says it like she has the answer already. According to her, nothing is ever Big Jack's fault. Goodness knows, he could part the seven seas all at once.

"Don't blame yourself. You did everything you could." Harlene had a rough early life, not much education, and raised a son while tending a disabled veteran for a husband. Without admiring her, I acknowledge her fierce loyalty to Big Jack, something I had never achieved with anyone. But she treated Jack like a bothersome salesman instead of her future boss. Biased robot that she is, she couldn't have failed to notice how much the store meant to him. "The rest is up to the doctors."

"Oh, but if you'd seen him, all pale and unconscious. He wasn't even breathing."

Her words throw ice water on my heart. In place of Big Jack, I see his son's face, ashen and still, as if he had fallen asleep in our garage, frozen against the driver's headrest. I shudder and pick up a pencil, doodling to distract myself, pressing down as I draw.

When the lead tip of my pencil snaps, my mind shakes off its inertia, as if I just woke up to an alarm. "Tell me something, Harlene." I wait for her to stop sniffling. "Who is Brett Kennedy?"

She gasps. "Don't mention his name around Big Jack."

Not that it would make any difference to him right now. "Why not?"

"He sold some company stock to that Dr. Kennedy last year, about this time. But something happened afterwards, I don't know what, and Big Jack has been furious about it ever since." She begins to whimper. "If he doesn't pull through, I don't see how . . ."

"We'll deal with it at the time, if it comes to that." I sit up straight, square my shoulders, and promise to call her the instant I hear any news. "Now, don't you worry. It's all in God's hands."

Perhaps not entirely. Who can guess what interference Saint Trixie might attempt? Maybe my mother-in-law misses the cantankerous old coot up in heaven.

Come get your husband anytime you want.

At least now I know what my next phone call will be. I root through the yellow pages like a pig under an oak tree.

Dr. Kennedy doesn't practice medicine, but higher education. I finally locate him in the history department at the University of Texas in Austin. He agrees to see me tomorrow morning at eleven o'clock. Better a short trip to the big city than a long visit to the funeral home. I cross my fingers.

The phone rings again. Judith Cromwell, my best friend and cousin by marriage, can't remember if it's her day to pick up Colton and her son Max after school.

"Your turn," I say. "Plus, I need you to keep Colton through dinner, if you can."

"Overnight, if you like, in case you're on watch."

Judith's kind offer to help with laundry or meals brings tears to my eyes. She and I have shared many trials, and I often wish we had grown up as sisters. In a crisis, Angelique can be counted on to provide any alibi, no questions asked, but Judith would help her friend hide the body.

"I guess word has already spread around town about Big Jack's accident." I glance at the kitchen clock and try to calculate how long the local buzz has been active. Judith could tell me, but I have a more pressing concern. "Do you know anyone named Brett Kennedy?"

"I've heard the name from Charlie." She giggles like a teenager in love. "He's never met a stranger and remembers everyone's face. I don't see how he does it."

I gather that her husband has had some dealings with the professor and later served up all the personal scoop to her like gravy. Judith sounds pleased to tell me Kennedy's military service broke up his marriage after the Vietnam War, but *before* he struck it rich.

"Charlie said she left him because he was a poor ex-GI." Judith's voice changes to singsong. "If she'd only waited."

"Your husband should have been a spy or a reporter, not a banker." I'm not above returning her tease.

"Why do you ask about this Kennedy guy?"

I share my plans with Judith, along with my anticipation that the professor will prove helpful.

"You're not serious, are you?" Ominous replaces singsong. "I'd leave that alone, if I were you."

"Why?"

"Give Colton more time to adjust. That's all he needs."

"What Colton needs is to know his father didn't kill himself."

"Colton will be fine. He's getting better every day. Expressing himself around here like he's normal. You'd be trying to kill a fly with a sledgehammer."

"What do you mean, 'normal'?"

"He laughs, he talks, he follows directions. Doesn't run with scissors and plays well with others. He's especially nice to Maddie when Max torments her."

"But—"

"Sally, you're seeing something that isn't there. Too much imagination killed . . . well, you know."

"Curiosity."

"What?"

"It was curiosity killed the cat."

"Just don't let your natural stubbornness lead you astray."

Add Judith to my strikeouts. Great. I had now hit 0-for-four. Maybe Jack would appreciate my baseball metaphor.

BY THE TIME I RETURN to the hospital, Big Jack has just entered the post-op ICU, sedated to the fingertips. The surgeon extracted the broken rib from his punctured lung, inserted a steel plate in his pelvis, and realigned the bones, both ulna and radius, in his right arm. The huge bump on his head had swelled outward.

"Good thing he's such a strong guy for sixty-seven," the doctor says. "We had to keep him under for quite a while."

"Is there any problem with his breathing?"

"Not since we put a chest tube in place. He's on oxygen, too, of course."

"I mean, earlier. From the accident?"

"Our neurological monitoring indicates there could be some brain damage, but we won't know much more until he is alert. We're watching him closely."

"Should I wait here until he wakes up?"

"We're keeping him sedated until he's able to breathe on his own and his pressure is stable. He won't even know you're in the room with him."

It takes all my courage, but I gut up enough to take a peek at Big Jack from the hallway. Bandages cover parts of him, tubes and wires stick out from different areas of his body, and hospital machinery hums and beeps like a trolley car. My stomach churns and I feel dizzy. When the ICU nurse asks if I'd like to go into his room, I decline. I can't get down the elevator and out to my car fast enough.

IN JUDITH'S AND CHARLIE'S KITCHEN, four noisy children and two adults chomp on fried chicken and corn-on-the-cob, while trying to answer homework questions. After my brief update, Judith makes everyone get quiet while she recites a quick prayer for Big Jack.

"Amen!" Charlie shouts, and the children, except Colton, reply "Amen" in chorus.

Judith holds out a plate of food, but I shake my head. "Thanks, I've got leftovers at home I need to get rid of."

In the car, I give Colton a few more details about his grandfather's condition. "He's still unconscious from the surgery, so he's not in any pain." Not enough to worry Colton, I hope. "If you'd like to go see him, I'll check with the doctor to find out when he'll be ready for company."

No answer.

"I picked up your new camera this afternoon. When does photo club start?"

The silence continues.

"How was school?"

"Thursday."

"You've got photo club tomorrow?"

He nods.

When I grow tired of using a verbal crowbar, we ride in silence for a while, until I turn onto our street. "By the way, I ran into Mike Avery today."

Colton stiffens as he inhales sharply and holds it.

"He offered to take you fishing with his nephews sometime." I press the button to raise the garage door and wait for it to creep open, panel by panel. "They go someplace down on the Brazos. Sounds like fun." I pull forward and turn off the engine. "Maybe he can help me with–"

"I hate to fish. I'm not going anywhere with that guy. Ever." For the second time in one day, Colton gets out of my car and slams the door behind him.

It's not as if I expect Mike Avery to replace Jack, but how can I get everything so wrong? My son refuses to answer my easy questions. What I think Colton will enjoy, he declines. I feel small and stupid until I remember Angelique's prediction. His disagreeable behavior points toward meltdown, and I will have to act fast.

Everyone else is wrong. Colton needs closure with his father's death. All the more reason I should speak to Brett Kennedy. The way to help Colton is to get reasonable proof that Jack died by accident and not his own hand.

I hope my mother hears me because I will need her help.

CHAPTER FIVE

The next morning as Colton and I prepare in silence to leave the house, the phone rings. Harlene needs me to drop by Big Jack's office before I visit him at the hospital. I dread spending any more time with her than absolutely necessary.

After I drive Colton to school, my return route takes me past the Hot Crossed Buns Diner. No silver pickup stationed in front. I wonder how Lois took the news.

Once I arrive at Big Jack's office, I park at the back of the building. A young man sits smoking on the edge of the loading dock, his plaid flannel shirtsleeves rolled up. It's amusing he is so oblivious of the cool air, until I recognize him, not as much from his unshaven face as by the black snake tattoos on his forearms.

After Jack fired Harlene's son Lamont and turned him in for selling pot, he was sentenced to two years in the Huntsville prison, because he was on probation at the time for the same offense, plus his rap sheet included stealing cars. Skipper, as everyone except his mother calls him, was released a year ago, right before Jack died. A week after the funeral I discovered Skipper seated in the break room, free on parole that Harlene had somehow persuaded the prison board to grant. By then, there was no Jack around, however, to throw his criminal ass off the property.

Although I hadn't seen him since that day, if I happen to find out now that Harlene sneaked him back on the payroll, I won't wait for Big Jack's recovery before I dismiss him. As if Skipper reads my thoughts, he glowers at me. I walk faster toward the entry.

Harlene's efficient manner has revived enough to assemble the documents Big Jack failed to sign yesterday, each page in order, starting with the one granting me power of attorney. "Last year Big Jack directed his lawyer to draw up, uh, as soon as . . ." She uncaps a pen. "He already signed, in case he ever needed it, but he didn't want to bother you with it."

"Why not one of his daughters?"

Harlene places the sheet of paper in front of me and hands me the pen. "I have my instructions." She taps her notary stamp on the inkpad and waits.

Her unwillingness to reply further gives me my answer. A survivor of the Great Depression, Big Jack never borrowed a dime in his life and didn't trust people who asked anyone for money. Something his children no doubt regretted discovering.

After she notarizes my signature, Harlene goes through the pile like a dealer at a blackjack table. The document placing my name on his bank account precedes a stack of checks. As I sign one by one, she stuffs them in envelopes with ten-cent postage stamps already affixed. It will do no good to offer to drop them at the post office. When it comes to Big Jack, Harlene never delegates even her smallest duty.

She flips to the final page of a group of papers stapled together. The line for the lessee's signature, or his representative, is left blank at the bottom. Above it, blue ink scrawls from other hands, including Brett Kennedy's, catch my attention. When I recognize my father's, my breathing comes to a halt. "What's this?"

"It's a contract to renew a lease."

"Why is my father's signature on it?"

She hesitates. "Nate Wallace is . . . he's majority owner now."

The pen slides out of my hand. "Was Jack aware of this change? How did it happen? I'd like to know when this all came about." Earth and sky have exchanged places.

"Sally, you know I can't talk about—"

My breath returns with force, and I pound my fist on the desk. "I want some answers!"

Harlene's eyes widen, but she says nothing.

I stare at the words typed below his signature. Nate Wallace, principal owner. Clutching the document, I stand up and head for the door. "I just obtained the power of attorney. If you won't tell me, I'll find someone who will."

By the time I arrive at the hospital, I can't explain to anyone how I got there. How dare Big Jack hand over his business to anyone except his son! Confusion and rage overpower my aversion to the smell of rubbing alcohol, and I stomp into the ICU.

Overnight, Big Jack has turned pale and shrunken, as if the tubes have siphoned his power instead of nourishing him. Standing next to him, I feel no pity, but rather the urge to howl. I shake the papers in front of his closed eyes and grit my teeth.

"What the hell did you do to your son?"

BY TEN O'CLOCK, I leave Mason's Crossing and drive toward Austin. Usually I enjoy the short trip to the capital, because it offers a few skyscrapers and more lush green hills than Mason's Crossing. Over a crest in the highway, the road stretches out before me like a magic carpet leading to an exotic bazaar. As I arrive at Brett Kennedy's office on the UT campus, the tower clock strikes ten forty-five. Rather than wait, I bang my knuckles on the rippled, frosted glass set in the thick wood door.

A low voice answers, "Come in."

His puzzled frown tells me he expects someone else.

"Sorry, I'm early."

"Then you must be Sally Edwards." His accent reveals deep East Texas, as if his words have been dragged through soft bottomland.

Kennedy stands and motions me to a chair across from his large cluttered desk. With a flash of gray at his temples, he looks about ten years my senior. On the wall behind him hangs a diptych abstract in oil, wedged between overstuffed bookcases that reach to the ceiling.

I sit and shuffle the lease agreement and Jack's appointment book in my lap. Kennedy listens while I explain how I found his name yesterday and his signature today. I could pretend to be a student requesting assistance from a professor, but I don't have to. After assuring him of my power of attorney, I ask him if he will share what he knows about Jack's attempts at a business deal.

"Around fourteen months ago, your husband called me about some property, but I wasn't interested in selling it. He said he'd consider a lease. A short while later, he inquired if I'd like to invest in a retail operation he planned to expand." He punctuates his explanation with a series of shrugs, probably the same taciturn answer Jack received.

A few more questions reveal Big Jack's feed store sits on Kennedy's property on the outskirts of Mason's Crossing. Simple, but there has to be more to it. I feel he won't show me his hand unless I show him mine first.

"Dr. Kennedy, I picked up the lease agreement this morning. You signed the renewal a few days ago." I hold it up, as if he requires evidence. "Nate Wallace is my father. I need to know how he came to be the principal owner."

His eyes dart back and forth. After a moment, his jaw muscles soften. With a loud squeak, he pushes back his chair and limps toward the window.

I want to ask if he hurt himself, but remember his status as a Vietnam War veteran and think it best not to inquire. He probably wouldn't want my sympathy anyway.

Books cram the window ledge, and he stoops to blow dust from them. "Don't get me wrong. I thought your husband was a nice guy and he had some cash to invest, but I concluded he didn't have the *gravitas*, or the financial support required, to attempt such a project on his own."

I nod. Thus far, except for the cash to invest, I can't disagree with him.

"After I turned him down, I received a call from the elder Mr. Edwards–"

"Who was furious."

"Just the opposite. He offered to sell me the whole thing. Not only the feed store, but also the two businesses in town. Land, building, and contents."

My mouth drops open, but I can't connect any dots to my father. Why would Big Jack sell Brett Kennedy the entire business operation his own son deserved to inherit? What if Jack found out his beloved retail operation was snatched from his future grasp and decided . . . No, it simply couldn't be.

"Frankly, my business interests lie elsewhere," Kennedy says. "Plus I didn't want to get mixed up in a father-son falling out. The same day I rejected your father-in-law's offer, Nate Wallace contacted me. I wasn't previously acquainted with him, but he persuaded me to make the purchase."

My head starts spinning, just from trying to keep the facts straight. "If you didn't want it, why did you agree?"

"You'll have to ask your father about that."

"I'd rather hear it from you, if you don't mind."

"Because he offered to buy it from me immediately at a ten percent profit."

As if the floor has shifted, I grab the arms of my chair. The lease agreement and Jack's book slide off my lap.

"I hope it worked out for him, because I haven't seen Mr. Wallace since."

I can't figure out if I should blame him for his take-the-money-and-run maneuver. Staring at his face, I decide he merely calculated his gain and believed he had no obligation beyond cashing the check. No wonder he and my father came to such a quick agreement.

"Obviously all this catches you by surprise. Perhaps your father can explain it better."

He hasn't laid eyes on Nate Wallace in over a year and still doesn't get it. My father excels at disappearing.

Aunt Mary must believe I have talent, even for my young age of nine, because she signed me up for private lessons with an art teacher. This morning Daddy told her to buy me all the supplies I might need, and we were on our way to the art store. I wondered if she would let me pick out more than twelve colored pencils. I would like to have at least three shades of pink and one for flesh. The picture I wanted to draw was already taking shape in my imagination.

Inside the store were bins filled with brushes of all different sizes and tubes of paint with weird names like ocher and henna, stacked tablets of textured paper, rectangles of canvas stretched on wooden frames, and fresh chalk and charcoal with perfect flat ends. But where were the colored pencils?

The clerk showed us to an aisle with shelves on one side, hung on brackets against the white wall. He selected a box made of smooth golden oak and faced me to open it. The contents might as well have been Ali Baba's treasure. Pencils of every shade lined up neatly in three rows, forty-eight colors in all. He explained they were oil pastels and then led us to the aisle with the drawing tablets.

I tugged at Aunt Mary's sleeve. "May I please get two? A medium and a large one?" Those blank pages and I were going to become good friends.

She nodded, and I followed the clerk to the cash register, hardly believing she agreed it all will be mine to use as I wished. Daddy must have told her not to be stingy. I danced on tiptoes all the way to the car.

Aunt Mary gave the chauffeur the address of the studio, and I sat up straight on the gray leather back seat, patting my new satchel with the oak box and the sketchpads inside. She told me to be still, then mentioned the driver would be back to pick me up in an hour. She was going home to lie down until supper. Aunt Mary was never any fun.

At the studio we crossed through the doorway together. A very tall, slender woman with dark hair walked toward us, and I was fascinated by her jewelry, which jangled and swayed as she glided across the floor.

"You must be Sally," she said. "I think we'll have a good time together." She squatted in front of me until our eyes met. Hers twinkled like black diamonds. "I hope you'll tell me about yourself and share some of your creative ideas with me." A smile played on her lips. "You're quite imaginative, I can already tell. What's your favorite color?"

Her voice sounded kind and mysterious at the same time, but I heard something new. She was the first adult who had ever been curious about me. All at once, I wanted to hug her, leap into her lap, tell her a joke to see if I could make her laugh, show her my bedroom and my new black patent leather Mary Janes for Sunday, snuggle against her in the front seat of the car, demonstrate my back flip from the diving board, bring her daisies from the garden, give her a cherry off the top of my banana split. Maybe she would let me untie her ponytail and braid her long black hair, or try on her African wooden necklace with the carved giraffes and elephants and her shiny red leather pumps with the silver buckles.

Aunt Mary tucked her brown purse under her arm and placed her hand in the middle of my back to nudge me forward. "Sally, this is Mrs. Pierce."

The enchanting goddess stood up and my head tilted back to keep my eyes on her face. Her red lips parted into a wide smile, casting a net, and I was caught in it. She winked down at me. "Sweetheart, you may call me Angelique."

The hour passed too quickly and I couldn't wait for my next lesson. Like a turtle in the sun, I warmed to her compliments, as Angelique hung my weekly drawings around the studio.

One day my assignment was to draw a portrait of my family, at home or in the park. Since we all had never gone to the park together, I decided the use the upstairs sitting room as my scene. I drew Mother lying down on her sofa to one side of the pink marble fireplace. In a chair across from her, tucked in a gray lap robe, Aunt Mary read a Bible, while I lay on the floor in front of the hearth with my sketchpad open. I used my medium blue pencil to copy the striped wallpaper pattern. In her white apron, Mrs. Gussmann stood in the corner holding a tray with teacups. Outside the big picture window, Clyde waved to us from our small private airplane. The sky behind him was light blue, with streaks of yellow. Everyone was smiling.

When I showed Angelique my finished drawing, she inquired about each person as if I had painted a masterpiece for the Louvre instead of awkward lines and circles. She asked how I knew about the museum, and I told her Aunt Mary, Mother, and I went there last summer when Daddy had business in Paris. We had to come back early because Mother got sick, but Daddy stayed a few weeks longer.

Angelique adored my choice of colors and declared I was a natural at design. I told her about Clyde's gold front tooth and huge skinning knife he keeps hidden inside his leather boot, and she said she'd like to meet him some day, as long as I am with her for protection.

With a giggle, I assured her that Clyde wouldn't hurt anyone. I skipped over the part about Mother's black moods and Aunt Mary's sickly condition, but described them as very pretty in different ways, one blonde and the other brunette.

She squeezed me around the shoulders and claimed I had a terrific artist's eye and sense of perspective, very advanced for my age. "But where's your father? Shouldn't he be somewhere in your picture?"

I ran my fingertips over the paper, careful not to smear the lines, and touched each face. "No," I say. "Daddy's not home."

"Where did he go?"

"I don't know." I closed my sketchbook. "He's gone."

Brett Kennedy must read the disbelief in my eyes. "Please don't blame me for realizing a profit. I had no idea I was participating in family treachery."

My head throbs with jumbled thoughts. Someone knocks. His next appointment, an attractive coed, opens the door and pokes her head inside. "Oh, excuse me," she says.

He holds up his hand in her direction, thumb and fingers spread out to indicate five minutes.

When the door clicks shut, I shiver as if awaking from a trance and reach down to retrieve the book and papers. With my free arm, I push myself to my feet.

"By the way, I'm very sorry about your husband. I read about it in the papers afterwards." Brett Kennedy shakes my hand as he limps forward and guides me to the door. "I hope you find what you're looking for."

The slow walk to the car gives me time to sift the information, and my frustration grows. On the way home, I long for the peace of my greenhouse, but my mind won't stop struggling to comprehend all that happened. The feud between Big Jack Edwards and Nate Wallace started before I was born, but why did my father find it necessary to push their enmity to a higher level? Big Jack's holdings wouldn't amount to a drop in the ocean of my father's fortune.

I try to make sense of Big Jack's fury. Bad enough for him

to work for my father during the last year. When Big Jack suspected his son had plotted behind his back, he offered the whole operation to Kennedy to punish him. But Jack hadn't known that Kennedy would sell to Nate, and he didn't deserve his father's retaliation. Despite Angelique's suggestion, Jack had nothing to do with my father after all.

No wonder Big Jack doesn't want me digging up the past, the old hypocrite. His legendary temper went too far, and he made sure Jack suffered. How did he think Jack took it when he learned that his own father had sold the family business, including the store where he worked, out from under him?

My arms lock and the car nearly swerves off the road. Now I know a plausible reason for Jack to have killed himself. How will I ever explain this mess to Colton?

CHAPTER SIX

By the time I reach my house, I still can't figure out exactly what Jack knew and when. If my mother intends to assist me, I need a signal from her soon.

The morning's coffee left in the pot isn't worth drinking lukewarm. After a few minutes on the burner, it bubbles, hot and ready to pour into one of Grandmother Mason's china cups.

On my kitchen table, I spread out the same materials from yesterday. Starting over with a fresh No. 2 pencil, I flip to a clean sheet on the yellow legal pad and scrawl three names across the top: Big Jack and Jack on either side, separated by Brett Kennedy in the center. It makes sense to draw the first arrow from Jack to Brett Kennedy. My husband must have felt both desperate and disappointed at Kennedy's rejection. How else could he have wrestled free of his father's domineering authority?

I place a large 'X' through the center of the arrow. According to Kennedy, the next move belongs to Big Jack, with his sudden desire to sell fueled by rage. I sketch another arrow from his name to the professor. That link also receives an oversized 'X,' based on Kennedy's lack of interest.

Frowning, I raise the china cup to my lips and blow steam from the coffee's surface. After a sip or two, I pick up my pencil again and twiddle the eraser against the tablet. My stomach rumbles, and I glance at the toaster on the counter. Two forgotten bread slices have gone stale. My reflection in the stainless steel appears dark and blurry, even when I shift from side to side.

Under Kennedy's name, I write 'Nate Wallace' and circle the block letters, as if my pencil can restrict his influence. My father already possesses a vast empire of self-made wealth and power; he doesn't need Big Jack's piddling one.

My heart wants to whisper that my father did it for me, but I dismiss the emotion. Years of estrangement cement the wall between my father and me. He will not lift a finger to help me and I will never ask him. Even Mother's divine meddling cannot soften me.

Instead of an arrow, I draw a question mark between Brett Kennedy and Nate Wallace. I fan the pages of the lease agreement until I find when Kennedy finalized his purchase of Big Jack's enterprise: March 19, 1975, the very day Jack died.

Jack, why couldn't one of your cockamamie schemes have turned out? It would have meant so much to you.

I want the earth to spin backwards, to carry me through time and space to last year on that Tuesday. I will assure Jack it doesn't matter what his father thinks of him or how abusive he becomes. I will pour the whiskey down the drain before he drinks it and wait past midnight in the garage until he turns off the engine before letting him close the door. I will stand guard over him, protect his life and his future, do what he can't do for himself. I will overlook his weaknesses, forgive his debts, and forget his faults.

I will stop treating him with disdain and indifference.

Instead, hostility has now settled in like extended family that won't leave. Big Jack and my father feuded, but Big Jack should have known Nate will always win. Jack pounced on what appeared to be an opportunity to cut the ties with his controlling father, and somehow it backfired.

Now I let anger give me energy and purpose, and I feed it in return. Almost like it can climb up into my lap and eat off my plate.

After I draw lines between Kennedy's name and Big Jack's, add pointed end caps, and write last year's date under it, the arrows look lopsided. Ah, yes, connect the professor to my father.

Yet my diagram seems incomplete. I squint and reach for my coffee. When I pick it up, the handle comes right off. Not in pieces, but intact. The cup drops, without breaking, onto the pad of paper and spills coffee all over what I wrote. Each name disappears under a sea of dark liquid.

I dash to the sink for some paper towels and blot as fast as I can. As I jostle Jack's appointment book to safety, it falls open to the page with my father's phone number, three days after Jack's suicide.

With a wince, I realize what is missing from my diagram, now drowned in coffee. I should draw a line between my husband and my father, but I don't know where to place the arrow tip. Did Jack call Nate after he learned about the second purchase, or did my father contact him earlier? Perhaps Jack hoped my father could somehow rescue him from Big Jack's retribution. Could that have been Nate's intention? What passed between them on Jack's last day?

Maybe Jack didn't commit suicide after all, but only one person can help prove it now. If I want my father's help, I will have to ask for it.

Reeling, I head for my greenhouse, but before I'm halfway across the yard the phone rings and I return to my kitchen. The clock's face shows two forty-five, too early for the boys to be finished with photo club. When I pick up the receiver, Judith's voice screeches even before I place it to my ear.

"Sally! Can you come down to the police station right now?"

"Why? What's wrong?" I hold my breath.

"It's Colton and Max. They've been picked up for shoplifting."

I hang up the phone. Surely, I told her I'd be right there, but I can't hear anything over the loud humming in my ears.

THE CAR RADIO PLAYS Freddy Fender's "Wasted Days and Wasted Nights," but I clamp my jaw shut and flick the switch. Better to ride in anxious silence than be reminded of past mistakes.

Inside the police station, Judith Cromwell lounges on a long wooden bench against the wall in the lobby. The room is quiet, the office empty.

"What happened?" I stand in front of her and wait.

"I haven't talked to the James Gang yet. We'll find out when Charlie gets here." She shakes her head and stifles a giggle. "What possessed them to act so stupid?"

"Why are you laughing? On the phone you sounded upset."

"No, just in a hurry. I don't have time for this foolishness. I'm considering signing us all up for a nudist camp because I can't get the laundry done."

I laugh.

"Seriously. You don't know what washing a hundred pounds of smelly clothes every other day is like."

How would I know? She doesn't hear me sigh.

"I had to leave Maddie with her grandmother because Meredith is still at school. What could they be accused of shoplifting? Max isn't big enough to hide anything under his shirt."

Even seated, I am eight inches taller than Judith. Curly red hair wafts from her head like a flag, and her laughter is loud enough to summon taxis. I feel a twinge of envy that Judith and her husband Charlie remain in love, more than any couple I know. I like Judith for her stubborn refusal to take life in Mason's Crossing too gravely, probably because her 'people' aren't from Texas. She isn't weighed down by any expectations springing from tradition and heritage.

"This behavior has to stop," I say, "but I can't get Colton to listen to me."

"I'm sure it's harder without Jack."

"Actually about the same. Jack preferred to play catch with Colton rather than make him do his homework."

"Most of the time, I have to be the bad guy, too."

I massage my temples. "Who's back there with them?"

"Officer Avery. And the shop owner, I think."

I stand up and pace a few steps. When the door at the

entrance springs open, Charlie Cromwell bounds through it like a Labrador puppy. Our mothers were cousins, but it still irks me that he kept his distance at Jack's funeral. It wasn't like Jack died of the plague.

"Where are the ring-tailed tooters now?" he asks, grinning.

Judith's guffaw startles me as if she stuck me with a pin. "In the interrogation room," she says.

Maybe they have reason not to treat this stunt seriously, but I don't.

"Looks like Mike drummed confessions out of them," Charlie says, pointing behind us.

Judith and I turn to watch our sons emerge from the back hallway. Max's whole body trembles, while Colton coolly saunters across the room. Towering between them, Officer Avery escorts them to the swinging gate at the far end of the counter. Released into our custody, he announces with a stern voice.

Max bolts past me into Judith's outstretched arms and bursts into tears. "I'm so sorry," he wails, as both parents stroke his hair and pat his shoulders. "We didn't mean to break anything."

When Charlie puts his arm around them and all three ruddy foreheads meet in the middle of their family circle, I spin around to face the others. Expressionless, Colton stands quietly next to Officer Avery.

Max's sobbing is the only sound for a few moments, until a smallish man standing behind the officer clears his throat.

Avery glances over his shoulder. "Oh, yes," he says. "The damages." He places his hand, like a paddle, on the back of Colton's neck and steers him toward me. The other man follows, clutching a tall shopping bag. Broken glass clinks with every step.

"Gee, I'm sorry, Sally," Mike whispers. "I know you don't need any more trouble." He shifts his gaze to Colton as he squints.

I feel the color rise to my face like a wave of fever and my palms start to sweat. "Colton, what do you have to say for yourself?" I hope the firmness in my voice is obvious. "I think you owe this gentleman an apology, don't you?"

"Sorry, sir." His voice might as well be a recording.

Max raises his head from Judith's shoulder and chimes in, "We didn't mean to break your vase."

"It's art glass," the shop owner says. "From my gallery."

The sobbing recommences as Max gurgles an explanation through his tears. "We were playing catch with it. We weren't really gonna steal it. Were you, Colton? Tell him."

At that moment, I lose my grip on my purse and it lands on the floor with a thud. All eyes shift to me, but I can't utter a word.

Mike rescues me. "Nah, these boys aren't thieves. They just have a peculiar notion of fun." He holds up his forefinger and gestures for Max to come stand next to Colton. "Now, you two, listen up."

Judith and Charlie unwind Max's arms and give him a gentle push forward. He snivels and wipes his red nose on his sleeve. When he sidles next to Colton, the top of his head reaches the same level as my son's shoulder.

Mike explains the settlement. Both parents will pay Mr. Donatello right away for the value of the broken vase.

He won't file any charges because of their youth and status as first offenders."

I can't believe my ears. What will happen to Colton for his second offense, should there be a serious one? Or his third? I never want to enter Mike Avery's police station again as long as I live.

Mike gives a fleeting look toward the Cromwells and me, and then glares at the boys. "We're gonna chalk it up to high spirits and bad judgment." He shakes his head, the way a lion would ruffle his mane. "But you're not off the hook. Come Saturday at nine, you boys report for work in the alley behind Mr. Donatello's shop. You'll sweep and haul trash and do whatever he wants until the place is spotless."

When we nod, he turns to the gallery owner. "Now, Mr. Donatello, why don't you go ahead and shock these parents with the price of your vase . . . er, art glass?"

Reading the bottom line on Mr. Donatello's invoice feels like a punch on the jaw. My half of the debt exceeds what I spend on gas and groceries in a month.

"Mr. Donatello, may I speak to you privately?" I take a few steps toward the corner of the lobby.

I ask the owner to accept a small payment now and work out terms with me for the balance. At first, I detect a slight hesitation on Mr. Donatello's part, but a nod from Mike smoothes the deal. Another rescue. Does he ever climb down off his white horse?

Before she got too sick, my mother expressed her fondness for Mike Avery. She believed he would become mayor of Mason's Crossing someday. Has she decided to work her juju through him?

Mr. Donatello departs the police station with his shopping bag of art glass shards in one hand and Charlie Cromwell's check for the full amount of their share in the other. Colton holds the door open as Charlie and Judith carry a limping Max through it, then he follows all three of them to wait outside.

Whirling around, I catch Mike staring at me. "What was that all about?"

"According to the owner, the boys–"

"Why did Mr. Donatello need your approval before he accepted my offer?"

Mike runs a finger around the inside of his collar and loosens his tie. "How about some coffee?"

"What right have you to interfere?" The instant the words leave my mouth, I feel the sting of ingratitude, like biting into something sour. Today isn't the first time Officer Avery has stepped between Colton and an angry property owner. I try a gentler tone. "Mike, please remember, Colton is *my* business, and no one else's."

His office phone rings, and he holds up a forefinger while he backs around the counter toward his desk. I can't keep Colton waiting. As I stride through the exit, he says into the phone, "No, it's all settled."

Once outside, I can't tell if the bright sunlight has cast too much warmth for early spring, or if the sight of my son with the Cromwells overheats my body. When I approach their group, Colton and I don't look at each other. Probably best for the time being.

Max stands between his parents, arms linked to them. Judith has finished drying his tears and smoothing his hair, and his face now shows a half-smile of relief mixed with a trace of contrition.

"How long is he grounded?" I ask.

Max's improved demeanor disappears as if I have kicked him in the shins. I glance at Colton, who has turned his back.

"We're going home now," Judith says, as she pats her son's cheek. "All he needs is a good supper and a hot bath before he goes to bed."

I arch my eyebrows. "So you're not punishing his misbehavior?"

Max wails and Judith hugs him tighter, while Charlie charges to his defense. "Max didn't do anything. He just got swept away by Colton's–"

"Not according to Mike Avery," I say. "He got the story from the proprietor."

"Look, we agreed to pay for half, but we all know your son's the one who broke the vase."

Colton turns his head toward Charlie. "Art glass." At the corner of his mouth, I detect a hint of amusement.

A year ago, I would have climbed all over him for his insolence, but Colton's behavior since Jack's death has made me hesitant to discipline my own son. Maybe I have made a mistake in holding back.

As Charlie tucks his son into the back seat of their car, Judith touches my shoulder. "We'll talk later," she whispers.

They drive off. Without looking at Colton, I use my words like a fist. "Get in the car. No photography club, not today, not ever. Give me back the camera so I can return it."

"Too late." His face muscles harden into a smirk. "I threw the box and the receipt away."

"Then I'll keep it. You'll never be allowed to use it."

HATRED NOW HAS A PARTNER at my house: silence. After we arrive home, I confiscate the camera and tell him he is grounded indefinitely. Colton retreats to his room while I escape to my greenhouse. I flip the switch on the automatic sprinklers to the off position. Twice I count the trays of begonias and check the angel wings for roots. My mind fixes on repotting geraniums and clipping dead branches from a hanging basket of bougainvillea, and soon my breathing follows a rhythmic pattern.

By the time dusk approaches, the greenhouse has worked its magic. In complete calm, I return to my kitchen and open the refrigerator door. Nothing appeals to me, but I pull out some containers of leftover meatloaf and mashed potatoes. I dump French cut green beans from a can into a pot and turn on the gas burner.

Looking around my kitchen, I smile as I contemplate the improvements I've made to this house over the years. Mother left it to me, but she never managed to finish plans, much less a single project. She and Grandmother Mason would be proud of me, if they could only see it now.

When the aroma of garlic and pungent meat sauce fills the kitchen, I step into the entry and yell "Dinner!" up the stairway. No way will I knock on Colton's door. The calm has disappeared.

The food grows lukewarm before I decide to eat without him. I pick apart the slab of meatloaf. The green beans might as well be plastic sticks. If I had opened a bottle of wine before I started reheating the food, it would be half empty by now.

When I take my last bite, his bedroom door opens and his footsteps tread down the stairs toward the kitchen. I chew slowly while he pours a large glass of milk. My gaze follows his movements until he sits at the table across from me.

"Food's probably cold," I say, looking down at my plate.

"S'okay."

"Colton, you don't seem to understand." I study his face. "Your little stunts this past year have cost me a pretty penny, but they were accidents. You broke that vase on purpose."

"Art glass."

I want to smack him, but I pound my fist on the table instead. "Now it's in pieces, thanks to you, and I can't afford to reimburse Mr. Donatello right now."

"So what? Big Jack will pay for it."

"We don't take money from Big Jack to pay for anything. Besides he's in the hospital."

"Dad did."

"Did what?"

"He took money from Big Jack. Last year I heard him talking on the phone to someone about it. A lot of money."

"You heard wrong."

"I was standing right there listening. You were in the greenhouse or somewhere else."

"Regardless of what you *think* you heard, he's not writing checks for anything until—" I put down my fork and glare at him. "What makes you think Big Jack would ever foot the bill for your foolishness?"

"I overheard Officer Avery tell Mr. Donatello my grandfather would pay for it."

Despite my protest, doubt surrounds me like a wave of noxious air. "Officer Avery is fully aware of Big Jack's condition. How could Mike promise–" I blink. Which grandfather?

"Why don't you ask him?"

I decide to do just that. Right after I ask my mother what the hell she is up to now.

CHAPTER SEVEN

Colton and I finish out the workweek like programmed robots. By Saturday morning, we have hardly uttered more than a dozen words to each other. Prickly silence accompanies us as we strap on our seat belts and I start the engine.

When we arrive at Mr. Donatello's gallery, we park next to a limo with Louisiana plates, no doubt belonging to one of his fancy clients from New Orleans. Mike Avery stands in the hallway outside the office chatting with the owner. "Hey, right on time," he says with a smile.

Mr. Donatello retrieves a push broom from a storage closet and escorts Colton out the back door to the storeroom. Their voices exchange instructions and questions.

"Isn't Max coming?" I ask.

Mike shrugs. "He knows he has to be here now." He takes a few steps into the gallery's display area and stops in front of an oil painting of indeterminate subject. "How 'bout all this modern art? Sheesh, I couldn't hang some of this stuff in my house without getting nightmares."

"What *do* you like?"

"I dunno. Scenery, I guess. As long as I can tell a tree's a tree."

"Mike–"

Before I can continue, all five Cromwells burst through the front entrance as if responding to a fire alarm. "Here we come," Judith sings. "We aren't late, are we?"

Officer Avery points to the back door and they head toward the hallway like cattle through a chute. As they stomp past, the office door slams. Good for Mr. Donatello. He has learned his lesson.

"Mike, I need to ask you something."

He listens while I explain that Colton had no knowledge of my arrangement with Mr. Donatello. When I come to the part about the payment, he begins twirling his hat around one finger. I ask him to repeat his exact words to Colton about the money, but he demurs.

"You probably heard Big Jack offer to pay for Colton's accidents before," I say, "but I never accepted. Besides, he can't write any checks now. I've got his power of attorney, but Harlene has the checkbook. Why did you tell Colton his grandfather would pay for the damages?"

"I, uh . . . well, there might be another explanation."

"Hello, Sally," a voice calls from across the room. "Ooh, isn't that color divine on you?"

I spin around to see Angelique float into the gallery, glistening like molten gold. Behind her, denim-covered legs support a large framed painting that wobbles behind her through the door.

"I'm so glad you're here," she says. "I don't remember if I

told you Mr. Donatello ordered this one." Angelique points to the canvas, as her helper sets her painting at his feet. "This kind gentleman offered to carry it inside."

I all but jump as I recognize the man who grins at me.

"Hello again," he says.

Angelique leans toward him, her earrings swinging to and fro as if they can hypnotize. "Tell us your name, you darling young man."

"Brett Kennedy," I answer.

"Timing really is everything," Angelique says in her husky voice. If anyone else winked and gushed a cliché like that, I would gag. From her, it sounds natural, even intriguing.

The back door opens, and squeals and laughter blow in from the alley. Charlie enters the gallery, with six-year-old Maddie dangling from his hand. "The chain gang is hungry. Who wants a breakfast taco from Hot Crossed Buns?" He scans the room for takers. "Oh, hey, Brett." They pump hands. "I didn't realize you were joining our party."

"I'm just here to pick up a new piece of artwork." Brett shakes his head. "But today has started off very fortunate for me." When Brett smiles at me, Mike Avery's black leather gun belt creaks as he straightens his back.

"Oh, yes, let me introduce you to Officer Mike Avery, a good friend of our family." I can picture redness creeping up my neck and onto my face, spreading like an oil spill.

After they shake hands, Mike excuses himself. Angelique takes Brett's arm and mine to tour us around the gallery. By their nodding and pointing, it's evident he shares her wide knowledge of the art world. We stop in front of the painting Mike found so troublesome.

"This is the one I've purchased," Brett says. Pride covers his voice like a tarp.

Angelique purrs and twitches like a cat pawing a toy. "You have a marvelous eye, Brett." She turns toward me. "Sally, what do you think?"

Is she trying to induce me to approve of the painting or the purchaser? "Marvelous, especially in the eye of the beholder. Why don't I get Mr. Donatello for you? I think he's in the office."

I tap on the door and detect some rustling noises, and then metal clicks against metal. "Mr. Donatello?" I try the handle. The door is locked.

A man's voice answers. "He's not here."

My hand lingers on the doorknob, and I wait, all but certain I heard wrong.

It was still dark outside, but I woke up thirsty. I looked at the clock beside my bed. Clyde taught me how to tell time last month. The big hand was near six, just like me. That cut the hour in half, he said. The little hand was stuck between the two and three. Morning was hours away.

I tried to swallow, but my mouth was too dry. Aunt Mary was right. Clyde and I shouldn't have eaten all that popcorn before bedtime.

The door to my bedroom was shut, and I crawled up on a chair to unlock it from the inside and crossed the hall to the bathroom. The drinking glass on the lavatory sparkled like crystal in the moonlight. I pulled up the little step stool so I could reach the faucet and filled the glass. I stood on tiptoe to peek at myself in the mirror. The light was not bright enough to check my front teeth, which were getting loose. After two full gulps, I swished my mouth, gargled, and tossed the leftover water down the drain.

When I reached the doorway, I didn't move. A door opened down the hall, but no one closed it. I remembered the rules. Always keep your bedroom door shut at night, Daddy told me.

Maybe someone was too sleepy and forgot. I passed Aunt Mary's room, where she was probably already tucked in tight behind her closed door. She always poked the side edges of her blankets under the mattress, so she wouldn't fall out of bed, I supposed.

The hall looked different in the dark, with too many places for someone to hide. I stopped and turned around, ready to run back to bed. Silly me. Daddy and Clyde wouldn't let anyone scary into our house. I turned back and kept walking.

Now I spotted the problem farther down the dark hall. A pale beam of light shined from the doorway to my mother's room. I loved her bedroom, with its watery blue walls and silk comforter floating like a raft on her huge bed. Whenever I bounced on her bed, it was like a beautiful lake, calm and smooth, unless she had been cleaning out her closets. Then there was no room for me because she tossed her clothes and shoes all over the bed and the floor, and later the maids had to come in and put everything back.

Mother might need my help or just a drink. She didn't want any popcorn earlier, but she could have gotten thirsty like me. Maybe she pressed the buzzer during the night and the maids hadn't come yet. The buzzer looked like a doorbell connected to the wall by a wire and sat on her bedside table. I pushed it once just for fun, and a few minutes later Mrs. Gussmann came running into the room. I didn't get in trouble, but she warned me never to do it again. Mother laughed, although I could tell Mrs. Gussmann meant business.

I peeked into Mother's room. With the moonlight behind him, a very tall man cast a shadow across her bed. She was sound asleep, so I kept extra quiet. He picked up her medicine bottle from her bedside table and emptied the pills into his palm. As he counted them, I recognized my father's steady movements, but I couldn't see his face.

The doorknob was cold against my cheek, so I covered it with my hand and hung on, resting my chin in the crook of my arm. My eyelids got heavy watching him replace the pills and set the bottle on the table. When Daddy turned on the lamp by her bed, my eyes popped open.

Mother didn't move, not even an inch. He stared at her blonde hair, grown long enough to cover her pillow like a shawl. He picked up a thick length of it and twirled it around his fingers, then let it fall, one strand at a time. The way the light shined through it, her hair looked like spun gold.

As Daddy twisted sideways to turn off the light, Clyde's big knife dangled from his left hand. He tossed it and caught the handle mid-air in his right hand, as if it weighed no more than one of Mother's slippers. He pulled on her hair again and raised the knife, then cried out words I couldn't understand. He cut off a thick piece of her hair and threw it on the floor behind him.

I gasped and stepped backward, yelling, "No, Daddy! No!" I covered my face with my hands and felt tears on my cheeks. The door slammed, and I was left standing alone in the dark hallway. Only the sound of my screams broke the peaceful night.

Moments later, Mrs. Gussmann put her arm around my shoulder and pulled me into her marshmallow of a bosom, all but smothering me. "Gracious me, what happened?" she said.

Mother's bedroom door opened and I grabbed for Mrs. Gussmann's waist and took hold of the sash of her robe. I sputtered and sobbed, but she couldn't make sense of my effort to tell her what I had seen.

My father's voice took over. "She's had a nightmare. Will you tend to her, please, Mrs. Gussmann?"

"Of course, sir," she said. "Come along with me, Sally. We'll sit in the rocking chair until you go back to sleep."

Hanging on tightly, I kept my eyes closed, and she guided me down the hallway back to my room as if I were blind. "You're getting too heavy now for me to carry," she cooed. After shushing me several times by saying I had a bad dream, she sang lullabies and rocked me until I fell asleep.

The next morning I woke up in my own bed to the sound of a drill. Outside my door, a man with a leather tool belt around his waist was attaching a plastic box to the wall. It resembled the buzzer on Mother's bedside table. How did he expect me to reach it from here? "Good day to you, miss," he said as he nodded.

I padded down the hallway, with a heavy feeling left over

from my nightmare. The door to my mother's room stood open. One maid was stripping the linens from the bed while the other ran a carpet sweeper back and forth near the bedside table.

The first one shook out a pillowcase. "Why would she do this to herself, the nut ball?"

"You just answered your own question," said the other.

I waited in the doorway. "Where's Mother?" I asked. They both jumped at the sound of my voice.

"Gone to the hairdresser," said the first one.

"Yeah, she's given herself a new bob," said the other.

"Was that his name?" And they both giggled.

I closed the door. There was no point in asking anyone what happened. Nobody paid any attention to me anyway.

Right where I stand, I want to pound on the door until the owner of that voice emerges from the office. The words -- no, the *sound* of them -- push my heart into a spin. I try to move, but my feet won't take orders. I let my hand linger on the doorknob, willing the person on the other side to show himself.

Mother or angel, whoever you are, work your magic. Help me. Make him open the door.

The power of the impulse fades and I step backward. The person in the office stands up and moves against the door, as if listening for me. I can hear him breathing.

"Thank you," I say, as I walk away. Even if I admit to myself I recognize the voice, I'm not waiting to find out if I'm correct.

Once Mr. Donatello comes in from the alley, Angelique and Brett keep him occupied, too busy for me to hand him my first installment. By the time Charlie returns from the diner, Mike has set up a makeshift table in the alley and we eat buffet-style. At Charlie's insistence, Brett and Angelique join us.

Judith and Charlie supervise Max and Colton's return to work as I clear away the mess from the meal. When I pick up the garbage bag, Mike offers to carry it to the dumpster.

"Thanks, I need to find Mr. Donatello anyway."

"He's inside. Try the office."

I smile at Mike and shake my head. "I already did. He's not . . . someone else is in there."

Mike's eyes widen. "Did you see who it is?"

"Mystery client, I guess," I call over my shoulder. "He wouldn't open the door." I feel the upheaval in my heart again when I pass the office.

I locate Mr. Donatello in the front of the gallery. Brett and Angelique have propped several paintings together against the wall where the light shines brightest.

"Here's my first payment, sir." I hold out the check. "I appreciate your cooperation."

He holds his hands up and flutters them as if shooing a fly. "No, no. It's all been taken care of."

"Who paid you?" My voice is loud enough for Angelique

and Brett to turn and look at me.

"I . . . I cannot say." He takes out a handkerchief and mops his forehead. "Please," he says to Angelique, "go get Officer Avery."

"Mike paid you?" I circle him like a panther stalking prey.

He moves a sculptured figurine from its pedestal to the floor, and then scoots it behind a cabinet. When he backs up a few paces, I follow, cornering him.

"Mike doesn't have that much money," I say. "Who paid my share?"

Angelique returns with Mike and the Cromwells. Mike's face looks stern, while Judith and Charlie stare at me, evidently puzzled by my loud voice.

"What going on?" I ask Mike. "Have you taken up money laundering?"

"Sally, someone is looking out for you, now that Jack and Big Jack–"

"What does this have to do with either of them? I can take care of myself. Always have." I poke him in the chest. "You went behind my back. Who? I want a name!"

He sighs and looks at his loafers, then glances toward the limo parked outside.

I whirl around just in time to see a well-dressed man wait for the uniformed driver to open the passenger door on the far side of the limo. He appears as dark-haired and handsome as I remember. The years have not lined his face. I watch my father duck his head and climb into the back seat.

My heart starts spinning once more, rolling through a sea of emotions. Caught between the urge to make him face my accusations and the exhaustion from keeping my hostility well fed, I can't tell which way to turn. Even if I might want to start fresh with him, there is nothing I can do about it. Mother is no help to me at all.

My feet might as well have grown roots through the gallery floor. I stand motionless until the limo backs out of the parking space and heads north on Mason Boulevard. It carries the one man I despise more than Big Jack. I can picture my father, seated in the back on comfortable padded leather, counting his millions and congratulating himself on how he manipulated my life again.

Does he always have a hand in something involving loss and death? My mother and I have endured enough. Why doesn't she send him a message to leave me alone?

Angelique puts a hand on my shoulder. "Sally, are you feeling all right?" She hugs me sideways and gestures for Brett to bring me a drink of water.

The moment I shake my head and shrug off her consoling touch, my ingratitude smacks me. "I'm fine. Can we speak later?"

I paste on a smile and turn my attention to Mike Avery. Better if I take a few deep breaths first, otherwise I'll do more than poke him in the chest. When I look at Mr. Donatello, he takes a step backward. "Sir, may we use your office?"

He mops his brow with his linen handkerchief and waves us toward the hallway, as if he is a maitre d' seating his favorite customers. Perhaps nothing in his office needs protection.

I scowl at Mike and turn to stomp down the hallway.

Mike scampers to catch up with me. "Sally, Nate only wants–"

"In here." I yank the office door open and march inside. A mixture of cigar smoke and fresh carnations lingers, and my father's presence twines around my senses like ivy. I struggle not to feel like a helpless child.

A pair of large overstuffed Queen Annes, exactly the right size for my six-foot-four father, partner with two smaller straight-backed chairs. Mike waits in the doorway until I select a wooden chair, not comfortable but also recently unoccupied.

"Well?" I cross my arms and wait.

Mike drops to the edge of one of the Queen Annes and lays his hat upside down on the marble coffee table. Leaning forward, he gently rubs his palms on his khaki knees. "After Jack died last year, Nate asked me to let him know if you or Colton ever needed anything."

"So you've been ratting on my son and me to my father?" I sit up straight and glare at his face, almost wishing I could blister his skin.

"He doesn't want to interfere, just help out."

"How?"

"By relieving you of the necessity to pay for certain things."

"What things?"

"Colton's accidents, mostly. And the damages."

I stand up and pace toward the antique roll-top desk against the opposite wall. "So whenever Colton gets into trouble, you call my father and he sends a check to cover the cost."

As I turn to face Mike, he leans back into the folds of the chair. I tick off the damages on my fingers. "He paid for some guy's fence, another man's roof, the ice cream parlor, and the cabin at the church summer camp. Everywhere

Colton gets a little destructive, Daddy steps in to fix it. Buy people off."

"Also the sprained ankle." His Adam's apple bounces up and down. "He paid for most of the hospital bill."

"He owns the land under our little hospital and sits on the board. I guess they'll take his money." I return to the wooden chair.

"Are you even madder at me now?"

"Is that what you're worried about?" I sit down and fold my hands in my lap, trying to remember where my fury belongs. "I'm not angry with you, but I want you to promise communication with my father will stop. Concerning Colton and me, that is."

Mike takes his time explaining how and why he owes allegiance to my father. "My mother always claimed she couldn't have raised me without Nate's care and protection. She was a widow, you know." The late Mrs. Avery worked in an insurance office, her long-term employment procured by my father's influence.

I study the man across from me, near my same age. Tall, dark hair, no extra weight, just like my father. "Mike, are we related?"

He laughs. "No, but I wouldn't mind if we were."

I detect a slight blush on his cheeks, but his tanned olive skin makes it difficult to be certain.

"I found out my own father died a few years after I started college," Mike says. "You knew him, better than I did. Clyde Farraday."

Since their days together laboring in the cotton mill and all through my father's climb to millionaire status, Clyde Farraday had served as best friend, bodyguard, major-domo, and probably hit man. Throughout my father's business empire, Clyde passed down word from Nate and it stood for absolute law. He was tough as ox hide, scarred from knife fights, fearless down to his toes, and loyal as a Bluetick Coonhound.

At the sound of his name, I don't know which tightens up more, my lungs or my throat. I'd give anything to see Clyde Farraday again. "So that's where you got all those cute freckles. Did your mother confess before she died that Clyde was your father?"

"Nate told me. Last year, when all this mess started." He strokes the stubble on his chin. "Sally, may I ask you something?"

I nod.

"Why don't you ever see Nate? What did he do to make you dislike him so much?"

If I share with Mike Avery what I repeated to myself a thousand times, will it ease the hurt that sticks in my heart like a splinter? Or will it fan the hot coals of my hatred? Either way, I have no control over how I feel about my father, but I know the pain can't get any worse by answering Mike's questions.

"When I was younger than Colton, he sent my mother away, and then she died. He could have kept her at home, where I needed her. He hired housekeepers, nurses, drivers, nannies, always a huge staff. Okay, she was a little *touched*, even manic at times, but she died of a broken heart in that hospital, I know it. He might as well have killed her."

When Mike reaches for my hand, I feel the splinter in my heart move. Maybe it will work its way out all by itself.

CHAPTER EIGHT

Brett loads his new painting into his vehicle and departs the gallery. Within twenty minutes, Angelique says her goodbyes as well. Mike leaves to begin his afternoon rounds, and I return to the alley to help supervise. By one o'clock, Mr. Donatello decides Max and Colton have fulfilled their obligation, and the Cromwells and I thank him for his generous treatment of our sons. As we stroll out together with their noisy brood, I decline their offer of a trip to the movies. No fun allowed since Colton is grounded until further notice.

Colton and I climb into my car. I let the keys dangle in the ignition without starting the engine. "Let's go visit Big Jack." I want to see if that shameless old man has the guts to admit what he's done to Jack and hope the sight of his grandson will make him feel twice as guilty.

Ready to witness an explanation, I drive to the hospital. "Yesterday Big Jack showed signs of improvement, but you'll notice his appearance is slightly altered. If he isn't awake, we don't have to stay."

Colton shrugs. "Guess we'll see."

I should quit expecting more reaction from Colton. If it's his way of punishing me, I can't figure out what I've done to deserve it. Silence doesn't always feel better than anger.

The head nurse at the ICU station informs us Big Jack has been moved to a regular room. "We don't call the families. Perhaps his doctor's office tried to reach you."

"I'm not sure he has one." I blink several times. "But maybe I should look into getting one of those new telephone answering machines anyway."

She snaps the hinge on her clipboard. "Pretty expensive, aren't they?"

On the elevator, only the hum of the cables accompanies our silence. When the door opens, I point to a sign on the opposite wall. "Six thirty-eight, to the right." Down the hall a short distance, I push the door open and stand back while a Candy Striper passes us carrying a tray. "He's all yours," she says.

Big Jack reclines at an angle in the bed, his bandaged left arm hooked up to an IV. Even with the extra swaddling of white surgical pads, he appears pale and shrunken.

Seeing him with his eyes closed makes me push my hostility aside. If I'd found him sitting up after a big lunch, watching sports on TV or flirting with the nurses, I would confront him with a list of his sins and ask how he could justify his final abuse to his son, harsh enough to break Jack's spirit forever. Perhaps it's better that Colton doesn't see anything except an injured grandfather.

"Big Jack, are you awake? We've come to see you, Colton and I."

He opens his eyes and his gaze jumps around the ceiling. "Eh?"

I touch the sheet covering his ankle. "Here we are. How are

you feeling?"

Big Jack frowns and stares at me. His face muscles twitch, as if he's trying to keep his mouth closed. After several seconds, he says, "Oh, Sally, it's you."

Considering everything he's endured in the past few days, it's unrealistic of me to expect to hear his usual "Sally-Girl." The bump on his head provides the most color anywhere above his neck, and I wonder if the pain medicine works well enough. Maybe repetition will help his alertness. "I've brought Colton." I nudge my son forward in range of Big Jack's view.

"Who?" He closes his eyes again.

"We should go," Colton whispers.

I take a few steps closer, until I stand even with Big Jack's head. "Don't worry." I lean over next to his ear. "I'm taking care of your business now until you recover. I'll handle the lease contract and everything else."

His eyes pop open. "Sally?" They roll back in his head before settling on a framed print on the wall. "I . . . something important to tell you."

"Yes?" Poised to hear him admit his treachery, I stand up straight and glance at my son. Colton stares at Big Jack's face, hard enough to bore a hole. He looks away when my father-in-law reaches for my hand.

Big Jack takes several labored breaths, as if gathering his strength. "Tell Jack to stop by to see me on his way home from work."

As I gasp, Colton bolts from the room.

"Go back to sleep," I say and leave.

Saint Trixie, this guy is yours for the taking.

ON THE DRIVE HOME from the hospital, I anticipate Big Jack's questions to increase as his condition improves. Since his fall has rattled his brain about Jack's death, no telling what else he might not remember. Armed with power of attorney, I can delve into his business dealings over Harlene's objections and hope for answers elsewhere.

Unless his mind can knit itself back together like his bones, he will be no help in reconstructing the events of Jack's last days. I can demand an explanation for Big Jack's sudden sale of his business, but what good will it do? If they argued and one of them stomped out, Big Jack might be unable, or unwilling, to relive those moments. I dread breaking the terrible news to him a second time that his only son is dead and probably committed suicide.

Caught in the middle, I can't prove Jack's death was unintentional without getting more information, but Big Jack will likely tell me something to confirm a motive for suicide. Did Jack kill himself because his son-of-a-bitch father sold the business out from under him? I pray I can get the whole story from another source.

Colton's voice breaks into my thoughts. "Do you blame Big Jack for Dad's death?"

"Why do you ask such a silly question?"

"You've been griping out loud for the last two minutes."

"What?"

"You shouldn't speak that way about Big Jack."

"Colton, there are things you don't know about Dad and your grandfather. I'm trying to sort out how Big Jack reacted after Dad tried to do something new with the business."

"You always make everything too complicated. Can't you just leave all of us alone?"

I feel like slamming on the brakes, just for the jolt it will give him. "Look, I have to find out why your father died. I *know* it wasn't suicide."

He snorts. "Can you prove it?"

"Not yet, but I'm getting closer to the truth."

"And you're driving everyone else crazy."

I suck in my breath and hold it. No matter how much Colton or anyone else might try to persuade me, I can't give up. No one will go crazy by my search for the truth. I am *not* my mother.

Once we arrive at home, it occurs to me if Jack had a secret contract drawn up for Brett Kennedy, the last place he'd leave it would have been the store or the office. He wasn't stupid enough to risk that Harlene or his father might see it.

After a quick snack, Colton withdraws to his room, giving me freedom to explore Jack's desk. He'd never been much of a correspondent, not even birthday cards to immediate family. Jack didn't save much paper either, but I pray to uncover documents or even helpful notes.

In less than a week, everyone in my family has gotten angry with me for asking questions about Jack. Colton is partly right. Things are complicated, but through no fault of mine.

Last spring, I'd searched his desk to retrieve property tax records and his checking account statements. Why hadn't I emptied out his desk and gotten rid of it? Or discarded everything in his office? But then, I never would have found the appointment book a few days ago.

The third drawer held what few files he kept, but nothing else except a handful of receipts and the expired insurance card for his truck. As I slide the hanging file folders toward the back, I notice a paper lying flat against the bottom of the drawer.

Saint Trixie, what kind of disorganized boy did you raise?

Without daring to blink, I turn the paper over and shuffle through legal-size pages stapled together. In several lines of the contract, Kennedy's name appears as a major investor. The proposal shows intention to relocate the sporting goods business to one of Kennedy's warehouses in a commercial area undergoing a facelift, situated between Mason's Crossing and Austin. Contracts with athletic departments of several school districts and universities provide the basis for the marketing plans. On page four, Charlie Cromwell's name pops up as the representative of the local bank to provide any necessary financing.

The last sheet contains lines for signatures, but no one can complete it with that big black "X" streaked through the page. At the bottom Jack had scrawled, "Call Nate Wallace."

According to Brett Kennedy, Big Jack called him immediately after Brett refused my husband's proposal. Easy to imagine how my father-in-law had learned what Jack planned. His office walls had ears, eyes, and tentacles, all named Harlene. Once she disclosed Jack's plot, Big Jack took his revenge for his son's disloyalty.

At first, Brett showed wisdom to turn them both down. Who would want to get caught in a family crossfire?

I rub my forehead. I can picture my husband telling his

father to stuff it up his rear end sideways, like he'd wanted to for years, but he had no safety net in place, no signed contract. When confronted by his father, Jack must have spilled his ideas like a bag of pinto beans.

Adding my father to the equation makes it more difficult to interpret. I fan the pages of the contract again until I reread Nate Wallace's name on the last page. It's enough to make me drop the contract on the desk.

Now that Mike Avery has assumed the role of white knight, I wonder if he knows about Brett Kennedy. When I introduced them to each other at the art gallery at few hours ago, they gave no indication they had already met.

I stop and chastise myself. So many names make it sound like a conspiracy theory. News travels fast in Mason's Crossing. It won't help to contact my lawyer or my pastor. I need to speak to someone who knows all the players, but can remain neutral.

I pick up the phone and dial.

"Of course, dear girl," Angelique answers. "Come right over."

"I want to get your impression of Brett Kennedy."

"That will be quite easy. He's sitting right here on my terrace."

For Angelique to give him the time of her day, he must be a well-mannered Southern gentleman, for starters. That much I had observed myself. But for her to invite him over probably means neutrality is already a lost cause.

Upstairs, I knock on Colton's door. No answer, but thumping vibrates the walls. I rap again harder and ease the door open, just enough to peek around the edge. With his back to me, he reclines on his bed, his bare feet propped against the wall. No wonder he can't hear me through his headphones, with "Eli's Coming" at full throttle.

Last year, I would have tousled his hair and he would have laughed, but I can't risk such affection now. The time has come for me to assert my parental authority. I cross my wrists behind my back and step over the pile of discarded clothes and books until I turn to face him. Like Big Jack, he lies there with his eyes closed, but he's enraptured by the joy of the music, and I hate to break the spell.

My heart is heavy. Everybody in Mason's Crossing knew how well I handled the death of a parent, but I would have given anything to save Colton from learning the same excruciating lesson.

Before I can shake him by the knee, he opens his eyes and stares at me. No surprised expression, as if he anticipated my presence. I tap my ear, and he pulls one side of the headphones toward the top of his head.

"I'm going out for a short visit to Angelique's. Can you manage to stay put until I get back?"

"I don't drive, remember?"

As if I am ready to draw a pistol, I shove my hands on my hips. "Why don't you get started on your homework? Isn't something due on Monday?"

"It's spring break, remember?"

"Well, try to do something productive while I'm gone." I turn to go, but spin around. "By the way, I found something else that might help prove Dad didn't kill himself."

I can save my breath. He puts his headphones back on and closes his eyes. His right foot thumps the wall like a bass drum.

Our interview is over, and I am dismissed. The little shit.

Fuming all the way, I drive to Angelique's. Two vehicles, one I don't recognize, sit parked in the driveway. The other belongs to Raúl, her occasional live-in restaurateur boyfriend. As I enter the front door, he is putting on a chef's coat. "Off to the kitchen. Busy night ahead." He flits past me, jingling his car keys.

"Of course, it's Saturday. Good luck." I wander through the house and find Angelique and Brett on the terrace, a tray of margaritas on the table near them. They huddle against the far wall, heads leaning together. Angelique's earrings swing to and fro, close enough to graze Brett's cheek. His hand grips her elbow.

"Don't say anything to Raúl," Angelique says.

I hesitate. Do I detect electricity in the air, or is it my imagination? When they see me, they both stand erect and smile.

"What's up?" I try to sound cheerful.

Angelique holds out a bowl. "Try some of Raúl's new mango salsa, too. Just the right combination of sweet and spicy to sweep you off your feet." She gives Brett what I interpret as a meaningful glance, and I'm not sure if she means food or men.

"Talented guy," Brett says.

I hope my face doesn't register surprise, as I look from one to the other. Maybe Raúl should skip the restaurant and see what's cooking here.

By patting the cushions, Angelique chooses our seats, placing Brett in between us. When she disappears to the kitchen for more drinks, I turn toward him. "I've been thinking about what you told me the other day."

"Regarding your husband?"

"Also his father." I set down my glass. "And my father."

"I'm sorry if I made it difficult for you."

"Not at all." I take a deep breath. "You told me Nate Wallace contacted you the same day you refused to buy my father-in-law's business. Big Jack never would have revealed his intentions to anyone. How did my father know to call you?"

"He didn't call me. He–"

Is he trying to trick me, or is my mind doing the job instead? "But you said–"

"Nate Wallace dropped by my office, same as you did. Very impressive gentleman, I must say."

My father in Austin last year? Why didn't I notice the sudden drop in air pressure or temperature that always seems to accompany his presence? "So nobody told you anything about my father?" I ask.

He shakes his head. "It was the first time we had ever set eyes on each other. He's not an easy man to forget."

Brett Kennedy is not the only man who ever thought so.

I stretched out on the floor in the downstairs parlor, turning the pages of my picture book. I could make out several letters and sounds, but not read whole words yet. Aunt Mary sat directly in the afternoon sunlight and knitted another wool lap robe. She'd made lots of them by now, all brown and beige or dark green. She knitted them big enough to be blankets and sent them to the USO office for people she calls "our brave men in uniform." Even though Daddy kept telling her it has been over for several months now, she worried about the war in Europe. Aunt Mary didn't want anyone to get sick while they were still away from home. But if they did, she wanted them to have one of her blankets so they'd feel better.

I turned the page and giggled at the picture of a dog and a cat riding in a pirate ship hanging from a hot air balloon. The dog wore an eye patch and the cat had on a black hat in the shape of a triangle. They didn't know a unicorn was flying under them, about to pop the balloon.

Mrs. Gussmann entered the room. "Excuse me, Miss Wallace. There's a man to see Mr. Nate."

"Someone here?" Aunt Mary put down her knitting needles and I sat up straight. We didn't often get visitors to the house.

"Who?" I asked.

"A . . . gentleman who says he knows Mr. Nate, um, from the early days."

Aunt Mary didn't like to speak to strangers. "Can't you just give him the office address?"

"I would, but he seems like, well . . . with that one eye . . ."

I closed my book and stood up. I hoped to catch a glimpse of a real pirate. "What does he look like?"

Mrs. Gussmann's voice dropped to a whisper. "Like he could use a meal. And a shave."

Aunt Mary picked up her knitting again. "Please offer him

something to eat and send him on his way. He sounds like a bum."

"That's what I thought at first, until he asked about you." She nodded like she knew a secret. "He mentioned 'Nate's sister, Mary Wallace.' Those exact words."

Aunt Mary tossed the knitting into her basket next to the chair and stood up. "Me? How does he know my name?"

I thought maybe the man was a magician, which was just as good as a pirate. No one from anywhere ever knew Aunt Mary. According to Mother, she came to us right before I was born with nothing but a ratty old suitcase and a bad case of the sniffles. I turned to Aunt Mary and tugged on her arm. "Let's go ask him."

I followed her into the entry hall, peeking around from behind her skirt. You can't be too careful around pirates. Besides, I'd been told to let the adults do the talking, but Aunt Mary wasn't very chatty. A man with red hair stood near the front door, looking up at the chandelier. Before he noticed us, he gave a low whistle.

I almost crashed into the back of her when Aunt Mary stopped at the edge of the Persian carpet. As I stepped out from behind her, she put her hanky to her mouth. "May I help you?"

The man stood at attention like he was going to salute. Aunt Mary stiffened when he walked toward us and held out his hand. "Pleased to meet you," he said. "I'm Clyde Farraday."

Since Aunt Mary didn't move, I reached out and shook his hand, the way Mother had taught me. He looked like a nice pirate.

When he grinned, his gold front tooth shone like a nightlight. "You must be . . .?"

"I'm Sally Mason Wallace."

"Nate never told me he has a daughter."

The redheaded man really was a magician, as well as a pirate. How else would he have known who my daddy was?

"Mr. Farraday, is there something I can do for you?" Aunt Mary sounded tired.

"Uh, yes, ma'am. I was hoping to find Nate at home."

"Did he know you were coming?"

"No, I just got released."

Aunt Mary gasped. "From where?"

I looked down at his boots. There was a hole in one of the toes, but no sock poked through.

"The Navy." Clyde winked at me with his good eye and I grinned at him. I couldn't wait to ask him about his adventures, especially the big scar on his face, probably from when another pirate tried to cut off his ear and poked him in the eye. He looked from side to side and shook his head. Maybe he didn't care for the new paintings Mother told the man from the store to hang in the entry hall.

"My brother is still tending to business, since his work day isn't quite over yet."

I thought Aunt Mary didn't like the man because he didn't have a job like Daddy.

She turned her head and patted the back of her tight little bun. "Perhaps you'd like to call on him at his office."

"I'd be glad to, 'cept I got no car."

Aunt Mary called Mrs. Gussmann into the entry and asked her where the chauffeur was. Gone to run errands for Mrs. Wallace, she said. Aunt Mary seemed disappointed.

"I don't mind waiting," Clyde offered.

"Inside?" She sniffed and glanced around, like she was trying to find some clean place to sit. She shouldn't worry. Clyde's pants already had picked up enough dirt so he wouldn't mind sitting anywhere.

"I'm used to being outdoors. How about I hol' up on the front porch 'til the master returns?" He chuckled. "It's where I left my duffel bag anyway."

Aunt Mary looked like she might faint. After Mrs. Gussmann closed the front door behind our strange visitor, Aunt Mary and I returned to the front parlor. Pretty soon, her medicine made her sleepy again and I slipped out of the room. There was enough sunlight left for me to see the outline of Clyde's head, resting against the window.

When I opened the front door and went out on the porch, he sat up. "How're you, little lady?"

We talked for a while, and Clyde told me things I had never heard before about my father. "Your papa was a skinny teenager, but he worked real hard. He could lift a bale of cotton twice his weight. Well, almost, anyway."

"Did you know my mother, too?"

"Nah, it was before he got married."

I asked him about being a pirate and hoped he would talk about his adventures sailing the ocean.

He looked up and down the porch and said, "Piracy must pay pretty well."

Before we had a chance to get to know each other better, tires screeched in the driveway. My father jumped out of his car and ran across the lawn. I wondered why Daddy was so happy to see me, but he didn't even notice me.

"Clyde, is it really you?"

"After all these years, here I am, like I promised."

They shook hands as if they were having a wrestling match, and then my father did something I'd never seen him do with anyone. He put his arms around Clyde's shoulders and gave him a big hug, almost lifting his feet off the floor. Then I knew Clyde really was our extra special friend. I was glad he'd come, but I also wished my daddy would hug me that way.

What silly smiles. As they slapped each other on the back, they headed for the front door. Clyde must have been a really good magician because he made Daddy laugh.

Maybe he also made me disappear.

I have other questions for Brett Kennedy. "Who told my father about Big Jack's offer?"

Brett sighs and peers up at the clouds. "I'm afraid my answer will make it worse for you, and I don't want . . ." He runs his fingers through his thinning hair before he looks me in the face. "Your husband did. Look, if you want to learn any more details, you'll have to ask your father."

My erect posture gives way as if he had dropped a heavy weight on me. I don't know whether to laugh or cry. Jack's struggle to be free of his father led him to throw himself into Nate Wallace's web. My husband wasn't a brilliant man, but this move scaled new heights of stupidity. How could he do that to me?

Angelique sashays across the terrace with a full pitcher and an ice bucket on a tray. She sets the tray on the table next to Brett. "Have you invited her yet?"

I sit up straight. "Invited me where?"

Brett grins and wipes the back of his neck, even though a light breeze cools the terrace. "The Pioneer Festival in Mason's Crossing starts tomorrow. I know it's kind of late, but I wanted to ask you to come with me. I bought VIP tickets and a whole table of seating."

He might as well be speaking Mongolian. I must appear puzzled, because Angelique repeats my name, but I can't answer her.

"A date, Sally," she says. "He's asking you on a date."

Widowed for one year and three days, and now a man I hardly know asks me out. What would my mother say?

I can almost hear her telling me to concentrate on Colton's behavior and solve the unanswered questions about Jack's death. She assures me I don't have to go out with Brett Kennedy to get his help.

Temptation steps into my path. Too many years have passed since I spent time with a man who is attentive and intelligent. Maybe Brett's wealth will make him interesting instead of conceited. I can overlook that fact that he isn't taller than I or as handsome as Jack. Is it too much to expect that he will turn out to be a good dancer?

Before I answer, I point a finger from Angelique to Brett and back. "What about the two of you? I saw you together just now, as if . . ."

Brett frowns and shoots Angelique a questioning look.

She lofts her throaty laugh and shakes her head. "I tripped on my high-heels and Brett caught my arm before I fell. Can't go around spilling drinks on my own terrace, now can I?"

"It would be best to tell Sally the rest of it, don't you think?"

I stare at her margarita glass and wonder if she could possibly have drunk more than she realized, like last Christmas when she stood under the mistletoe for an entire three hours, sipping mulled wine between smooches from everyone who attended her open house reception. She spent all the next day in bed, her feet as hung over as her head. Now I check for extra brightness in her eyes and cheeks too rosy.

With a sly grin, Angelique arches one eyebrow. "You know how handsome men make me swoon."

I've seen her react that way often enough, but her adjective lets Brett off the hook. While not unattractive, his looks can be described as average in every way.

"Angelique suffered a dizzy spell," Brett says. "She almost fainted."

I stand up and move next to Angelique. Silly to think I can protect her. My breathing grows shallow, as if there isn't enough air to go around.

"What will you darlings wear to the Pioneer Festival dance?" Angelique pulls a cigarette from her gold case and holds it near her cheek between two artfully cocked fingers. "The invitation reads 'cowboy chic,' but that term is an oxymoron."

I touch her arm. "You told Brett not to mention something to Raúl."

She bends her head toward Brett as he flicks and steadies her lighter. During the first long exhale, she smiles as if she's indulging a child. "He'll only worry. And you shouldn't fret either. I merely stood up too quickly, that's all."

Despite our protests, Angelique insists she doesn't need to go for a check-up. She steers the conversation back to the motion on the floor, as she puts it. After a few minutes of her wheedling and cajoling, I accept Brett's invitation, and before I leave, we settle on a time for Sunday afternoon.

In the distraction of the moment, I forget my purpose was to get Angelique's impression of Brett Kennedy. His concern for her health and safety, plus his hesitancy to reveal circumstances I might find uncomfortable, gives me enough insight to relax. It is only one date, in front of everyone in Mason's Crossing.

I belt out "Country Roads" with John Denver on the radio all the way home, until I turn the corner to my street. I wonder how Colton will take it when I break the news that some stranger will be escorting me to our town's biggest social event. One my family's history makes possible.

Why can't I try to rewrite my past and weave a new future at the same time? *Mother, are you listening?*

The first opportunity to tell Colton of my Sunday plans comes at the dinner table. It is what any responsible single parent would do.

"So what?" Colton takes another bite of grilled chicken.

"You don't mind I have a date with–"

"I told you I don't care. Do what you like."

"I just wanted to be sure you didn't object."

"It's your life." He carries his dishes to the sink. "I'm going with the Cromwells anyway. Max and I are running the ring toss booth for the church youth fellowship."

"You're supposed to be grounded–"

Colton shoots me a quick glance. He looks away so fast, I can't tell if I read fear or the usual anger in his eyes.

"–but I can make an exception, since it's for the church."

"As long as I don't have fun, right?"

How much trouble can he get into with all those friends and neighbors around? Mike Avery's presence should provide a big deterrent, if nothing else.

"It's your last chance for a while. Have all the fun you want."

Maybe we both will. We can certainly stand a little playtime for a change.

CHAPTER NINE

Folks in Mason's Crossing always go all out for the Pioneer Festival. Usually I accept a major volunteer role, but the planning committee chair had given me a lighter load this time. Before Christmas, I made a few phone calls to ask the local wholesale nurseries to supply potted plants for decorations, and my responsibilities ended. No one took me seriously when I said I'd rather be busier.

As we enter Mason's Park, I give Brett the lowdown on what to expect. The pavilions offer booths with local dishes, drinks, games, and prizes. Children can watch puppet shows or last century's craft demonstrations while licking something that drips onto their shirts. Women in period calico costumes churn butter and stitch quilts. In mock street gun battles, gray-uniformed Rebel soldiers fire at Yankees and carpetbaggers to remind us of our survivor roots.

Judith and Charlie commandeer the section with the ring toss and other carnival attractions. Colton seems absorbed in hanging stuffed animals from the rafters, while Max sets up wooden pins on a table against the back tent flap. The line of children waiting their turn at the booth stands five deep and growing. Brett and I wave as we amble past. I can tell he makes an effort to downplay his limp. So much for the dancing.

Brett's VIP tickets include a buggy ride along the path around the lake. He chooses sunset for the cooler air and tucks the woolen blanket around me, keeping his hands discreetly out of my lap. He tells me about his parents and their farm, and how he learned to shoe horses and milk cows. His mother has been gone two decades, and his father died a few years ago. When Brett could afford it, he bought his dad a tractor. "My father never owned one before. He always had to rent from the neighbors."

As we come around the last bend by the lakeshore, the strains of electric guitar waft across the water. The band is setting up on the stage by the dance floor. I gaze at the stage lights reflected on the lake and try not to appear wistful.

I feel a twinge of envy, not for the tractor, but for his opportunity to give his parent something he needed. "Your father would have been proud of you, I'm sure."

"He owned the land to begin with, bought with his sweat. I simply stumbled, almost literally, into the petroleum underneath it." He pulls the reins until the horse stops in front of the attendant, and then takes my hand to help me down from the buggy. My pulse quickens as we stroll toward the dance floor. The twinkle lights in the trees come on right as we sit at the table he reserved ringside.

"Are we too close to the band?" he asks.

"If you're not sitting in front of the speakers, you won't go deaf, at least not right away," says a man's voice behind us.

Mike Avery, dressed in long johns, a Hawaiian shirt, and

khaki slacks, leans over the back of a folding chair. Brett invites him to join us. Mike pulls out the chair next to me and sits down. "I wasn't sure you'd come this year."

"My plans weren't firmed up until yesterday." I glance at Brett.

"Mike, what are you drinking?" Brett stands up. "I have a whole roll of drink tickets I need to use up."

"Cold beer, thanks."

He leaves to get our drinks, and Mike and I grow quiet. After a few moments, I compliment him on his colorful shirt, and he describes his 'Elvis' routine. "I always take requests from the audience, so be thinking about what you'd like to hear. You might end up with one of those fake orchid leis around your neck."

"What I want to hear isn't set to music."

"What do you mean?"

"Do me a big favor, will you?"

"If I can."

"Help me put together Jack's last day. I know he contacted Brett and my father. What happened afterwards? I believe my father knows something, but I can't ask him."

"You can't or you won't?"

I shake my head. "Brett has filled in a few details, but I need your help."

"Is that why you're here with him?" He toys with the sugar packets and rearranges the salt and pepper shakers on the table. "I thought you might come with your other friends."

"He asked me yesterday." Why do I need to explain my actions to Mike? It's not like he has claims on me. "I want you to reopen the case. Or at least help me figure out what really happened."

Brett reappears and sets three longneck Lone Stars and a bowl of unshelled peanuts on the table. Their roasted aroma tickles my nostrils. Mike rises from his seat, picks up his bottle, and salutes Brett with it. "Gotta start the music now."

"Opening with 'Jailhouse Rock'?" Brett grins. "I hear it's your specialty."

Mike climbs onto the stage, as couples stroll out to the dance floor, ready to burn some energy on boogie. I yearn for Brett to hold out his hand and lead me toward the center of the crowd. While we wait for the percussion to make the air throb, he rotates his chair around for a better view.

Mike changed the opener to "It's Now or Never." Several couples misstep from the first beat. Brett catches the rhythm and taps his fingers in fast quarter-time. At first it's strange to do no more than watch others. I figure Brett's dancing days must be over, so I bounce my foot and sway in my chair, trying not to be too obvious.

During the break, we enjoy a barbecue dinner with Brett's other guests, Angelique and Raúl, a couple of history professors from UT, and Mr. Donatello and his wife. Before dessert, the band launches into the "Jailhouse Rock" number everyone expected earlier.

At the first strains of "Are You Lonesome Tonight," Brett admits he can't resist the chance to hold a lighthearted woman in his arms, and we ease our way onto the dance floor. He hopes he won't embarrass himself, but I say his moves are easy to follow. The truth is he dances at attention, as if he never left the army.

By the end of the song, we slick each other with compliments and return to our table. Before we can take our seats again, Mike comes up and taps Brett on the shoulder. "Mind if I enjoy the next one?"

Brett looks at me and I nod, hoping his feelings aren't bruised. He retreats to the sidelines and swigs his beer. He joins Raúl, and they share a loud guffaw at something Angelique says.

I smile up at Mike. "Aren't you supposed to be singing?"

"They can handle this one without me." He holds out his arms and I step nearer to him. Before the music starts, he lifts my left hand to his shoulder and puts his arm around my waist. I place my right hand in his, unsure what tune I'll hear or how fast we'll move.

For a moment I forget to wait for the downbeat. The feel of Mike's muscles through his shirt and his arm around my back remind me of what I've been missing. Our touch fires a little spark of awakening, and I look up into Mike's eyes. His expression tells me I'm a desirable woman, and I'm curious to know how his flesh would feel against mine. Music or not, I'm tired of life as a widow and ready for a change.

The bass and the piano begin in slow waltz time, and I press against him, resting my chin against his shoulder. He pulls me in tighter and bends his head down until his chin warms my cheek. The fresh aroma of Ivory soap should relax me, but I picture him pulling off his undershirt instead. I wonder if he senses the electric tingle that starts at my heels, travels up the backs of my legs, and spreads from my torso all the way to my collarbone. If I turn my head to the right, our lips will meet.

Couples crowd us on the dance floor, as the substitute Elvis croons, "Can't Help Falling in Love." For both our sakes, I wish the song didn't remind me of Jack and our wedding reception. Someone might as well dump a bucket of cold water on me.

I lean back "So, Mike, will you help me?"

He looks down at me and studies my face. "You can't let this go, can you?"

I shake my head.

"Okay, I'll see what I can do. Nothing official."

"That's all I ask."

The next number begins and he doesn't release my hand. Jitterbugging to "Hound Dog" proves too much fun to abandon the floor. The memory of getting breathless from dancing with Jack resurfaces.

The Terpsichore muse must have tripped the gravity switch because Mike moves as nimbly as any accomplished dancer and manages to look graceful over every inch of his tall frame. While twirling and catching me, his eyes never leave my face.

The song ends. He leans forward to kiss the back of my hand and then returns to the stage with one broad leap. When he faces the microphone, he looks anywhere but at me.

As I join Brett at the table, two faces on the other side of the seating area catch my eye. Harlene huddles with her son Skipper at the table Big Jack reserved and paid for long before his accident. With a sneer, Skipper lifts his beer bottle and tips it toward me.

I shudder. What a nasty gesture.

On stage, the Pioneer Festival chair takes the microphone from Mike and announces her gratitude to the committee by asking all of us to stand up. When she pulls out a long list to read off the names of sponsors, including Brett and both sides of my family, I excuse myself and head for the ladies room. Beyond the caterer's area, I detour around the back of the building to catch Mike as he exits the stage.

I motion to him, and when he approaches, I grab him by the wrist and pull him into the shadow of a doorway. "Did you see who's here?" I whisper. "Skipper!"

Mike's face registers puzzlement. "What about it?"

"How did he get here?"

"Looks like he came with his mother. Maybe he used Big Jack's ticket."

"Do you know what he's been doing since he got out of prison?"

"He reports to his parole office in Austin on a regular basis. I hear he's living with his mother and looking for a job. I get updates."

Mike's calm demeanor doesn't help my agitation. "I think he's up to something criminal. I saw him on the loading dock behind the store the other day."

"Was anyone with him?"

I shake my head.

"All by himself, he couldn't be selling drugs at that moment, could he? Sally, you didn't really witness anything."

"There's more." I hesitate, because I don't want Mike to think I am seeing a felon behind every bush. "He had to know Jack turned him in. You heard Jack's testimony at his trial. After I saw Skipper last week, I realized he got released from prison a few days *before* Jack died."

"And now you think, out of revenge, Skipper had something to do with Jack's death?"

I clutch Mike's shirt and my lip quivers. "It's possible, isn't it? Can't you find out?"

As he puts his hands on my shoulders, tears trickle down my cheeks. I didn't mean to cry ever, especially since Jack's funeral. Why now?

"Sh-sh-sh," he murmurs and presses my head against his chest. His hand feels warm on the back of my head, and I let him stroke my hair and brush it off my shoulders with his fingertips. "There, now," he says.

Before I can stop myself, I tip my head back and, reaching my arms around Mike's neck, pull his face down to mine. My lips find his, and the hunger I ignored grows. The spark I felt earlier flares into white heat. I lean into him against the doorframe, wanting each curve of my body to recede into his solid strength.

Even if I caught him by surprise, his reflexes match mine, and he wraps me in his arms and holds me, until we almost crush each other's lungs. I struggle for breath as his lips travel down my neck, and I am just about to twine my fingers through his hair when high-pitched screams and trampling feet race toward us.

We freeze, not breathing, not daring to look at the children or the teenager who chases them. I pray the shadows conceal us enough to keep our innocence intact. A kiss is harmless enough.

After the intruders disappear around the corner, I step back and smooth my blouse. Mike might as well be a marble statue. I can't see his face or hear his breathing. I shake out my hair. "Sorry, I shouldn't have thrown myself at you like that."

"My fault." His loafers crunch on the gravel as he walks away.

I wait a few moments, and then turn in the opposite direction toward the ladies room. Even with the dim light overhead, the mirror reflects my glowing face. A few splashes of water cool my cheeks enough to reduce the blush, and I hope no one will notice I have been crying. Or passionately kissing someone.

I return to the table and ask Brett again to take a stroll over to the arcade. We find the Cromwells and Colton at the church booth. I gesture for Colton to come out from behind the counter and we step a few paces to one side. "Officer Avery is going to help me put together the missing pieces about Dad's last day."

I can't bring myself to tell him I refuse to communicate with my father about his part in Jack's final business effort. Better not to mention someone my son will never meet. For a moment, Colton stares at his shoes and then retreats to the booth.

A light breeze blows across the lake and I shiver. Brett weaves my arm through his, and I appreciate his thoughtful gesture. Putting his arm around me would be a bit much too soon, in front of my son. Especially tonight.

We have scarcely taken more than a few steps away from the booth when Mike calls my name. I turn around just in time to see Colton leap over the counter and crash into Mike, knocking him to the ground.

Judith screams and Charlie tries to pull Colton off Mike. Brett dashes to help Charlie, and they yank Colton upright and pin his arms behind him, as he keeps squirming and kicking.

Mike jumps to his feet and dusts off his shoulders. He glares at Colton. "What's the matter with you?"

I try to move, but my feet might as well be staked to the

path. "Colton, what's wrong? Why did you knock Officer Avery down?"

My son's body goes limp and he collapses to the ground, sobbing. I can't understand his words, jumbled through his tears, and I don't dare touch him or try to comfort him in any way. I stand there looking at him, as if through a glass window, unable to reach him.

Angelique breaks through the line of children and adults surrounding Colton. She bends over him and speaks in a low voice only he can hear. Holding him gently by the arm, she raises him up. She mouths to me that she will take him home to stay with her overnight. He allows her to lead him away from the glare of the lights and the heat of his actions.

"I'm so sorry, Mike," I say. "I don't know what's gotten into him."

"I can't ignore an assault on an officer of the law, especially in front of all these witnesses. Bring Colton to the station tomorrow."

"You want him to come there?"

When he nods, my words hiss like steam from a broken pipe. "I can't believe you're so insensitive. You know he's having problems. Grieving out of control. How can you make such a demand? After everything he's gone through, I expected you to be more understanding." All our passion is cast aside, not to mention his kindness.

Mike turns and walks away.

No way can my father pay anyone enough to fix this damage.

CHAPTER TEN

With Colton taking a timeout to stay overnight with Angelique, my house seems roomier than usual the next morning. I wander through the silent spaces and wish Mondays didn't trouble me. The whole week looms ahead like a flat, empty highway. Nothing I do makes much noise, and even if it did, there's no one to hear me.

The truth about a watched pot also applies to the telephone. I linger in my kitchen and wonder why Judith hasn't called to commiserate with me over last night's debacle. When the phone finally rings, the caller brings a welcome surprise, a chance to revive my passion for landscaping and earn some money.

"Yes, I can start right away." I grab a pencil. "What did you have in mind?"

The man rattles off a short list of commercial properties that need new designs and plantings. When I suggest a bid with preliminary sketches, he claims the board of directors will be happy to review my proposal and grant a decent allowance.

I ask him to name the properties specifically and jot them down, along with the addresses. "Are there sprinkler systems already in place?"

"If not, you can install them, can't you? Just add it to your estimate."

At the bottom of my note pad, I write his name and the property management company address. "I'll need to get measurements, but I still require some rough idea of a budget. No one likes unexpected expenses, and you'll have to sign the work order."

"Okay, put together a list and a timeline, and after our meeting I'll send you a purchase order."

We thank each other and hang up. I skim my notes again and tap my foot at the prospect of the thousands of dollars in gross billing, right in time for the next quarterly tax payment. Tapping gives way to gliding around my kitchen island, as I hum "Laughter in the Rain." For the first time in months, I really do feel like laughing out loud.

The euphoria lasts a few moments longer, until I remember I have to take Colton to Mike's office. How could I have been so rude to Mike? Resolving the events of last night will take more than apologies.

We stretch Mike Avery's patience too thin, my family and I. How many times has he smoothed over Colton's difficulties? What else did Nate Wallace ask of him?

Mike probably believes Jack really did commit suicide, but at least he agreed to take another look at the circumstances. Whether he includes Skipper in his inquiry remains to be seen.

Although Colton embarrassed me, I can't blame Mike for his reaction. He isn't the type to let emotions change his mind, but maybe by the time we arrive at the police station he'll have regained his empathy and cut us both some slack.

I just wonder what Mike said to Colton to set him off like that. Of course, he doesn't know my son as well as I do, so I should cut Mike some slack, too.

My thoughts stall as I sit down, and I break my inertia by dialing Angelique's number. Two rings, and she answers.

"How's Colton?" I ask.

"Still in bed." She flicks a lighter. "Why don't you come over now? There's something I want to share with you."

"What can you tell me about Colton I don't already know?" She enjoys his frequent company, but he hasn't spent time at her house or taken art lessons from her like I did when I was his age.

"Not him."

ON RARE OCCASIONS I find Angelique dressed in her work clothes. In tight denim jeans, she looks sexy as ever, and the tails of a white oxford cloth shirt tied under her bust reveal a flat torso a woman of any age would envy.

Evidently she has been rearranging paintings in her studio all morning. She lifts a large portrait and angles it toward the light from the clerestory window. "Remember this one?"

In oils, she captured the colorful image of a young woman by a wooden gate, with a country lane behind her and a floral meadow across the slatted fence. The breeze billows her long blonde hair and the coral ribbons of the straw hat she holds at her side.

"How could I forget?"

"You haven't changed much at all."

"Aren't we sentimental today?" I zigzag my way through several easels until I stand next to her. "How old was I when you painted that?"

"Eighteen, maybe? Had to be before you married Jack."

"Everything has changed since then." I turn away from the canvas. "I can't look that far back now."

"It might be a good idea to take a short walk down memory lane." She waves me to the chair under the skylight where her models, including myself, usually sit. "Colton is upstairs, sound asleep." She settles sideways on the settee cushions and wraps one leg underneath, while spreading her arms across the back. She might be Queen Sheba awaiting a royal visit from Solomon. "You know I've always claimed you as the daughter I never had."

"So you're going to tell me something I need to work on?" Has anyone loved me for as long as Angelique? One by one, the others who truly cared for me–Grandma Mason, Mrs. Gussmann, Clyde Farraday–all disappeared from my young life.

"I hate how much you suffered during the past year, but I thought maybe time would work its magic and things would get better."

"They're getting worse lately, especially for Colton."

"He seems to be one frightened boy."

I cock my head to one side, as if I didn't hear correctly. "What is he afraid of?"

"Something you might do."

"Did he tell you that?"

She shakes her head.

I jump to my feet and stride toward the window. "I'm his mother. I'm *not* scary."

"We both know from experience the two aren't mutually exclusive. Please hear me out." Angelique follows me, takes me by the arm, and leads me to sit again. "How did you react when your father moved to the ranch?"

When Nate made decisions that altered my life, I learned the hard way I had to fight.

I couldn't concentrate on my studies for all the squealing in the hallway of the Tri Delt house. One of my sorority sisters just surprised us with news of her engagement, and the celebration launched at our Monday night meeting showed no signs of abating. By tradition, the president kept the secret until she passed a candle around our circle and the lucky girl blew it out.

Two weeks until midterms, and I had a bear for a chemistry professor. So far, she liked me well enough, and I intended to ace the exam and maintain my 'A' average this whole sophomore year. But hydrocarbons weren't nearly as exciting as two-carat solitaires, and I'd rather have joined the fun.

As I stretched for perhaps the fifth time, I decided the UT Academic Center would make a better place to study. If I sat away from the entrance, I'd avoid any distractions, especially Jack. His study habits were almost non-existent, and I refused to let him disrupt mine with his fraternity party spirit. He could wait until Saturday night to try to get me in the mood for a keg social prior to the football game.

Before I had a chance to pile up my books and notes, my phone rang. My father was calling about Thanksgiving, to let me know where we'd been invited this time. Since my mother died four years ago, we hadn't spent a single holiday at home. Quite often, the Cromwells graciously included us, except for last November when we traveled to London. Not a roasted turkey to be found in the whole damp country.

"What's up, Daddy?"

"I thought you'd like to know," he began. "I've bought a ranch."

"Really." I couldn't get enthusiastic about remote acres devoted to the tending and feeding of livestock. Besides, my father bought and sold properties all the time, and I'd never paid much attention. "Where?"

"West Texas, mostly in Pecos County. Between Fort Stockton and Alpine."

"Sounds like it's near nowhere."

"It seemed to be a good idea." He mentioned mineral rights, productivity estimates, and an airstrip.

Good for whom, I wondered. "Well, I hope you enjoy it." I yawned.

"That's why I'm calling."

"Good grief, are you going to suggest we spend Thanksgiving *there*? Why can't we just stay home this year? We can order all our meals catered." My father and I were still learning to get along without Mrs. Gussmann, who retired last summer after knee surgery. From climbing too many stairs, she claimed.

He cleared his throat. "I'm going out there in a few days and I have a lot of business to keep me busy for a while."

"How long?"

He didn't give me a direct answer, and my patience slipped away. "I'll just stay home. Mason's Crossing is barely awake these days, but if I get bored, I'll find something else to do." If I visited friends in San Antonio or Austin, he wouldn't even be concerned.

"We have to make other arrangements. You'll like the ranch."

He didn't sound angry, but I matched the frosty edge in his tone. "You can't force me to come out to Fort Pecos, or wherever your new ranch is." I clamped my jaw, hoping he heard stubbornness in my voice. "I won't go."

"You can't stay in Mason's Crossing."

"Why not? I'm almost twenty." If I sounded ungrateful, I didn't care. Responsibility for myself made me that way. "It's a big house, but I can manage."

"I sold the house."

The floor might as well have collapsed. I clutched at the wall to keep from tumbling and slipping down what felt like a rocky ledge.

My father was a demon, tearing my life apart piece by piece, year after year. I waited until my voice returned, determined not to submit to his control the way my mother did. He tried to convince me the realtor's offer was too good to pass up, but I wasn't listening.

"You go to the ranch by yourself." I clenched my teeth. "I'll make my own arrangements." Without waiting for his reply, I hung up. I tasted bile in my throat, but I tamped it down and picked up the phone again. I dialed Jack's number. "Hey, is that offer still good?"

He wanted to know which one.

"Come pick me up and I'll tell you."

Always ready for distraction, Jack agreed to drive over immediately.

I would say yes and tell him I want three carats, not two. My dorm room seemed sweltering and cramped, barely space for one, not two. My stomach heaved, and I vomited that evening's meal of King Ranch Chicken Casserole into the trashcan.

I stare at Angelique. "How could he leave me at college with nothing to come home to? Where did he think girls in my sorority went during school holidays?"

"Probably to the Riviera or somewhere else in Europe." She tucks a strand of hair behind her ear. "He had no experience with females that age, except your mother. And we both know how that turned out."

"My point exactly."

"He didn't act very fatherly, did he?" She coughs and struggles to regain her voice. "But the important point is how your relationship with him changed."

"Nothing changed. He *never* loved me."

"Maybe not the way you needed, but he tried. And failed. Because of his mistakes, you cut him out of your life completely." Angelique enumerates the other people I axed, starting with my husband. "For you, who can possibly measure up?"

I protest that my sense of loyalty isn't on a par with others. If people, even family members, demonstrate they lack faithfulness, then I have a hard time seeing them as worthy.

"Now bring Colton into the picture," she says. "He keeps messing up."

"I wish I knew why his accidents are getting more serious."

"Can you see how he might be frightened you will shut him out?"

I shake my head. "He's my *son*."

"And Nate's your father." She lights a cigarette. "If you can see it through Colton's eyes, it's not that complicated. What's to stop you from treating him the same way?"

As I argue that my son knows I love him, my tongue feels thick, and I can't seem to swallow.

She leans forward and chops her palm with the edge of her other hand, ignoring the ashes that fall to the floor. "You've perfected the art of disconnection. Colton needs to be reassured of your capacity to love, no matter what. Show him you can reconcile with your father. Call Nate and talk to him."

Angelique's paintings grow watery as tears prick the edges of my eyelids. I blink several times and gaze at the high ceiling. After a moment, I look at her. "No."

"But Sally, detachment isn't–"

"It's impossible."

"What's impossible?" says a voice behind us.

We both stand up quickly and turn toward the door. Leaning against the doorway, Colton munches a croissant, wearing his clothes from yesterday, not a care in the world. Angelique and I exchange frowns that mean uh-oh, but he gives no indication he overheard us.

I face him. "Please thank Angelique for her hospitality and let's get ready to go visit Officer Avery. We need to be there in fifteen minutes."

"Impossible." He shoves the second half of the croissant into his mouth and saunters down the hallway toward the kitchen.

I clench my jaw and stare at Angelique for a few seconds. "I'm going to my car. Will you send Colton out as soon as you can?"

God help me, she's right. I have already begun to disconnect from my son, and not even my mother can stop me.

Fifteen minutes dissolves into twenty, then twenty-five. After we leave Angelique's, I refuse to speed, even though Mike can't issue tickets from behind his desk at the station.

Once we arrive, Colton maintains his cool behavior. How have I spawned such an actor? He apologizes without prompting and shows no reaction when Mike imposes a probationary period.

Last night, I would have sworn Mike warmed up to my lapse of decorum, but now he seems distant, his words curt. He excuses himself to answer the phone. After he returns to the conference table, I inflict an indifferent smile on him, but he doesn't look at me.

He pulls out a pocket calendar. "That was Nate. At my request, he's agreed to return to Mason's Crossing for an informal, er . . . chat. Are you available tomorrow afternoon? Two o'clock."

My body freezes. "My father's coming *here*?"

Mike huffs and rolls his eyes. "You want me to take another look at Jack's suicide, don't you?"

I glance at Colton and something in me rallies. Damned if I will let my father's presence keep me from finding out the truth about my husband's death. My son deserves to know, and so do I. "Fine. I'll be here tomorrow at two o'clock."

"We're meeting at the hospital instead. Big Jack seems to be feeling well enough to answer a few questions."

I clutch the edge of the table. "The hospital?"

Colton fidgets and hiccoughs, his cool demeanor stripped away. "You can't make me go back there."

I feel like a tennis ball in a madcap match. "You'll stay with Angelique. She needs help moving boxes." I point to the exit. "Please wait for me outside."

After the door clicks shut behind Colton, I frown at Mike. "Have you lost your mind? Being in the same room with my father could give Big Jack a heart attack."

"I talked to him already. For what it's worth, Big Jack appears ready to clear the air." He scratches his chin. "What will seeing your father after all these years do to *you*?"

I stand up, unable to tell if Mike's expression conveys genuine concern. He isn't the type to tease. "Don't trouble yourself. I can handle it."

"One more thing." He clears his throat. "I also invited Brett Kennedy to attend our little gathering."

"The more, the merrier. See you tomorrow." I turn to leave before Mike figures out what a brave liar I've suddenly become.

CHAPTER ELEVEN

I wake up tired. Sleep eluded me throughout the night, except I remember waking from strange dreams: basketball hoops, ocean liners, campfires, department stores. Freud would have a field day.

After a breakfast of coffee and half a piece of dry toast, I head out the back door to my greenhouse. The cool morning air sends shivers up my arms, and I hurry inside where it is warm.

My stomach won't stop churning, no matter how many times I pinch the begonias or inspect the geraniums. Pacing back and forth doesn't help.

The calm I always count on from working in my greenhouse won't come. I can't settle down.

In perfect detail, I recall the last day I saw my father, almost fifteen years ago. Bright sun, high clouds, light breeze for that January afternoon in 1961. We drove to church together, he in his tuxedo and I in my wedding gown. Not much conversation, as usual.

I could only guess why the custom originated, but in our family, the father of the bride always escorted her from home to the church. Maybe it was a preventive measure in case the bride bolted from the groom and his relatives. If we carried on such a heritage, there was probably more than one good reason for it.

Daddy's new Lincoln crowded the space in Angelique's driveway. In the sunlight, the elongated four-door sedan gleamed shiny black, just like the one President and Mrs. Kennedy rode in.

It was his fault we had to break with tradition. Angelique's house had been my home base ever since I accepted Jack's proposal. Except for the fact I'd rather have been planning my debutante ball, she and I had a terrific time over the last three months, choosing gowns, color schemes, invitations, menus, flowers, and musicians. She knew more about throwing a grand reception than anyone else in Mason's Crossing.

As punishment, I spent as much money as I could, but Nate never raised an objection. He paid every invoice covering the ceremony and the party at the country club, without a word of criticism. The bride's cake alone cost over five hundred dollars because Angelique insisted on a fourth tier, topped off by a pair of hand-carved sugarcoated doves. By the day before the wedding, the thought of lovebirds made me want to puke.

Angelique said he probably had no idea how much a wedding

should cost, and I thought he felt relieved he had no part of the decisions. The chances we would have taken his suggestions were non-existent anyway. I hoped he felt really guilty.

Trying not to squirm, I sat carefully in the front seat, with my cosmetic bag in the space between us. The antique ivory Alençon lace on my dress, ordered from Maison d'Orleans in Paris, wouldn't show any wrinkles, but I didn't want the delicate seed pearls to snag on the upholstery. I slipped off my matching *peau de soie* pumps and wiggled my toes. I wasn't used to wearing stockings and had bought a girdle to hold them up.

After starting the engine, he fiddled with the radio dial. "I think you should have waited."

"For what?"

"Until you graduate. There's no reason to get married now."

I reached over and flicked off the radio. "The wedding cake was iced this morning, and my dress was altered several weeks ago. Don't you think your suggestion comes a little late?"

"I mean, why didn't you wait to see if you could find . . .?" He steered the car out of the driveway. "It's only the middle of your second year in college. What's your big hurry?"

How did he have the nerve to ask me that? "I need some place to go during Christmas and spring break, other than Europe or the beach. I'm too young to sign a lease for an apartment."

"I would have rented you an apartment if you'd asked me." He shrugged. "Or you could come out to the ranch."

I all but snorted and wanted to ask why I should live under the same roof with him ever again. "What about next summer? Where should I go then?" I popped down the visor and opened the mirror. A fancy little light came on, and I checked my lipstick.

"What would I do at the ranch the whole three months?"

"Laze around. Catch up on your rest. You've been studying too hard."

How would he know? "Thanks, but you'll have to come up with a better reason than that." If my sarcasm pained him, I didn't care. I didn't tell him about my plans to attend summer school.

We arrived at the side entrance to Hillside Methodist Church, a classic red brick colonial in the center of town. Great-Grandfather Mason had donated the land and his son later paid for the heating and air conditioning systems, but it was Aunt Mary who saw to my baptism and kept the family in regular attendance. She made sure all our significant events were observed in the shadow of the church's wings. The ones I remembered best were the funerals.

I opened the car door and lifted the edge of my skirt. "I'll meet you in the narthex just before the ceremony begins."

He nodded and drove the Lincoln around to the front of the church to park in the nearly empty street. I stare at the baby blue stretch limousine reserved for the bride and groom, hoping Jack and his mother didn't follow up on their idea to rent him a tuxedo to match. Twice I told them black only, and even wrote it down for him.

I climbed the limestone steps to the second-floor bride's dressing room, where my dozen bridesmaids had smuggled a cooler with six iced bottles of Taittinger. All Tri Delt sorority sisters, they cheered when I came through the door and handed me a glass of champagne.

Angelique helped the hairdresser attach my veil. "I'm glad

you didn't go with the one covering your face," she said. "It's not like Jack needs to be kept in suspense."

"He should know by now what he's getting for a wife." I had already fussed at Jack for getting sunburned while playing golf at the groom's party on Thursday. Didn't he realize how unpredictable Texas weather could be?

"I have something for you." Angelique dug a wad of tissue paper from her evening bag and unwrapped something sparkly.

"A sixpence for my shoe? It's the only thing lacking." While the lace was old, my dress was new, and the garter halfway up my right thigh was pale blue like the limo. I had borrowed an heirloom linen handkerchief from Charlie Cromwell's mother, another family tradition.

"Something old," she said with a smile. Her lip quivered. "It's from your mother." She handed me a heart-shaped diamond solitaire dangling from a gold chain.

"It's gorgeous! How is it you had this?"

Her eyes shone like the unusual gem dangling in front of me. "Before she went into the hospital, Weesie asked me to keep it for you." Angelique unlocked the clasp. "I've been hanging onto it all these years." She stepped behind me, careful to avoid the train of my dress, and reached over my head. Once the necklace was in place, she faced me again. "You look beautiful, so much like her, especially now."

We held each other by the forearms, like comrades before battle who pledge victory or death together. "You've been a wonderful . . ." I tightened my grasp. "I didn't miss her when I was with you."

"It's been a joyful time for me, as well. You've given me

something I never had before."

"What's that?"

"Since my own two weddings transpired without any planning, and I never had a daughter, I had no hope of helping to make anyone's dreams come true. Now I have."

"It sounds lame, but I couldn't have done it without you."

Angelique kissed my cheek. "The music must be starting by now. I'll go find a seat in the sanctuary."

"Remember, you're the last one up the aisle before the processional. The head usher escorts you." At the rehearsal last night she demurred, but Angelique deserved her place of honor in the front row.

After we picked up our nosegays one by one from the florist, I followed my bridesmaids into the hallway. The strains of Bach's "Jesu, Joy of Man's Desiring" reached my ears as we descended the stairs to the narthex. My sorority sisters swirled into a sea of deep raspberry red, dotted with pale pink rose bouquets. The music changed to Pachabel's "Canon in D," and they unrolled in waves of two abreast down the aisle toward the altar.

I touched the diamond pendant, thrilled to have something to remind me of my mother. When the last pair of bridesmaids passed through the center doors, the figure of my father came into view.

He stared at the necklace as he approached me. "Where did you get that?" I could swear he winced.

"Angelique brought it to me. It was Mother's."

"I know." He extended his left elbow toward me. "She wore it at our wedding."

It wasn't like my father to remember details of past

events. He could quote the Dow Jones averages from last week or last month, but he didn't recall where we spent Easter last spring.

"Was it Grandmother Mason's?"

"No." He faced forward, as the trumpeter began Mendelsohn's "Wedding March," joined by the organist. "I gave it to Weesie the day we were married."

The two ushers stood at attention as they held open the doors to the sanctuary, and Daddy waited for me to take his arm. With the final pair of bridesmaids in position, the minister gestured for the congregation to rise and look at us, expectation on his face. The trumpeter's notes reached their introductory climax and the organist plunged into action. It was our cue, learned last night at the rehearsal.

Instead of starting down the aisle, I handed one of the ushers my bouquet, reached to the nape of my neck, and undid the clasp. Letting it dangle from my fingertips, I dropped the pendant and chain into Daddy's hand. "You can keep it." I should have known he would find some way to ruin my wedding day.

Once I retrieved my bouquet, I took his arm and we set off, a slow march away from my past and toward the man who would share my future. I couldn't hesitate now, even though I was unsure of the wisdom of the trade I was about to make.

I remember refusing to be surprised that Daddy left town the day after my wedding, without saying goodbye. Whether he departed for his ranch or one of his offices in Dallas or New Orleans, I didn't know. Or care.

Now the prospect of being in the same room and exchanging words with him sucks up the usual serenity I feel in my greenhouse. Anxiety takes over. How will I look and sound to him after all these years? Will I remind him of my mother? Since I have no answers, I hope Mike knows what he's doing.

No point in letting an entire afternoon go to waste fretting over the inevitable. I return to the house and sit at my desk to call a few wholesale nurseries for inventory and prices. Almost an hour passes when the doorbell rings.

Judith, along with Max and Maddie, stands on the front porch. She grins. "I know Colton is grounded, but can he have company?"

I open the door and wave them inside.

In the entry hall, Judith drapes her arm over Max's shoulder and pulls his head close to her lips. "No fireworks, understand?"

He cackles like a Saturday morning cartoon villain. "Wanna check my pockets for matches?"

She kisses his forehead. As Max darts up the stairs, Judith and her daughter follow me into the kitchen.

Maddie dangles a headless Barbie doll in one hand. "Mommy says she's out of her head," the child lisps through missing front teeth.

"Barbie is my alter-ego," laughs Judith.

I hand Maddie the remains of an open package of graham crackers and tell her to play outside where we can see her through the window. "You can sit in the glider with Barbie."

When the door closes behind her, Judith turns to me and purses her lips. "I want to speak to you about Colton."

"You, too?"

"He's been putting you to the test. Maybe grounding him isn't the best choice right now. He needs more interaction with other people."

Without returning her smile, I tilt my head toward her.

"He's very well-behaved at our house and when he's out with us in public. It's only when he's—"

"With me? What about the times he got into trouble away from home? Like the cabin at church camp he set on fire? Or with Max at the art gallery?"

"My point is, I think he responds well to being in a family situation. Having a father figure around."

"You mean Charlie?" I all but choke. "You said yourself he's an overgrown playmate to your three kids. Almost like you've got a fourth one."

She giggles. "I know, but he goes to sleep later."

I can't help laughing along with her, until I sober up at the thought of my options. "I wish I *could* find someone to help me with Colton, but who can manufacture a family? Mason's Crossing isn't exactly teeming with eligible men over the age of thirty-five."

"Or any age. What's Brett like?"

"Quite nice and a real gentleman, but not very exciting."

"Maybe dull is what Colton and you need for a change." She shakes her head, then looks up at the ceiling. "There's Mike."

I squint at her. "Mike who?"

"Are you blind or just stupid? Maybe both? Don't you realize Mike Avery has been in love with you for years?"

"You're exaggerating. He's very friendly and provided a lot of help, that's all. Only because someone else asked him to."

"He'd have stepped up to your plate whether Nate Wallace prodded him or not."

I stare at her. "How did you find out—"

"Everyone's known it." Judith shrugs. "Except you."

"Why didn't you tell me?"

"I figured you'd put a stop to it, but frankly I couldn't see the harm. Besides, what your father does with his hard-earned bazillions is his business. Mike's very generous, too, but in other ways."

"Colton doesn't seem to like him, remember?"

"You're the heiress-with-the-mostess in five counties. At least all Mike wants to get his hands on is you."

I shake my head. "You're seriously delusional."

Her merriment proves contagious and I forget my anxiety until they leave. My spirits take a deeper plunge, and I almost wish they hadn't come, or that she hadn't mentioned Mike's crush on me. Our little moment of unguarded passion shouldn't be enough to encourage him and we could probably continue our friendship without complications.

Something Judith said begins to fester, like a splinter under the skin. What else would there be for a man to get his hands on except me? Every woman wants to think of herself as a prize catch. Minus a huge fortune plus debts mounting up, I will make a tenuous partner.

EACH TICK OF THE CLOCK winds my gut tighter. By noon, I decide to take Colton back to Angelique's. We find her resting on the terrace. "Help has arrived." I point to my son.

Her eyelids flutter, then open as she lets out a long sigh. "Good. I'm feeling listless today. Barely enough energy for a catnap."

"Let Colton do all the work." I give him a wry smile.

"Good luck with your quest for proof." Angelique shifts her weight and lets one arm dangle from the chaise. "Tell Nate I said hello."

"You can tell him yourself, can't you? Everyone but me seems to be in touch with him."

Colton narrows his eyes and glares at me, heaving a snort as he walks away.

I recognize contempt when I hear it. I follow him. "What's wrong?"

Silence.

"Is there something you want to say?"

He whirls around to face me and spits out his words. "You can't stop screwing things up. Everyone hates what you're doing. You don't even have a decent relationship with your own father."

His stormy words feel like a door slammed against my face, and I can't let him get away with it. "You don't know what you're talking about."

"No one believes anything you say. You're full of shit."

Lunging toward him, I draw back my hand, palm open. He doesn't cower, but stands waiting, as if he wants me to slap him. I let my hand drop and turn to leave. Another time, another year, his disrespect will rain punishment on him, but I figure he'll change his mind if he ever meets Nate Wallace.

WITH JACK'S APPOINTMENT BOOK in hand, I arrive at the hospital early to seize the advantage and determine what Big Jack's stamina will allow. Muted male and female voices come from his room, and I hesitate. So much for early. After a moment, I knock and push the door open. "Big Jack?"

Harlene stands next to the bed, leaning over Big Jack, a little too close to suit me. They glance up as I enter, and she snatches a pen and a few papers from his meal cart. Someone–Harlene?– had placed the tray on the floor, his lunch half-eaten.

"Hello." I give her a mirthless smile. "Having a hard time getting him to hold a pen?"

"Sally can sign 'em." Big Jack flops his head back on the pillow. "My goddamn fingers won't close."

"Not with a right arm broken in at least two places." I brush past Harlene and fluff his pillow. "Where's the comb I brought you? Your hair needs grooming." Winning a turf war against Harlene will give my day a turn for the better.

Channeling Saint Trixie, I fuss over my father-in-law, a weird maiden voyage for both of us. "There, that's better." I turn to face her. "Now, what can I do for you, Harlene? Big Jack says you need my signature on . . . what?"

"Inventory records and payments. I have accounted for every item delivered myself, since I'm the only one in the office these days."

"You're one of the special people Big Jack trusts to hold down the fort." I hold out my hand for the pen and papers. "This will just take me a minute, then you can be on your busy way."

She exchanges lingering looks with Big Jack and takes her sweet time about offering me the documents, as if they are her children leaving for summer camp for the first time. I pretend to double-check her math and then sign each one at the bottom, along with the corresponding payment draft. Harlene thanks me and departs, trailing the scent of 'Jungle Gardenia'.

"Let's get some fresh air in here," I fan the room with the door. "Company is coming soon and we want to–"

Big Jack groans. "Where is Mike Avery? Let's get this over with. I wish I hadn't . . ."

"You'd prefer people not see you in your condition, right?" I pick up the tray from the floor and set it on the cart. "Frankly, you don't look so bad. You're on the mend."

"After what Nate Wallace stole, I don't want that bastard anywhere near me."

"I know exactly how you feel, but I saw the agreement." I scoot the cart across the room and swivel his wheelchair toward his bed. "It was a legitimate sale."

"I'm not talking about the business. I meant Weesie!"

I freeze, as the wheelchair escapes from my grasp and bumps the bed frame.

Louisa Mason Cobb Wallace. No one had ever been permitted to call my mother by her nickname except people she loved deeply. Her parents. My father.

Big Jack sits up and swings his legs one by one over the side of the bed. "Help me here, will you? Get my pants out of the closet."

Sliding khaki pants up over my father-in-law's knobby knees affords me another first. He seems too preoccupied to be embarrassed, and I wonder if, in his absentmindedness, he has mistaken me for someone else.

"I'd rather walk," he growls.

"Of course you would. Think you can manage it?"

"Get my shoes."

"It looks like all you have here is slippers." I hope he doesn't take my answer as argument.

He slides one foot to the floor, as if testing the water, and changes his mind. After setting the wheel locks, I steady him as he rises and shifts his weight to the seat.

I try to see him through other eyes, as a younger man. Big Jack had been in love with my mother? Did Saint Trixie or my father know? Before I can get any words out, someone taps on the door.

I stare at the door, waiting for it to open. "Come in," I call. Nothing.

Louder. "Come in."

The door swings toward me and I hold my breath.

The figure of Mike Avery consumes almost the entire frame. "Ready? We're meeting in the conference room down the corridor."

In the hallway behind him, a commotion of male voices catches my attention. As I strain to peer over his shoulder, Mike steps to one side. My father's head inclines toward Brett

Kennedy. When he turns forward, our eyes lock.

I expect to be zapped by electric current, but nothing happens. Neither of us blinks. I feel no magnetic power, no pull of attraction. Nothing until I detect a white hot ball of fire where my heart should be.

Oh, Mother, what have I gotten myself into?

CHAPTER TWELVE

My father stands against the wall next to Brett Kennedy in the hospital hallway. With his black wool topcoat draped over his arm, he makes no move to shake my hand. "Hello, Sally. It's been a long time."

A lifetime. Mine, a life I had to make for myself, settling for a different family instead of the one I was born into. Crumbs, not the feast it should have been. A mountain of losses, a pile of regrets, a carefree youth stolen and replaced by responsibilities and longing. We had mutually separated, and yet somehow he again finds a way to manipulate my life.

Feeling choked, I realize I had fooled myself. Indifference had only masked the anger, not erased it. I study his face, searching for signs of aging. His skin lies smooth across his cheekbones, his forehead unfurrowed. Didn't pain and loss have any effect on his appearance, or had his own indifference kept him youthful? Squinting, I nod.

"Excuse me," says Mike's voice behind me.

I move to one side of the doorway.

Mike wheels Big Jack toward the door. "Everyone, follow me to the conference room." He leads us down the hall, my father immediately behind them, while Brett and I bring up the rear.

It's not as if I expect great balls of fire to come shooting toward me, but the atmosphere between the two older men is charged. There can't be that much distrust and animosity without some level of combustion. Nate stays behind Mike and the wheelchair, out of Big Jack's line of sight. Big Jack faces forward, struggling to sit up straight.

Mike thanks everyone for coming as he tucks Big Jack under a corner of the table, his back to the window. "Let's keep this friendly and remember"–he glances at me–"it's strictly informal." He takes a notepad from his pocket and clicks his pen. "Be prepared to talk about when you spoke to Jack during that week and what you discussed. Sally might have questions for you."

In turn, I study each face. These three men had all been involved in my husband's attempt to start a new venture. One would have quashed it completely, the second couldn't resist the temptation to ride along for profit, and the third had pulled all the strings. I wish I felt anything but pissed off at each of them for the part they played in thwarting Jack's life. And his future.

Brett waits to see where the rest of us choose to sit. My father moves to the far end of the table, opposite Mike, as if they are partners. I walk to a chair across from Big Jack and lay my husband's appointment book on the table. Brett follows me and pulls out my chair before he seats himself next to me. Maybe Brett intends to be a buffer between my father and me, the way he stepped in between Big Jack and Nate when he brokered the sale.

With a nod at me, Mike picks up the appointment book and fans the pages. He asks each of us to match dates and notations with conversations, offers, signatures, and meetings. A whole week, the last of Jack's life, unfolds before me with no surprises. Doesn't anyone know what really happened?

Clicking his pen, Mike flips to the next page of his notepad. "Now, I want each of you to think back about your talks with Jack. Anything lead you to believe he was upset or depressed?"

I try to remember even one thing Jack and I discussed. Arguments, money worries, what was for dinner. Nothing comes to mind. The bastard kept his plans well hidden from me.

Brett wags his forefinger. "Not when we first spoke. Later Jack admitted he and his father had had a serious disagreement. Very contentious." He stares at his hands, and then looks up at Nate. "It's one of the reasons I turned him down."

"Big Jack, you have anything to add?" Mike fixes his gaze on my father-in-law, while I wonder what he can possibly say in his own defense.

"We argued. That's all." Big Jack spews the words out, like the snap of a wet towel.

"What about?" I'm not letting him off the hook that easy.

"He wanted to spend too much on another of his cockeyed schemes. I wouldn't go for it."

"Is that when he started contacting other people?" I want to make him squirm and don't care if it happens in front of my father. "As potential partners?"

"I told him he had to give me back the money he took."

"You mean, the money you gave him?"

"I didn't give him any money. On his last day at work, he took $18,000 from the office safe. I told him he'd have to pay it back."

I sink back in my chair. Is this the money Colton was talking about the other day, when I didn't believe him? Without grasping all the implications of Jack's actions, I can see his behavior those last days as desperate. But desperate enough to steal from his father? If Colton knew about it, no wonder he didn't want me to dig all this up. He's been fighting me to protect Jack.

"Nate, it appears you might have been the last one to speak to Jack." Mike leans back in his chair and tugs at his belt buckle. "What was your impression of Jack's reaction to the news you'd bought the whole enchilada?"

Jack's David to my father's Goliath, maybe? Except Goliath would win this one. I am disgusted just hearing about it.

My father places his hands carefully on the edge of the table as if he's hiding the cards he'd just been dealt. "Disbelief at first. He thought he'd be out of a job the next day."

"What did you tell him?"

"I offered him his same job at a slightly higher salary, with a chance for advancement. I planned to make him area manager in the event of improvement and expansion." Nate throws a quick look in my direction. "He knew there'd be hurdles, but he seemed pleased."

My father's voice reveals his unemotional, matter-of-fact demeanor, a practiced response to every event, whether crisis or routine. He used the identical tone when he informed me my mother was all packed for a visit to the sanitarium. I don't cry this time either.

We must have been getting ready to take a trip somewhere because somebody's luggage waited in the front entryway. No one told me where we were going, but I supposed Mrs. Gussmann had already instructed one of the upstairs maids to pack for me. I climbed the stairs to my room, to be sure my doll Esmeralda came along. Three years ago Mother's cousin, Audrey Cromwell, ordered it for Christmas from a doll maker who created it to look like me. Esmeralda and I also had seven matching outfits. Despite what Clyde said, nine wasn't too old to be playing with dolls.

My room looked just as I left it this morning, clean and everything put away. I wondered where my suitcases were. Maybe someone carried them to the trunk of the car already.

I tucked Esmeralda under my arm and wandered down the hall to Mother's suite. Grunts and groans came from beyond her bedroom. I tiptoed toward her dressing room and peeked in. She straddled a bench, pulling on a knob to her highboy. The bottom drawer wouldn't open, and she used language that would earn me a spanking. When she noticed me, she asked me to bring her a hammer. She needed lingerie for the trip.

I was not allowed to give Mother any tools, nor was anyone else, but I went downstairs anyway in search of someone to help. To my surprise, our pilot Danny waited in the entry hall.

"Hello, missy." He doffed his cap. "Coming for another ride with me soon?"

"Of course." I tried not to make a face at him, since I hated that nickname. The Negro servants called me Miss Sally, but everyone else just used my name. "Can you please come help me?" All the same, I thought he was very cute, with broad shoulders and close-cropped blond hair. He won some medals in the last war and was very proud of them. Mrs. Gussmann once said he acted like he was the Lord's gift to women, but I didn't know what she meant by that.

I took him upstairs to my mother's dressing room. His eyes widened when he saw my mother in her pale pink dressing gown, barefooted and with her blonde hair hanging down.

She asked him to get the drawer unstuck and he moved the bench out of the way. She and I stepped back while he braced his foot against the front of the dresser, next to the stubborn drawer. Standing on one leg, he gave a mighty pull, once, twice, and the drawer popped open. He flew backwards, dragging the drawer with him and scattering Mother's underwear all over the floor. Danny flopped on his back and a pair of blue lace panties landed on his face.

Mother shrieked with laughter, holding her tummy and leaning against the wall. I started to giggle, until the figure of my father blocked the light in the doorway.

"What is going on here?' he barked.

Like it was a giant leech, Danny snatched the underpants from his face and turned sickly white. "Oh, sweet Jesus," he gasped. "Mr. Wallace, I swear I was just helping your missus get a drawer unstuck." He jumped to his feet. "I was downstairs when your daughter came to get me."

I felt sorry for our pilot. Daddy shouldn't have been mad at him, because the troublesome drawer wasn't his fault. Daddy glanced at me, and I nodded, but he glared at Mother. Then he turned to Danny. "Your only concern here is to take the luggage to the airstrip and stow it in the plane. Wait for me on the front porch."

Danny raced out of the room and I edged toward the door. I didn't want to witness my parents arguing. It would make for a bad beginning to our trip together.

My father picked up a white bra and tossed it at my mother. "Please get your clothes on. We're leaving in ten minutes." He talked through clenched teeth, but his manner was calm.

She shouted at him that she wouldn't go and didn't need any check-up at the clinic in Baltimore.

I put my fingers in my ears, but I could still hear her.

"You want the doctor to come here again and give you another treatment?" Daddy spoke softer than she did, the kind of tone that perked up everyone's ears because they didn't want to miss a syllable.

He might as well have thrown a blanket over her. She rubbed her wrists and frowned, as if she was trying to remember where she left her gold cuff bracelets. Her voice grew quieter, like she was telling a secret, as she promised to get dressed and meet him in the entry hall.

Daddy turned to leave and stopped when he saw me. "Oh?" He glanced at Mother, uncertainty on his face. "How long have you been standing there, Sally?"

He didn't wait for my answer, as he left the room in two quick strides.

Mother dropped to the floor and shoveled her lingerie back into the drawer. I knelt to help her, but she told me never mind. Scrambling to her feet, she sent me out so she could change into a traveling suit.

I went back downstairs to the entry. Daddy must have stepped outside. I checked the ID tags on the only two bags remaining. They belonged to Mother. Danny probably stowed mine already.

The front door swung open, and Danny came in to gather up the two bags. He must have been still embarrassed, because he didn't look at me.

"May I come sit beside you during the flight for a little while?" I asked. "I like to watch the instruments."

He looked puzzled. "I didn't think you were coming on this jaunt." His hands were too full for him to close the front door after he took the bags outside.

His words pierced my heart like icicles. Why couldn't I go along on the trip? It wasn't fair to leave me behind.

In a panic, I looked to the left and right. Daddy wasn't in either room. A door closed upstairs. The grandfather clock's first chime startled me, and I ran to my father's office. He talked quietly into the phone and snapped his briefcase shut at the same time. When he hung up, he stared at me.

As if he could read my thoughts, he said, "Not this trip. You're staying home." His voice was calm, as if he had just given Mrs. Gussmann his order for dinner.

Tears pricked my eyes and I blinked several times to make them quit. "But I don't want to get left here. Mother needs me to go with her."

He hefted his leather case off his desk.

I fought back the sobs and swallowed hard. "How soon will she be home?"

"I'll be back in a few days." He walked out, leaving me to gaze at the portrait of Mother hanging over the mantel. It was painted when she was young and beautiful and healthy.

While I still stared at her portrait, the front door closed.

School and Mrs. Gussmann kept me busy, so several days passed before I realized how long they had been gone. By the dinner hour of the third day, I was excited to learn the plane had landed at Daddy's airstrip. Downstairs, I waited for the sound of his car in the driveway. I wanted to show Mother my book report and what I'd been drawing while she was away. Daddy came in the house alone.

I stood on my tiptoes, but couldn't see over his shoulder. "Where's Mother?"

He sighed and placed his briefcase on the table in the entryway. "She has to stay at the hospital."

"For how long?"

Daddy rubbed his chin, his fingers covering his mouth. "For a long time."

When he said she was sick and the doctors told him a cure was impossible, I felt like I had stepped into a flowing stream and the water rushed by faster than I realized. I was about to lose my balance and get swept away, taken far from the shore I have always known.

Mike shuffles his papers. "Did you and Jack discuss anything else that last evening, Nate?"

I didn't know he is allowed to address my father by his first name. Besides Mother, Clyde was the only other person I ever heard call him Nate. Perhaps logical, since Clyde was Mike's father.

"He expressed concern over telling his wife about the sale of his father's company. He worried Sally would leave him." He glances toward me and speaks more softly. "Again."

Mike's eyebrows shoot up and his eyes shift sideways at me.

I swallow hard and wonder how red my face has turned. "It was only once . . . before Colton was born." Does my father also know I returned because I discovered I was pregnant? He has no idea what it requires to keep a marriage together for the sake of a child. His fortune let him take the easy way out.

Mike returns his gaze to Nate's face. "You mean because her husband would be working for her estranged father?"

Is Mike trying to pin Jack's state of mind on me? My husband and I never discussed any of his arrangements concerning Brett or my father.

As Nate nods, Mike purses his lips. "Did he mention Big Jack's reaction to finding his son and his company under new management?"

Nate inclines his head toward Big Jack. "He told me they

almost came to blows. His father fired him, then kicked him out of the office."

Big Jack stirs in his wheelchair. "He was *my* employee. It was strictly business between us. I had every right to . . ."

So that's what Big Jack has been hiding. He will never be anything but a vicious, malevolent bastard who deserves to die alone. How could he make his son suffer so?

Mike rubs his palms together and takes a deep breath. "It seems we have several reasons why Jack may have felt despondent, despite the benefits of new ownership. Possibly the good news didn't outweigh the bad, at least in *his* mind." He looks at me and hands me Jack's book. "Unless you can give me any other insight, I'll have to stick with the original ruling from the county coroner."

Gasping, I grab the edge of the table until my knuckles hurt. "But Mike, the appointment book–"

"Doesn't prove anything." His voice softens. "It seems like Jack became overwhelmed at the impact of such a big change. Sally, please accept that." He puts his hand on my arm, but I jerk it away. "That's not to say anyone's to blame. Jack probably just didn't see a way through. The money situation, or whatever you want to call it, was extra pressure. He went out after his last day at work, had a few too many drinks, came home late, and left the motor running when he shut the garage door."

"You're wrong. Jack made plans for later. Days after he . . ." I wave Jack's book at him, while my thoughts choke off my air and I can't get a breath.

"May I see that, please?" says Nate.

Brett asks my permission and then hands it to Nate. Not even our fingertips touch.

After flipping a few pages, Nate looks at me. "Jack wrote Colton's name on the Sunday following the day of his death, maybe for a father-son event." He holds out the appointment book toward me. "Is it possible your son could add something?"

Brett intercepts it for me and I pass the book to Mike. "You've got to speak to Colton. You can make it part of his probation."

Mike doesn't move. "Are you suggesting I try to trick him?"

"He won't discuss anything with me. Maybe you can get him to tell you what he and Jack talked about that night."

Mike glowers at me. "Have you forgotten that he knocked me down at the festival, or did you think he was playing tackle?"

"Use your official powers of persuasion. Tell him he can't evade your questions or pretend he doesn't remember."

"What makes you believe he might know anything?"

"I already mentioned, Colton told me Jack called home around nine o'clock that night, but he wouldn't tell me what he said, except that he'd be late." I gulp and try not to hiccough. "Please, Mike." While he strokes the stubble on his chin, I go numb all over.

Mike shoots a look at Nate, who gives a tiny nod of his head. If I had blinked, I would have missed it.

"Okay," Mike says. "Tell Colton I'll need to see him at the station tomorrow."

A rush of warm air flows over me and my muscles relax, but I refuse to acknowledge it as gratitude. If my father manipulates Mike to dig deeper, I can't object.

Everyone in the room seems to sigh in relief, but a knock at the door makes me jump. Brett rises from his chair and pulls it open. He answers a question from a uniformed person in the hallway, and then motions to Mike. "Someone to see you."

Mike excuses himself and steps out into the hallway. The rest of us wait in silence, gazing anywhere but at each other.

When Mike returns, he seems shaken. "Colton called the hospital looking for us."

I grab my throat. "Is he all right?"

"Angelique fainted. He says she's still woozy, but she won't let him call an ambulance. Unless anyone has something to add . . ." He takes his keys out of his pocket.

"I'm coming with you." I pick up my purse and head toward the door.

I count on Big Jack's relief to have us out of his way, and on Brett to understand our hurry to reach my son. My father shouldn't expect me to treat him any differently than he acts toward me. I don't say good-bye as I leave the room.

CHAPTER THIRTEEN

Mike and I speak very little during the ride down the hospital elevator. Since he already agreed to interview Colton, I figure I'll wait for the outcome before badgering him further. Later I'll sic both Saint Trixie and my mother on Colton if their powers can do any good. For now, I have to count on Mike to probe the stubborn reaches of my son's memory.

Mike presses his palm against the rubber seal as the elevator doors part. "I wonder if Angelique has put on more makeup so we won't notice she's turned pale and weak." He tries to smile. "Can't you just see her flopped on her fainting couch?"

"I'm not sure what to expect."

He nods, and we fall in step together out the elevator doors and down the first floor hallway. Our strides match in length and pace.

Images gallop through my mind, getting worse by the moment. What if Angelique has fallen and Colton can't lift her up? Did she stop breathing? "I'm just hoping Colton hasn't, well, maybe he kept his cool." I grab Mike by the arm. "What if we dispatch an ambulance before leaving the hospital and–"

"She'd send it back without setting foot in it." He holds the emergency entrance door open and we cross the parking lot. "Look, we have to join forces and persuade her to get a checkup."

Mike is more worried than I first thought. He climbs into his cruiser, leaving me to stand next to my unopened car door and wonder how on earth we will ever talk Angelique into seeing a doctor for professional purposes only.

After following him across town, I park next to his squad car in her driveway. Her front door stands wide open, while laughter ricochets from the back of the house, interrupted by an electronic whirring noise.

Angelique looks up as we peek through the kitchen door. "There you are, darlings. How about a virgin daiquiri?" A long, slim cigarette dangles from her fuchsia-tinted lips.

"New gadget?" Mike asks.

Colton flicks the toggle switch to Angelique's stainless Hamilton Beach blender, and frenzied pink slush comes to a standstill in the glass container. He sips from a large stemmed goblet, his eyes daring me to stop him.

"Isn't Colton a little young to tend bar?" I scan the counters for a bottle of rum, not that I suspect Angelique of corrupting my son. But in her condition, whatever it might be, he can easily sneak something past her. I check the ashtray to be sure all the butts wear pink lipstick.

"Strictly in training." Angelique's throaty laugh collapses into a deep cough. For a moment her face turns the same shade as her lips, then she says, "We'll add the alcohol after he goes to bed."

"Thanks, but I have to work tonight," Mike says. "Where's your phone book?"

She directs him to the drawer in the corner, and he waves through the pages like a traffic cop during rush hour. When his hand rests near the center of the book, he picks up her phone.

Angelique sets her glass on the table. "What are you looking for?"

"A specialist."

"I don't know what for." She throws her head back and glances away, arms crossed over her chest.

I sit next to her at the kitchen table and put my hand on her arm. With a slight wince, I realize it is the same appeasing gesture Mike tried on me at the hospital. "We're concerned about your health, Angelique. You need to get a checkup to find out why you're short of breath so often."

My luck fares no better with Angelique than his had with me. She pulls loose. "Let's all go to dinner. My treat."

"Here we are," Mike says. "Cardiopulmonary." He dials the number and drags the phone into the hallway. After a few muttered negotiations, he returns to the kitchen, phone cradled on his shoulder. "They have a cancellation tomorrow at eleven."

"I'm not going."

He speaks into the receiver, "Yes, that will be fine," and hangs up. "Sally, Raúl is out of town for a few days. Can you take her to the medical center or shall I?"

Angelique shakes her index finger toward Mike. "You call them right back and cancel that appointment."

For a split second, I peer at Mike and speculate whether he learned from my father how to finesse such bossy interference. "I can drive her."

Mike sits on the other side of Angelique and takes her hand in his. "Sally and I are ganged up on you this time. No more pretending or hiding your symptoms. We need you to take better care of yourself. You're too young to–"

At the sound of glass crashing to the Saltillo tile floor, I turn around to stare at Colton.

He ignores the broken container at his feet and the glass shards sticking up like icebergs in a frozen pink lake. His face looks suspended, as though he fears Angelique will disappear if he blinks. "You can't die." His lip quivers. "You can't leave me."

All their argument, the clink of stemmed glassware, even the ticking of her kitchen clock melds together into a whisper. Then absolute silence commands the room, until all I can hear is the thudding of my own heart.

Has all I lost and suffered at his age given me a hard shell? I should be able to express those fears to Angelique, but his feelings bubble up faster than I can sort my thoughts. Maybe I tamp my own emotions below the surface, where they won't impede my actions. If only I had spoken similar words to my mother when I was Colton's age. Would it have made a difference?

Mike stands up. "Colton has a–"

"Oh, hush." As if a young lieutenant has asked her to dance, Angelique rises from her chair and steps over the spilled daiquiri and broken glass. She puts her arm around Colton's shoulder and squeezes him close enough to kiss him on the cheek. "You precious boy. Of course I'm not going to leave you. Don't you worry." She glares at Mike and me. "The doctor won't find a single thing wrong with me."

Mike and I look at each other and sigh in tandem. How

did a thirteen-year-old boy succeed where two adults hit a brick wall? Maybe my mother worked her spell through Colton this time.

AFTER MIKE DECLINES HER OFFER for dinner, he leaves to make his rounds, while Angelique, Colton, and I beat the evening crowd to the Hot Crossed Buns Diner. Our favorite waitress Lois drops menus at our booth, out of habit more than the possibility we need to view the selection. Colton's double grilled cheese sandwich, a peach half stuffed with cottage cheese, with French fries on the side, makes up his standard order for perhaps the thousandth time since he learned to read.

"When are you graduating to chicken fried steak?" Angelique asks him.

"As soon as I'm big enough to play football."

"Basketball isn't satisfying enough?"

"You can't knock people down in basketball. Not without getting a penalty."

She cackles while they exchange more quips, and I envy their camaraderie. How did I lose touch with my son, even when he sits across the table from me? Jack's death came between us instead of driving us closer. Changing the ruling from suicide to accident will be the best thing for us. I need no more proof.

I sit through dinner without saying much, as they chat about their favorite TV shows. He likes "Rockford Files" and "MASH," while she prefers "Mary Tyler Moore" and "Police Woman." She assures him he can stay up late at her house and watch "Mannix" or "S.W.A.T." Although she smiles at me, I dodge the issue of parental permission. It is easier to avoid

Colton's ire by keeping silent than endure his angry outbursts and huffy demeanor. Good thing the parking lot activity picks up soon. Observing people arrive gives me something to do.

Angelique motions for Lois to bring her coffee. "Colton, are you staying with me again tonight?"

With a grin, he nods.

"I don't know about that," I say.

His smile disappears as if I unplugged it, and Angelique twists sideways toward me, one eyebrow raised a smidgeon.

"Why don't *you* come spend the night with Colton and me instead?" I ask. "The guest room is ready, clean sheets already on the bed." While Angelique sips her coffee, I wait. "That way, I can drop Colton at Officer Avery's headquarters before I take you to the specialist in the morning."

"How come I have to go there?" His face freezes.

"He wants to ask you some things about Dad's final week. What you remember, what Dad talked about, how his mood seemed to you." I can't bring myself to mention the cash Jack took, despite that Colton overheard Jack's conversation and probably knows more than I do about it.

"Are you coming, too?"

I hate to give my son another chance to reject me or take his hostility out on me. Perhaps I should tell him he will remember and talk more if he and Mike meet alone. Yet I can't interpret the feelings behind his question. "Legally I might have to. Do you *want* me to be there?"

"No." He grows fidgety and runs his fingers along the edge of the table. "This is your stupid idea. I don't want to go at all."

"You have no choice. It's part of your probation, even if it's unofficial. Maybe you can be part of the solution and help make things better for us. Besides, I already gave Mike permission to speak to you as a family friend."

He collapses against the cushioned divider and stares at his empty plate. His breathing grows shallow and labored, and for a minute I think he might vomit.

"Colton," Angelique says. "Why don't you go to the bakery and pick out some cinnamon buns for us for breakfast? Get whatever you want and tell Lois to put it on my ticket."

He bolts from the table like a bobcat escaping from a cage.

I sigh and wonder how long before Colton and I can speak about teenager problems and fun stuff, go to the new mall or a movie together, and decorate eggs for Easter. Will everything awful that happens always be my fault?

Angelique emits a dainty cough while I drum my fingers on the tabletop, staring straight in front of me. I squirm. "You want to say something. Go ahead."

"It's hard for Colton to feel like you're listening to him."

"I hear every single word he utters." I unfold and refold my napkin. "Especially the hateful ones."

"You're only listening with your ears. What does your heart tell you?"

"Colton is angry that Jack's dead, and somehow I'm to blame."

"Quit focusing on yourself for a minute and take a good look at Colton. Do you think he feels responsible somehow for Jack's suicide?"

"We don't *know* it's suicide, not yet. I'm trying to find a way for us both to feel better, despite losing Jack in such a dreadful way." I frown. "How can Colton be responsible for Jack's actions that night? He was in bed asleep."

"I don't mean he had anything to *do* with it, but sometimes children believe they can or should be able to prevent something from happening to their parents." The spoon clinks twice as she stirs her coffee. "It's their childish fantasy, an unrealistic view of their powers. Like children of divorced parents feel it's their fault, or that maybe they can get their parents back together again."

I study my fingernails, as my breathing grows shallow. I know what that kind of responsibility feels like.

I put on a clean frock and pulled my hair back neatly in a ponytail. If my father saw how well I managed, maybe I could persuade him to bring Mother home. He already noticed I was tall for the age of ten.

The grandfather clock in the entry hall chimed six times. I sat on the bottom step of the main staircase and waited. He'd realize that she was better off at home because I could take care of her. He'd change his mind and believe I would never again do anything to upset her.

While my finger traced the pattern in the Persian carpet, I planned her meals and selected her clothes. I scheduled outings to our gardens, with the pond and the tempietto beyond. She would sit resting on the terrace and I'd pick her favorite flowers and lay them in her lap. She'd wear white, always white, with a wide-brimmed straw hat. I really liked it when she smiled at me and patted my cheek.

By seven o'clock, Mrs. Gussmann bustled into the hall. "There you are, child," she fretted. "Did you know I've been keeping your dinner warm for you?"

"Sorry. I wanted to wait here for Daddy."

"What's that red streak on your face?" She rubbed my forehead with her thumb. "You must have been leaning against the newel post."

"Is Daddy home yet?" There was a chance he might have entered the house from the side door leading to the courtyard by the garage. "It's getting dark outside."

"Come along to the small dining room and have your supper. Your father won't be home for a while longer."

I trudged behind her, practicing my speech under my breath.

"What's that?" Mrs. Gussmann's hearing has gotten worse lately. She forgot to ask me to repeat myself. Maybe her memory has slipped as well.

In the informal dining room, she pulled a chair out for me and I sat at one end of the huge oak table. From the kitchen, she brought a plate of roast beef with mashed potatoes and green peas and set it in front of me. I wondered how Mother would like the gravy. After my third bite, I strained my ears toward the front of the house. A door slammed, and I jumped up and dashed back to the entry hall.

There stood my father, sorting the day's mail, briefcase at his feet, frown on his face. He glanced at me, and I could tell he was tired by the way his mouth drooped. Without saying anything, he tossed the mail onto a table and stooped to pick up his briefcase, but I was too quick for him. Smiling up at him, I grabbed the handle and then followed him into his office.

Mrs. Gussmann had already switched on the green-shaded banker's lamp on his mahogany desk and I hauled his briefcase to the center and laid it flat on top. I expected him to sit behind his desk, but he chose the leather sofa instead. With the *Wall Street Journal* across his lap, he propped his feet on the coffee table.

"Daddy, I already finished my homework and didn't need any help."

He shuffled the newspaper.

"Clyde says I must be getting smarter, or probably just more grown up."

"Maybe so." Yawning, he turned the page.

"I picked out my clothes for school every day this week, without Mrs. Gussmann." I scooted around the end of the sofa and stood at the edge of the coffee table. "Would you like me to order dinner for you? I can ask one of the servants to bring it in here."

He shook his head. "Not now."

I launched into my prepared speech, but before I could get out my logical explanation, he said no. No matter how many times I apologized or said it's my fault, his answer was always, "No."

"You don't realize Mother needs me."

"I believe *you* think so."

"You don't know how mature I've become, how capable I am. Look at me."

He glanced around the edge of his newspaper. "I see you."

"I promise never to make her cry, ever again." I stamped my feet.

He folded up the newspaper and tossed it to one side. Several sections slid off the slippery leather sofa and landed near my ankle. I planted both feet firmly on the floor, but he rose to tower over me. He glared down at me. "Don't ever bring this up again."

If I believed I held the power to make Daddy change his mind, I must have imagined it, but I couldn't give up. The very idea of losing was hateful and I shoved it from my mind. I kicked his newspaper under the table and stomped out of his office.

I stare out the window into the diner's busy parking lot. "Colton treats me like I'm the enemy. It's so . . ." Not fair because Colton fails to realize a big difference. Unlike my father's choice to banish my mother, I didn't decide to cause Jack's death. "I didn't do anything wrong."

"Can you see how he feels powerless?" Angelique asks.

"I can try to reinforce for him that he's not to blame for anything."

"That's a start."

I tell Angelique about the money Jack took. "Also Colton doesn't want anyone making his father look bad. That's why he's been so resistant to my efforts."

"Mike will be sensitive as well, when he speaks with Colton tomorrow. Try to remember Colton can't direct his anger at himself, so you're the next best target. Moms usually are."

"And he chooses me because I'm tougher than dirt and I'll love him, no matter what he does." As I speak those words, I pray they are true and hope my battle fatigue doesn't make me give up.

The sound of exploding glass, followed by a high-pitched scream, hits the room like a bolt of thunder. A split second without any commotion gives customers a chance to look around for a dropped tray or a brick through the window. Then the voices crescendo as everyone speculates on the cause of the noise.

Lois comes running toward our table, pointing to the bakery section. "Come quick," she pants. "It's Colton."

I follow her, but she moves too slowly, so I race around her before we get halfway across the dining room. In the bakery, Colton stands in front of the display case, holding a small loaf of bread.

Everything shifts to slow motion. I can't reach him fast enough. Blood from the back of his hand soaks into the bread and drips onto the linoleum floor amid the shattered glass.

"Colton!" I call. "Colton, what happened?"

"He put his fist through the glass," Lois tells me, but she sounds far away.

My son looks at me with his large sad eyes, dark and mysterious like Jack's, and opens his mouth. His jaw muscles move, but no sound comes out. Then his knees buckle and he falls faint to the floor, surrounded by the shards and blood, both arms stretched out sideways like wings.

Before I can bend down to help him, Angelique comes up behind me and puts her hand on my shoulder. "Let's get him up and out of here."

Squatting on either side, we clutch him by the shoulders and try to lift him, but his dead weight proves too heavy for Angelique. Lois appears offering ice cubes in a clean white towel and wraps his hand. Two men I vaguely recognize step forward to help, and they all but carry him out to my car. He doesn't resist when they buckle his seat belt.

The whole way to the emergency clinic, Colton doesn't speak. He says nothing when the doctor gives him a shot to deaden his hand, or when he stitches his flesh back together. In silence, he lets the doctor wrap a bandage around his hand, up past his wrist, and put his arm in a sling.

After the doctor places a thermometer into Colton's mouth, he motions me to one side. "Your son shows some signs of being in shock, but possibly not from the injury. He hasn't spoken one word." He fans the papers on his clipboard. "Something's not right. Any idea what's bothering him?"

I shake my head.

"No? Well, these episodes are seldom related to just one

incident. I'm going to recommend a drug test and a psychiatric consult. We'll need a urine sample. Sign here."

His words hit me like a shove to the chest. Colton on drugs? Impossible. Unless Skipper has corrupted him behind my back.

How could the ER doctor possibly believe my son requires a psychiatrist? Does he think I haven't done a good enough job maintaining a normal home life? I refuse to give my permission.

He doesn't get it, Mother. You're the only one in the family labeled as crazy. And that's how it's going to stay.

CHAPTER FOURTEEN

Once we leave the emergency clinic, Angelique points out I can't manage to pick up Colton's prescriptions and get him home without her help. She stays in the car, both of them in the back seat, while I collect his antibiotics and pain medications at the pharmacy. Ignoring the total amount, I tell the cashier to charge it to my account, sign the ticket, and drop my copy in the bag. I'll worry about the bill later, when I decide whether to buy groceries or go without heat for the next two weeks. The payment to the emergency clinic all but drained my checking account, and I feel too hammered by exhaustion to remember the balance in savings. I pray our health insurance will reimburse me for some of the expense.

As I steer my car into the garage, Colton moans. Angelique strokes his hair and croons, "There, there, sweet boy. We'll get you into bed right away so you can sleep for hours and hours if you feel like it."

It pains my heart to realize if I touched him and spoke in such endearing terms, he would shake me off and stomp away. We drag ourselves from the car and teeter into the house, with Colton clinging to Angelique as if he were blind.

"The pharmacist recommended not waiting too long between doses of painkiller," I say, as I flick on the kitchen light. "Besides, he said it'll help you sleep." For a moment, I consider swallowing one, too. No, I need to stay alert through what is bound to be an uncomfortable night for all three of us.

Angelique pours a glass of milk for Colton while I peruse the instructions accompanying the bottles of medicine. "We'll continue the antibiotics in the morning, but you should probably take a painkiller now." I hand him a white tablet half the size of my thumbnail and hope he won't choke on it. "If you wake up hurting during the night, the doctor said you can have another one." I slip the bottle into my pants pocket. "I'll keep my door open so I can hear when you call me." If he awakes in enough pain, he will have to speak to me.

Colton takes a big swig of the milk, swallows the pill, and turns toward Angelique. She links her right arm through his good left one and says, "Of course, I'll help you get ready for bed." They hobble out of the kitchen together, and a short while later the stairs creak. Whether they scale them slowly for his sake or hers, I can't tell.

"Good night, Colton," I call after them.

When did Angelique develop radar to answer his unspoken questions? To my knowledge, she had never helped a child of any age get ready for bed. Will she read him a story, too?

I catch my pique before it storms out of control. I should be grateful she came along to keep Colton steady, but it is hard to accept that someone with no parenting experience whatever can so easily replace me. Besides, if she spends her energy comforting Colton, it could be to her own detriment.

After I remember to close the garage door, I trudge across the patio along the back wall of the house until I reach the entrance to my greenhouse. Inside, I fumble in the dark for the light switch. As soon as the light sputters on, bright fluorescence bathes the greenhouse, distorting the pinks and greens of the begonias and geraniums.

There is no point in watering them again, so I occupy myself by rearranging terra cotta pots, short ones in front, taller ones behind. Soon I lose track of time in the rhythm of bending and lifting, enjoying the clatter of the pots, until Angelique's voice catches me by surprise.

"It's cold outside. Guess I can't smoke in here, can I?" She sets her pack of cigarettes and the lighter on the edge of the potting table.

I shake my head. "I'd rather you didn't smoke at all. Why don't you quit?"

"Too late now." She scans the area as she pats her sternum. "I need to sit down. I'm not used to all those stairs."

I clear off a bench for her. "Would you like something to drink?"

"Gin, if you please."

"I bet tomorrow the doctor will tell you to quit." I stand with my hands on my hips and eye her with amusement.

"With tonic and lime." She waits. "What, no fresh lime in the house? Bottled concentrate is okay."

"You know, smoking causes a lot more health problems than lung cancer."

"I'll settle for bourbon instead, if you have any Maker's Mark."

I fill a paper cup with water from the fountain against the wall and hand it to her. "I hope you follow his advice."

She sets it down on the bench. "Thanks, but I'd prefer to hear what Mr. Maker has to say."

Angelique picks up her Virginia Slims and lighter and steps outside. I watch to make sure she keeps steady on her feet. As if drawing an ace from a poker deck, she extracts a long cigarette from the pack and lights it. The smoke hovers above her head until a light breeze chases it into the dark sky overhead.

By the time she returns to the bench, I have moved to one side to restack the plastic bags of pine bark mulch against the wall, next to the fertilizer. One of the bags has torn at the corner, releasing the earthy aroma of fresh pine mixed with soil.

"Brrrr!" Angelique rubs her upper arms. "How can Colton change Mike's mind during their interview tomorrow?"

"I don't have any idea what Colton will say, because he has refused to discuss it with me." I wipe my forehead with the back of my wrist. "Around nine o'clock that night, Jack called home and spoke with Colton while I worked out here. All I know is, Jack told him he'd be home later and not to wait up for him."

"But your whole argument hangs on the fact that appointment book shows Jack made plans for later in the week."

"Mike is reconsidering whether all the mess with Jack's job, the money he helped himself to, and the blow-up with his father caused him to feel depressed enough to kill himself."

"Plus Jack was worried you'd divorce him."

"Maybe I should have. It'd be easier than dealing with his death, suicide or not."

"You don't mean that, do you?"

"Not really."

"What would Colton possibly have to say about Jack's state of mind?"

I sit down next to her and dust my palms together. "Very likely the last person to speak to Jack before he died was Colton. If he can convince Mike that Jack was *not* depressed, but rather looking forward to working for my father, where he'd have job security and get a raise, then Mike will have to rethink his conclusion."

"Assume Colton tells Mike exactly what you describe. Then you hope Mike can get the coroner to revise his finding?"

"I'm counting on it."

"But Sally, my angel, it doesn't work that way. The coroner's ruling is official, registered at the courthouse, and listed with the IRS. You can't expect a small town sheriff to get all those federal records changed just because you *know* something, which actually amounts to no more than a hunch. Mike doesn't have that kind of power and influence."

"But Mike wants to be on our team, and besides he has resources."

Angelique frowns and squints at me, as if she can't remember my name. "He's certainly stepped forward lately with solutions to your problems." Then her face muscles relax as her mouth forms a small 'o.' She points her index finger at me. "You mean Nate, don't you?"

My head might as well crack in two. The voice on one side screams, "No, never, not possible," while the other insists Nate can pull any string he wants and asks why not use him to get what I need. It is about time he shows up helpful on my terms for a change. Maybe I have been subconsciously maneuvering in that direction. Yet my heart refuses to let that line of reasoning prevail.

"Not him. Colton."

"That's a lot of pressure on one adolescent boy. Are you sure it's worth it?" She hugs her quilted Oriental waistcoat tighter around her torso. "Hasn't bringing this up had a negative effect on Colton? Look at all his so-called accidents recently." Her voiced softens. "Have you considered getting professional help for him?"

"Like my father did for my mother? We know how that ended, don't we? Colton's behavior will improve the instant the ruling gets changed from suicide to accident. Then we can get on with our lives and handle our grief in a healthy way."

"Why do you call it accidental?" Angelique wags her head until her earrings jingle. "Didn't Jack lower the garage door himself, with the motor still running?"

"But he had gotten so drunk, he didn't know what he was doing."

"Happy drunk?"

I stretch out my legs in front of me and raise my arms over my head, elbow joints popping. "If Colton confirms it."

"So now, since Mike doesn't quite believe you or the appointment book, you expect your son to provide the crucial testimony?"

"Sure, why not?"

"Have you forgotten about the money Big Jack demanded that Jack repay? What about the note Jack left in the front seat?"

I sigh and stare at my shoes. "Every word is burned into my brain. Thing is, it wasn't like Jack to threaten me. It's like he was talking to someone else. He was so angry."

"If it wasn't meant for you, who—"

I sit up straight and slap my thigh. "Big Jack."

"What?"

"Now it makes sense. After Big Jack fired him, Jack wrote that awful note to his father, not to me. Big Jack was the one who would have to learn to get along without him and see how well he managed alone."

"How can you be sure?"

"Oh, I'm absolutely sure. With that and Colton's official testimony."

"Unofficial or otherwise, maybe he's not up to it."

Before I can answer, Angelique and I turn our heads in tandem toward the sound coming from the entrance to the greenhouse. Pale and shivering, Colton stands there in his underwear looking up at the rafters as if he has spied an owl. His injured hand falls at his side, while the cotton sling around his neck dangles near his waist. He seems not to realize we are present, as he grunts and sucks in the cold night air.

"No quick moves," Angelique whispers. "Try not to startle him." Louder she says, "Colton, you're chilled." As I follow her, she walks slowly toward Colton, pulling her arms out of her waistcoat. "Did you have a bad dream? Let me wrap this around you."

After she covers him, she coaxes him into the house and back up the stairs. I watch from the doorway of his room as she pulls a tee shirt down over his head, tucks him under the sheet, and sits on the edge of his bed. We wait until the twitching stops and his breathing grows steady and shallow. She leans forward to kiss his cheek and pulls the blanket up over his shoulder, and then she tiptoes toward the door and takes me by the hand.

"He seems comfortable now, but I'm still cold," she says with a shiver. "Can you turn the heat up?" She drapes the silk waistcoat around her shoulders and rubs her upper arms.

"How about some coffee? I can make us some decaf." I stare at the lump under Colton's bed covers and wonder how long my son will sleep. "On second thought, maybe regular is better."

"Regular will keep you up all night."

"That's the idea."

Downstairs again in the kitchen, she suggests I call Mike and cancel Colton's appointment tomorrow. I agree to postpone it until we can evaluate his state of mind, maybe until the pain medication wears off. No point in asking him questions if he can't make sense.

"Someone will have to stay with him while I take you to the specialist." I drain the last of my coffee from Grandmother Mason's china cup.

"What about Judith?"

"I'll call her in the morning. Let's get some rest."

Poor dear Angelique. Up the stairs for the third time in less than an hour. No wonder she is tired and out of breath. A good night's sleep will work wonders for all of us.

But sleep is the farthest thing from my mind. Even when we are all in our beds, whispers from the edge of darkness call to me and help me keep my vigil.

Today I was up extra early to get ready for school while the house was still quiet. I should have read over my new spelling list one more time, to help me prepare for the sixth grade spelling bee. Also I wanted to draw a picture for Aunt Mary to cheer her up. The doctor has been coming each morning and again in the evenings to check on her. So far, Aunt Mary has been too weak to get out of bed.

Lately Daddy has looked really tired. It couldn't be from working too hard, because he hasn't left the house in three days. Maybe the doctor should give Daddy some of Aunt Mary's pep pills.

Yesterday I heard Mrs. Gussmann talking in the kitchen. She said she was conversing with the Almighty, but I thought she should wait until Sunday morning when God settles back on His throne and just listens. She also sang church songs like "Shall We Gather at the River" or "Precious Lord, Take My Hand." I hoped Mrs. Gussmann wasn't planning to go anywhere. Even though I was now eleven and grown very responsible, I didn't know how we'd get our meals cooked or laundry done without her.

Life has been pretty dull around our house and I missed Clyde. Since Daddy hasn't taken any trips this week, Clyde has gone to tend to business elsewhere instead of staying around Mason's Crossing.

Aunt Mary liked the seashore, where she lived when she was a little girl, so I got out my colored pencils in blue and tan, plus green for the palm trees. I sat at the table in my room and sketched the beach, with seashells, sand dunes, and waves crashing on the shore. The seagull in the sky was almost finished when a voice down the hall called, "Mr. Nate, Mr. Nate!"

Now that Mother was moved to the hospital, my bedroom door wasn't locked any more. I opened it and peeked out. The voice belonged to one of the new upstairs maids, and she raced to the banister and hollered down the stairwell.

I waited in my doorway as my father dashed up the main staircase. He must have spent the night in his office again. Mrs. Gussmann usually found him there in the morning after she made coffee. She always fussed over him about getting proper rest.

When Daddy reached the door to Aunt Mary's room, he told the maid to summon the doctor and Mrs. Gussmann. The maid headed for the back staircase, but he paused outside the room. I could tell by the way his shoulders moved that he was taking deep breaths. Without waiting for Mrs. Gussmann, he stepped into Aunt Mary's room and closed the door.

I tiptoed down the hall and put my ear to her door. Daddy and Aunt Mary didn't make any sounds. She must have been asleep.

I was still leaning against the door when Mrs. Gussmann came up behind me and rapped softly on it. She didn't often frown, but this morning her eyebrows were knitted together like dark clouds.

Daddy answered, "Come in."

Mrs. Gussmann turned to me and, with a finger to her lips, shooed me away from the door. She stepped inside, but I didn't feel like going back to my room to finish my drawing. I decided to give it to Aunt Mary after school.

Within minutes, the house came alive. Servants bustled about, carrying folded stacks of fresh bed linens, cardboard boxes from the storeroom, and even vases full of the daily fresh flowers Daddy insisted on, even though Mother isn't here to enjoy them. Most of the maids said good morning as they passed me in the hall, but no one offered to take me to school.

When Mrs. Gussmann came out of Aunt Mary's room, she stopped one of the maids to give her instructions for breakfast and answer questions. She shook her head slowly. "Yes, poor thing passed in her sleep."

Now I understood why Daddy didn't go to bed. He must have been worried about her dying during the night. I wondered if Aunt Mary had felt any pain. She was always grabbing her side and hissing. I thought maybe I should light a candle or something.

Mrs. Gussmann blew her nose. "The doctor told Mr. Nate on Tuesday she wouldn't last much longer. Her heart was too damaged from the scarlet fever she suffered as a baby."

After the maid headed downstairs to the kitchen, Mrs. Gussmann noticed me across the hall. "Oh, Sally, I guess you overheard."

I nodded, while Mrs. Gussmann gathered me up in her arms. I was tall enough not to get smothered by her huge bosom, but I didn't mind it when she hugged me. She smelled like cinnamon. "What's it like to die in your sleep?" I couldn't quite picture someone just stopping breathing without a struggle.

Mrs. Gussmann explained that God took Aunt Mary to heaven to be with her mother and her little sister, who both died of the Spanish flu a long time ago. "Your father is the only one left now."

"Why did God take her away?"

"He needed her more than we did."

I never thought about God needing someone, as if He was human like us. If she asked me who I needed, I would know just what to say. Angelique for certain, and definitely Clyde, too.

Daddy opened the door. "Mrs. Gussmann?"

We both turned at the sound of his voice.

"Please call the funeral home and tell them to send the hearse. Is the doctor here yet?"

Releasing me, she answered my father and said how terribly sorry she was for his loss. "Miss Mary will need clothes for the burial."

"Oh, yes. Select something appropriate from her closet."

Aunt Mary was the first person I knew who died. How were they going to get her out the door and down the stairs? I kept waiting for my tears to start. Someone should cry because she was dead.

Before lunch, I stood in my closet and wondered what Mrs. Gussmann would select for me if I died. Maybe my blue sweater and matching plaid skirt, a new uniform for the school I'd attend soon. She should probably choose a different outfit so people wouldn't get me mixed up with all those other girls.

Daddy stayed in his office until lunch. Reverend Atherton from Hillside Methodist joined us in the informal dining room and he told us how sorrowful he was for us. "I know you'll miss her every day."

I squirmed in my chair and wondered what to answer. It would have been impolite for me to say he's mistaken. How could Daddy miss his sister when he didn't spend much time with her? He didn't miss my mother either. I could tell because he never mentioned her name, except on the days before we flew to Baltimore for a visit.

If something like this ever happened to Angelique, I'd scream and cry and beg God to bring her back. But I never felt very close to Aunt Mary. In the years before she got too sick, she often accused my father of spoiling me. She complained he wasted too much money on me, like she didn't want me to have so many things. I guessed all that time she spent in an orphanage made her stingy. Had sickly Aunt Mary treated me the way Angelique did, then I'd miss her. I felt bad because I was supposed to feel sad.

Reverend Atherton patted my shoulder. "Your aunt was very special to you, I know."

I couldn't smile, but instead nodded at the minister, which amounted to the same thing as saying "yes" right out loud, and hoped I didn't go to hell for being a liar.

My father checked the time on his watch. "Is it possible to hold the service tomorrow?"

"That soon?" As Reverend Atherton swallowed, his Adam's apple bounced up and down. "What about your other relatives? Won't they need time to get here?" He expected our family to be like everyone else's.

"There is no one." Daddy wiped his mouth with his napkin. "I have to go to Cairo on Friday."

The minister looked puzzled. "Illinois or Georgia?"

"Egypt." My father's expression said business-as-usual. He wasn't worried if Reverend Atherton figured out he didn't care about anyone.

Twisting my lips and frowning, I tried to look sad and hoped Reverend Atherton was convinced. I didn't want him to think I was anything like my father.

CHAPTER FIFTEEN

Awake early, I'm glad to put yesterday behind me. For the last few days, it seemed I left a piece of me, if not my hard-earned money, everywhere I went: Big Jack's office, the hospital, the art gallery, Mike's office, Angelique's house, the emergency clinic, the bakery. Tuesday's people and events carved up a large chunk of my spirit, and I feel relieved Colton didn't call out during the night, for both our sakes.

While brushing my hair, I gaze out the dressing room window overlooking the back yard. Beyond the garage, the far edge of my greenhouse glows more than it should at dawn, and for a flashing moment, I worry Angelique's first cigarette of the day ended up on the window ledge, still burning. When I realize I failed to turn off the lights last night, I giggle in relief. How unlike me to be so careless.

Downstairs, I fill the coffee pot and leave it to perk while I tend to my greenhouse. The floor needs sweeping where the pine bark mulch spilled, and I move three more terra cotta pots to line up with the others. I inhale the warm humid air, satisfied the new sprinklers had dependably performed their overnight duties. Most of the geraniums and begonias will find a fresh, sunny home in the gardens of those office buildings I envision, and payment for such a big landscaping job will ease my financial burdens. With a smile, I turn off the lights.

In the kitchen, I set out two cups and saucers, remembering how much Angelique appreciates Grandmother Mason's china. Before I can decide between eggs or oatmeal, the phone rings.

"I figured you'd be up early, after what happened at the bakery last night," says Judith. "How many stitches did he get this time?"

"Not too many." I grimace as I realize the whole town buzzes with the news. "So glad you called. Can you watch Colton for me this morning?"

She can't come stay with Colton at our house, but she is willing to pick him up and take him home.

"Angelique and I are leaving here at a quarter 'til to be at the doctor's office by eleven. We can't exactly drag him with us. He's needs rest, and he's still too groggy from the meds."

"Hmm, busy day ahead. I've got orthodontist and gymnastics on my list, plus hair cuts for all three kids. Hold on." She drops the receiver and calls her children to breakfast. Picking up again, she says, "Meredith gets her learner's permit at the DPS by ten-thirty at the latest. Maybe sooner, unless we're in line behind every other fifteen-year-old in the county. I'll swing by and get him after that."

"I'm tired already, just listening." I try to sound impressed, or at least sympathetic. "Once Colton wakes up, I'll explain to him that he's to wait here. You won't be much later than eleven?"

"Yeah. Or so. I'll take them all back to our house for a good hot lunch."

"I'll guess he'll be okay for a few minutes by himself."

After we hang up, I ask Saint Trixie to keep an eye on her grandson.

You didn't do such a good job with Jack. Here's your chance to redeem yourself.

ANGELIQUE CRAVES COFFEE, no cream or sugar, followed by dry wheat toast smothered in peach preserves. When she finishes eating, she steps outside in the driveway to smoke and pick up the morning newspaper. I hope the neighbors don't object to seeing her in nothing but her flimsy silk caftan.

"I like to work the crossword first thing," she says when she returns to the kitchen. "It's one way I make sure my brain still functions." She hands me the front-page section with its headline about the new Alaska pipeline. "Wonder how all our Texas oil men will react to such a big development." She dabs the tip of her pencil on her tongue and settles in her chair. "What's a four-letter word for uh-oh?"

"I'm sure some of them are in for a shock."

"Hmmm. Not enough blanks, but I do think it starts with the same two letters."

Where others think nothing of a potty mouth reply, Angelique has never let a curse word or obscenity foul her ladylike lips. She gives me a crooked smile. "You-know-who will make another fortune on the deal before it's completed."

I sigh.

She rattles her paper. "When it comes to opportunity, Nate certainly has cornered the market."

I want to argue that his public success means nothing to

his family, that he was a complete failure at understanding the needs of his wife and his daughter, that there is no way to corner the market on forgiveness. Instead I slice a Gala apple and hand her a juicy section. "I have to give Mike a call."

"Don't you want to wait until after you talk to Colton?"

"I want to share my new theory with him about Jack's note. Besides, Colton's still asleep."

"Just now I saw him from the driveway, standing at his window. He waved at me."

"Then he should be downstairs soon."

"Shouldn't we see if he needs anything?"

"He'll let us know." I pick up the receiver.

"Maybe you should check. What if he can't get his shirt on?"

I replace the receiver in its cradle, but pick it up again immediately and begin dialing. "You go." After three digits, I hang up. "Sorry, I should remember not to over exert you. I'll help him."

"While I start the pancakes." She shoos me through the doorway. "Where are those mixing bowls? Oh, baby, how I wish my precious Raúl were here."

She remembers Colton loves pancakes, but does she also realize someone will have to cut them for him? It pains me that I already know Colton's choice. I clench my teeth and head for the stairs.

As I enter his room, he looks anywhere but at me. I explain the nurse's instructions. He has to bathe with his right hand in a plastic bag, sealed with a rubber band, held aloft away from the spray. While he showers, I sift through his drawer for tee shirts and pull out four of them. He shakes his head until I find the black one with the Rolling Stones logo. I leave the other three on the floor where he discarded them with the rest of his jumbled mess. During the hour it takes to get Colton cleaned up and dressed, he never utters a single word.

In the kitchen, Angelique chats and gossips enough for two people. When she reads Ann Landers aloud, she tilts her head toward Colton and snickers as if they share the secret handshake. He shoots daggers back at me every time I glance at him, and I feel neglected and left out. She would never cause such feelings on purpose, but he's an ace at it.

"Holy smokes, the hour!" Angelique says. "Please say you don't recognize me when next I appear. Glamour shall have transformed me." She stands up and calls over her shoulder as she drifts toward the doorway, "Colton, remember to take your pills."

I clap my hand to my temple. How could I forget? "Do you need something for pain now?"

He gives his right wrist a light shake, winces, and nods.

I hold out two tablets, a painkiller and the antibiotic, and wait for him to stretch out his left hand.

He doesn't move.

I set them on the counter. "Milk is in the fridge." I could add, "asshole," but don't want Angelique to overhear me on her way out of the room.

After I clear the dishes and turn off the griddle, I call Mike. We agree to wait to see how Colton feels by afternoon. I save my new theory until I see him in person, and I don't tell him Colton thus far has refused to speak. It sounds too crazy.

I wish I could understand my son's behavior better.

What keeps me on track is the hope that everything will change once we settle Jack's death as unintentional. Besides, I remember acting sullen at his age, especially after my mother died.

By ten-forty, Angelique hasn't reappeared, so I go upstairs and knock on her door.

"Come in, darling girl. I'm almost ready," she calls.

I open the door. Angelique sits on the edge of the bed, fully dressed, panting. "What's wrong?" I ask.

"Nothing. I can't find my other earring. It dropped out of my hand."

"Did you search under the bed?"

"Well, no. I . . . I'm afraid—"

"That's where it probably landed." I kneel down near her feet and pat the floor. "Slide over a little, will you?"

She raises her feet, and I spy the gold bauble on the other side of the bed, just beyond the white eyelet dust ruffle. "There it is!"

"Thank you. I'm vastly relieved. I thought maybe if I crawled under there, I wouldn't be able to get back out. Then you'd find me weeks later, all skin and bones and very thirsty. And craving a cigarette."

I retrieve the earring and hand it to her. "They'll make you take them off for the doctor's exam."

She sticks out her tongue at me, and I laugh. It's nice to find what you're looking for, especially when you can't locate it on your own.

My mother couldn't find her diamond brooch. She was certain she had it yesterday afternoon at tea. The problem was, nowhere in her room at the hospital could it have gotten lost. All the furniture was plain and beige, and there wasn't much of it. Her clothes hung in the closet, but it wasn't crowded in there. I knew because I looked in the corners and, now that I was twelve, I'd grown tall enough to see on top of the shelf. The diamond brooch was nowhere to be found.

Daddy said not to worry about it. He would bring her another one next time we visit.

I asked her where she went for tea, but her answer confused me. I didn't know they let her out of the hospital to go for tea at the Dorchester Hotel. Daddy shook his head.

This trip, I brought my sketchpad again to show Mother my drawings. She said she remembered Angelique, but when I passed on Angelique's greeting to her, Mother looked like she didn't know who I was talking about.

Daddy suggested we go outside and sit on the terrace. There were big wicker chairs with cushions and large woven backs shaped like fans. Mother explained they're called 'peacock style.' She grinned when I stood behind the chair and peeked through what were supposed to represent feathers.

Mother turned her chair away from the sun, and the

light that poked through it like little crystals gave me an idea. "Why don't I draw your picture sitting in the chair?"

She patted my cheek and I sat on the stone steps with my sketchpad in my lap. After I chose my first colored pencil, I could almost hear Angelique's voice telling me about negative space and light source. Mother made a good model, because she hardly moved at all. Her blue dress was a soft contrast to the white wicker, and her wrists were draped gently over the armrests. She took off her shoes and tucked one leg under her.

When an attendant brought two cups of coffee, Daddy disappeared behind his newspaper, probably because Mother had fallen asleep in her chair. They never talked much anyway. I decided to draw her face with her eyes open. I had gotten better at faces lately, using simple strokes for the nose and the chin. Since the front porch at home would make a better background than the hospital, I could save those details for later.

After about twenty minutes, I stopped to inspect my progress. I thought the dimensions and perspective were just about right. With a little more contrast, the filtered sunlight behind her would sparkle more. The last touch was to add a diamond brooch to her shoulder. She wouldn't mind that it wasn't exactly like the one she couldn't find.

This could have been my best drawing ever. I captured my mother's figure and expression perfectly. She looked beautiful and peaceful and happy. Maybe Daddy would want to frame it for his office wall.

"Okay, I'm finished!" I announced.

Daddy looked sideways from behind his newspaper. With a groan, Mother startled and sat up straight.

I stood up and turned my sketchbook around to show her. "What do you think?" I stepped next to her chair and held it out for her to look closer.

She smiled and praised my choice of colors. I felt really proud when she said how talented I was. As her smile faded, she frowned up at me. Her finger pecked the page like a nervous bird. Finally she asked me who the woman was.

"Can't you tell?" I struggled to keep my voice from cracking. "It's *you*."

She shook her head violently and said no.

"I'm sorry, Mother." I didn't want her to see me cry. "I guess I didn't–"

My father jumped up and called the nurse. "Put your stuff away now, Sally," he ordered.

Sobbing, Mother wrung her hands and asked for her diamond brooch. Daddy knelt in front of her, almost knocking me out of the way. "Weesie, don't do this," he said in a quiet tone, as he took her wrists and held them. "Not in front of Sally."

"I'm sorry," I repeated. "I didn't mean to upset her." Tears pricked the corners of my eyes.

Daddy didn't pay attention to me. He talked to Mother in a voice so low I couldn't hear what he was saying. She twisted to escape from his grasp, but he was too strong for her.

"Stop! You're hurting her!" I tried to pry his hands away and free her wrists, even after Daddy warned me not to interfere. She moaned as if she was in pain, but I was the one who winced.

Breathless, I pulled on Daddy's arm as Mother screamed. Without looking at me, he shook me off, all but shoving me against the other peacock chair. My sketchpad landed on the ground, and in the chaos, Daddy's cup tumbled from the little table and spilled coffee on my drawing. The colors ran in a puddle. It was ruined. Tears spilled down my cheeks, but no one could hear my sobs.

The nurse came and I looked away as she gave Mother an injection. Daddy finally stood up while the nurse studied her wristwatch as she took Mother's pulse.

After wiping my eyes on my sleeve, I ran back to Mother's room and yanked open her closet door. I lifted all the hangers from the rod and threw her clothes on the bed. One by one I shook them to be sure the brooch wasn't stuck in a pocket. Then I pulled her shoes off the shelf and turned them upside down, dropping them to the floor. I had worked halfway through emptying Mother's dresser drawers when my father appeared in the doorway.

Frowning, he surveyed the mess. "Sally, what are you doing?" Maybe he was worried I was going to turn out like her.

"Looking for Mother's brooch. It's got to be among her things somewhere."

He came to stand next to me, so close I detected the faint odor of cigars and carnation-scented soap. "It isn't here."

"How do you know?" I slammed the bottom drawer. "Did someone steal it?"

He sighed and picked up Mother's hairbrush. "There is no brooch. She's making it up."

"You hid it from her."

"She can't . . . the doctor says she isn't allowed to have any sharp objects."

I glared at him. "You're lying."

It was all my fault. I shouldn't have drawn her portrait with the brooch, so it wouldn't remind her of what she lost. If only I could find that stupid piece of jewelry.

Angelique and I stop at the door to Colton's room and I knock. He wears a headset as he lies sideways across his bed, long legs dangling to the floor. I tap him on the shoulder and say, "Judith will be here to pick you up in a few minutes. Try to get some rest until then."

When he sees Angelique over my shoulder, he peels himself from the mattress and ambles toward her. She stretches out both arms and hugs him. "Be brave," she says. "We'll both be fine." Her eyes glisten.

On the way to the garage, Angelique and I enter the kitchen, where the sweet toasty aroma of pancakes and maple syrup lingers. Colton has left the two pills on the counter. I stop and glance at the clock. Ten forty-nine. Shouldering my purse, I jangle my keys and press the button to raise the garage door.

"I remember driving *you* to the doctor's office once, a long time ago," Angelique says in the car.

"We found out I was pregnant." I smile at her.

"Beyond the realm of my experience or imagination, but utterly thrilling anyway."

We reminisce about that mysterious and joyful time all the way to the medical building and slip inside the door of the doctor's office at two minutes after eleven. In the lobby, I sit and pretend to read recipes from *Southern Living* magazine while Angelique fills out paperwork for new patients.

Another fifteen minutes passes while we wait. I wonder if Judith has arrived at my house yet. No point in calling there. Colton won't answer or speak to me if he did. Maybe I can phone Mike and ask him to find out.

As if by magic, a nurse in a white uniform appears at my elbow. "The doctor will see you now."

We both stand up, but Angelique steps forward ahead of me. "*I'm* the customer," she says to me. "You wait here."

"Make her answer lots of personal questions," I whisper to the nurse, loud enough for Angelique to hear. "Be sure she tells you everything,"

Once they vanish behind the doors to the inner sanctum, I ask the receptionist where the pay phone is located.

"Down the hall by the water fountain."

As I walk, I feel the bottom of my purse for a quarter but recognize only two nickels instead. Waving a dollar bill, I return to the receptionist to ask for change. She acts like I ordered one of her kidneys on shaved ice, but she gives me four quarters from her purse.

"I only need one," I say, nudging the other three toward her. To punish her huffiness, I leave my dollar on the counter. Good thing I don't require change for a hundred.

There is no answer at Mike's office. I hang up, retrieve my solitary quarter, and dial again. Still no Mike. I turn around, but return to the phone when I remember my neighbor across the street usually stays at home with her twin toddlers. She answers after five rings.

"Sally, you better get home right now. There are fire trucks in front of your house."

"Oh, my God! Can you see what's happening? Is anything burning?"

"There's smoke coming from the back of your garage, and I heard some explosions a while ago."

"Do you see Colton anywhere?"

"There are too many people, too much commotion. My kids are scared and crying."

"You tend to them. I'll be right there."

I toss the receiver at the switch hook and race down the hallway to the doctor's office. A silver-haired woman holds the door open for her husband, who blocks the entrance. Without stepping inside, I call to the frosty receptionist that I have an emergency at home. I'll send someone to pick up Angelique later or she can take a taxi.

All the way home, I pray Colton didn't fall asleep and get caught in the fire. Had he taken another pain pill and passed out? Maybe someone rescued him through the upstairs window. Where is Judith? What could have exploded?

Saint Trixie, you better have a damn good excuse for letting this happen.

By the time I turn onto my street, I can smell smoke. Three trucks are parked at my house, one in the circle driveway and the other two in front on the street. Hoses lead from the fire hydrant down the block, crisscrossing the shrubbery, and neighbors are gathered in the corners of their yards. I pull over to one side and get out of my car. Mike Avery stands on the front lawn, locked in deep conversation with the captain. The man hands him a plastic bag containing a hodgepodge of colorful fabrics, charred at the edges. I recognize them as remains of the three tee shirts Colton rejected wearing earlier. The captain turns around to join his men at the adjacent truck.

When Mike sees me approach, he waves me forward. His face muscles tighten as he slips his arm around my shoulder.

"Where's Colton?" I look up at him.

"We can't locate him. He's not in the house or the garage. We searched around the greenhouse and the backyard. One of the neighbors saw him leave the house about ten minutes before the first explosion."

"Explo–?" I can't make a whole word, much less an entire sentence.

"The blaze started in the garage and spread to your greenhouse. The windowpanes shattered after the fertilizer in your greenhouse caught fire. When the outside wall collapsed, the greenhouse caved in."

"But–" I put my hand to my lips, or maybe I feel my cheek for tears.

"He can't have gone far, if he's still on foot."

"But where's Colton? Is the fire–"

"The fire's mostly out now. Your house is not damaged inside. No smoke, no water got in, nothing else is ruined. The trouble is, we have reason to think it's arson."

"Who? Have you seen Skipper hanging around here?"

Mike holds out the bag of tattered and burned tee shirts. He doesn't have to say anything.

I shove his arm away and shudder. "No, no, it wasn't Colton!" I shout. "He didn't *do* this!"

"They're soaked in gasoline."

"My son did *not*"–my voice breaks as I sob–"burn down my greenhouse."

"Right now, he's a suspect. Or at least a person of interest. When I find him, I'll have to bring him in."

I shake my head as I clutch the front of Mike's shirt.

Mike gently pries my hands loose. "He'll have to answer some questions. No more hiding."

CHAPTER SIXTEEN

I stand in my driveway. As Mike's patrol cruiser pulls away from the curb, it's all I can do to keep from running after him, screaming my son's name. For a moment, I wait at the edge of the heat from the smoke-filled garage, wondering if I can simply faint and escape my misery. I head toward the house to call my lawyer.

"Mrs. Edwards?"

A young man's voice jerks me back. One of the firefighters needs directions where to relocate a damaged bench removed from what is left of my blackened greenhouse.

"Here, let me help you with that." I approach the garage, relieved for a distraction.

He holds up his gloved hand. "Sorry, ma'am, but you can't come in here."

My expression must relay my confusion, and I keep walking until he trots in front of me and halts. "The area's now under investigation," he says. "You have to stay clear of it."

Any other day I would argue about my rights as a homeowner, but Mike's suspicions, plus the bag of gasoline-soaked tee shirts belonging to Colton, force me into obedience. "All right.

You can set the bench on the patio behind what's left of the garage. Am I allowed in *that* section of my property?"

He nods, and I surrender the smoldering area to the professionals. The trip through my house, front door to back patio, takes less than a minute. As I inspect scorched terra cotta pots, smoke stings my eyes and my hands shake. I wipe my face, but can't distinguish sweat from tears.

While the firefighters continue their job, I wash whatever items they set to one side of the patio, as if I can rinse the damage down between the bricks. One thing cannot be salvaged: Jack's appointment book. I stare at the charred cover, soaked with water, the ink washed out and the pages stuck to each other like they had melted together.

The discovery is more than I can bear. I break down and sob as I rip the book apart along the spine, section by section, and throw the smeared puckered pages in the trash heap. Never had I felt drained by something more final, not even Jack's death. All my hopes and expectations snatched from my grasp and lost forever. Swept away by fire and an ocean of tears.

I forget about Angelique until she appears an hour and a half later. She hurries toward me with her arms outstretched.

I raise my palms toward her. "You don't want to get this . . . this grime on you."

Without hesitation, she enfolds me in a sympathetic embrace. "There, there, my sweet angel girl, I'm just here to be with you."

At that moment, she knew the perfect thing to say. Judith might have encouraged me not to worry or assured me everything would be all right, but I'd have sent her straight home without packing her overnight things. With my head nestled on Angelique's shoulder, a long howl threatens to erupt from my throat. I tell her about the loss of Jack's book. "How did you get here?" I finally ask.

"Mike sent Nate to pick me up from the doctor's office." She relaxes her grip on me and surveys the growing pile of charred lumber and broken glass. "What on earth happened?"

I swallow what feels like a lump of charcoal. "Somebody . . . the captain said someone started a fire in the garage, and it spread and ignited my greenhouse."

"Somebody?" She chucks me on the chin and raises my face to meet hers. "I thought maybe it was the new heater gone faulty." Shaking her head, she furrows her brow. "Arson! Who would do such a thing?" Her frown recedes as her eyes widen. "Oh, no. Not . . ."

How can I argue? I have my own suspicions, too, dragging my heart down into a blackened pit. "According to my neighbor, Colton left the house before the fire started. Mike has gone to look for him. Just to ask him some questions."

"Has Colton run away from home?'

I shake my head, but the truth is, I don't really know.

"Sally, what are you going to do?"

"The fire department won't let me–"

"About Colton." Her sympathetic tone now sounds serious. "If you can't figure out what's driving his crazy behavior, then, for God's sake, get some professional help."

"Do you think he's *crazy?*"

"Okay, poor choice of words. If he won't tell you what's bothering him, get him talking to an expert who can sort through all this mess. Someone without any connection to your family history." She pulls on her ponytail. "Have you asked yourself why he might have started the fire?"

I squint. "As of last Wednesday, it's been a year since Jack died. For the past week, Colton has seemed increasingly distraught at the mention of Jack's death. I've *had* to speak about it, because . . ."

Angelique nods but says nothing.

". . . he's grieving for his father so much, and he's angry that Jack isn't here to . . . to be his dad any more." My eyes search her face, as I silently plead for approval. "You can't say I am totally ignorant of his feelings, can you?"

Angelique brushes a strand of hair from my cheek and tucks it behind my ear. "Can you imagine what it must have been like for Colton–"

"To find Jack's body in the garage the next morning?" As the familiar sharp sensation pricks my eyes, I bite my lip. "No wonder he wanted to burn it down." I drop to a chair in the shade of the eave over the porch and put my head in my hands. Even rubbing my eyelids, I can't erase the vision of sooty residue.

Angelique sits beside me. She rests her hand on my arm, massaging with gentle pressure. "I know you love your home." Her hand grows still. "But maybe it's time to let it go."

I sit up and run my hand through my grime-dusted hair, wishing my mother were here to brush it for me, the way she sometimes used to do.

In my mind's eye, I entered the house through the front door for the first time. The curved railing of the front staircase seemed to lead to heaven, and echoes of distant laughter resounded from the high ceilings in each room. Light from the crystal chandelier scattered a shower of golden sparks across the polished oak floor. I glided through each doorway, expecting treasure, and somehow found Grandmother Mason and my mother as her little girl, smiling back at me, the way I remembered from old sepia-toned photographs.

I touched the doorknobs and reached for my mother's hand just beyond my grasp, gazed in the mirror over the mantel, and longed for her face to emerge from the shadows. Aromas from the oven in the kitchen beckoned me, and I licked my chocolate-smeared lips and crunch peppermint candy canes, as I awaited trick-or-treaters and St. Nicholas.

The shades over the windows dropped like sleep-drenched eyelids, while the scent of pine logs in the fireplace chased away the darkness and cheered the corners of the room. Night sang an encore, notes woven through the tall columns of the front porch, as the sun trailed its glory off the worn-out stage.

Later I carried a small bundle across the threshold, trussed in soft trappings, fresh and white as the bride I had once been, and watched for a sign of hunger. A tiny fist secured its future by gripping a strand of my hair and pulling me into its milky breath. I relinquished time and myself in the trundle of feeding and sleeping, mostly to watch God's promise to remember me, growing and thriving, even as my baby slumbered.

Pacing the gardens bequeathed blooms, not footprints, and shade to cool the heat of creation, season after season. With my hands, I dug in the damp ground and buried my soul, and waited for each new season's awakening to leave the protection of the earth's womb. Under my fingernails resided the energy of ownership, my house, my home, my heart. All of which tied me to my mother by an invisible cord.

I shake myself as if waking from a dream. With my fists relaxed, I look at Angelique and say, "I always thought"–my mouth goes dry–"I would stay in this house forever." Cupping my hands over my knees, I let my head droop. "You're right. Maybe it's time to sell."

Angelique slips her arm around my shoulder. "I know that's a big decision."

"I'm good at detachment, remember?" Sitting up straight, I look at her from the corner of my eye. "I should be good at it. I've had years of practice."

She smiles and nods.

One of the young firefighters approaches me with a toasted cardboard box. "I think this was in your storage closet in the garage. There's nothing in it we need for evidence." He sets it next to my feet.

"Thank you." The odor of charred fibers makes my nose itch. With my toe, I lift the flap and lean forward to peek inside. My doll Esmeralda stares back at me with bright blue eyes, her blonde hair drenched and her cheeks dusted with soot. I lift her from the wreckage and smooth her pink corduroy jumper and remember when she lost her shoes.

Daddy said I couldn't stay home by myself because I was only eleven. Also because Mother came home for a short visit from the hospital in Baltimore. The doctor sent two nurses with her. Since it was Mrs. Gussmann's day off and Aunt Mary was at the doctor's office, Clyde had to bring me with him on his errand to the airfield. I liked to ride in the car with him, just the two of us, because he talked to me more when no other adults were around.

Esmeralda sat on the front seat between Clyde and me. I didn't have permission yet to go for a spin with Danny, but I planned to ask Daddy when we got there. Last time he said yes right away.

Danny, our pilot, hasn't come to the house lately because Daddy has stayed in town all week. He saved his visits until my father was gone on a long trip across the ocean. He must have thought Daddy was still mad at him for breaking Mother's dresser drawer.

Mother liked for Danny to come roaring up the driveway on his motorcycle. She giggled a lot around him. I bet my father would have been surprised to hear her laugh so much. She also wore her new dresses when Danny was around. Mrs. Gussmann wondered how he got any work done, but maybe he dropped by to check on things, like Clyde did when Daddy was away.

I asked Clyde if he thought Daddy would let me go for a ride, but he didn't talk much and frowned a lot. He must have had something on his mind. He already said he's been working on a special project for Daddy, and maybe he wasn't finished with it yet.

I picked up Esmeralda and showed her the view out the side window. She couldn't count the horses in the pastures as we go by, but I could. I liked the times tables better, starting with my favorite number five. By the time I reached eighteen, I couldn't remember what came next. When I turned to ask Clyde for help, I accidentally dropped Esmeralda on the gearshift.

"Hey, watch it!" Clyde shoved my doll to the side. She landed face down on the floorboard.

Clyde had never yelled at me before, and my eyes got teary. Large drops spilled down my cheeks and I sputtered, "I'm sorry. I didn't mean to—" I scooted forward, as I tried to reach Esmeralda.

"Aw, don't cry." He stepped on the brakes and Esmeralda

rolled forward as the car came to a stop beside the highway. "I wasn't paying attention, there now." He pulled Esmeralda up by her hair. "Here's Esther for you, good as new."

I took my doll from him and cradled her against my shoulder. "Her name's not Esther." I choked the words out, trying not to blubber, but I cried as if my heart had broken. It wasn't like I hadn't heard anyone yell. Mother yelled at Daddy all the time, and sometimes at the servants. It was why they never stayed long, all but Mrs. Gussmann. Ever since he arrived, Clyde has acted like my special friend. He spoke to me the way no one else did. I laughed at the funny stories he told me when we were by ourselves. Except today there were no funny stories.

"Oh, now, stop that," Clyde handed me his hanky. His voice grew softer. "I didn't mean to make you cry. I'm just concentrating on something and I plumb forgot you was in the car with me." He patted my head. "Is Esther okay?"

"Esmeralda's fine." After wiping my eyes and honking into the hanky, I turned and sat facing forward in my seat again.

Clyde steered the car onto the road once more and we drove to the airstrip. Daddy paced up and down outside the manager's office. Clyde got his duffel bag out of the trunk and I waited in the front seat. Daddy walked around to the back of the car to speak to Clyde, but I couldn't hear what they said. When Clyde set the bag down, it clunked like there were heavy tools inside.

As Daddy walked by, I leaned over the edge of the open window and asked him if I could go for a ride today.

"What?" He frowned and glanced at Clyde.

"Can I, um, may I go for a ride today?"

"Sure, Clyde will take you. Just wait here or go play in the office until we're ready to leave. Miss Weatheridge will give you some pencils and paper."

"Not Clyde. Danny."

But my father had already walked away. I opened the car door and followed him toward the office, but decided to look for Danny in the hangar instead. I wanted to be sure he knew I was allowed to take a short ride before his big trip with Daddy. Maybe he would do a crazy-eight loop, like I'd seen in the Saturday cartoons at the movie theater.

Daddy and the manager were talking to Danny in the manager's office. There was a big window looking out into the hangar and Danny stood with his back to me. I tiptoed past toolboxes and storage bins. Daddy's airplane was already parked on the airstrip next to the hangar.

Before I had taken ten steps, Clyde came around the corner from the airstrip and waved at Daddy. Then he went out the side door toward the car. All Esmeralda and I needed was the pilot.

I tucked my doll under my arm and headed for the plane. The passenger door was unlocked and I climbed in the front seat. Danny had called me 'his little co-pilot' last time, even though I didn't do anything for the five minutes we circled around the airport. Maybe I'd learn to fly when I got older. I put Esmeralda in my lap and twisted sideways to find the seatbelt. It wasn't too tight when I strapped it around both of us.

Danny tapped on the glass on the other side of the cockpit.

I grinned and gave him a thumbs-up, the way I'd seen Clyde do.

He shook his head. "Mr. Wallace says nobody's flying

anywhere today." He opened the door and picked up a large envelope from the seat.

I felt like someone had just broken my favorite crayon on purpose. Frowning, I stuck out my lower lip. "But . . . but I really wanted–"

"Okay, okay, how about a quick spin on my motorcycle before I leave? Let me get the right packet from the manager, kiddo, and we'll zoom."

While Danny went to the office, I took Esmeralda to the parking lot and waited next to Danny's motorcycle. I liked the red and orange flames he had painted on the tailpipes. "Vroom, vroom!" I imitated the sound of the motor for Esmeralda.

Danny returned with another envelope, which he tucked inside his jacket. He threw his right leg over the seat and pulled the motorcycle upright, releasing the kickstand. With Esmeralda snuggled under my arm, I jumped up and down with excitement. He started the engine and let the wheels roll forward a few feet, then he took my arm and swung me up behind him, as if we were riding a horse together.

"Uh-oh!" I squealed. "Esmeralda's shoes have fallen off."

Danny started to take off, but stopped when my father appeared, waving his arms like a traffic cop.

"Not this trip, Sally. You have to get off the motorcycle."

"But you said–"

"Get off now!" He grabbed me by the arms and tried to pull me from the seat, but I held tight to Danny's shirt. "Damn it!" He let go of one arm and pried my fingers open.

"No! No!" I screamed as he lifted me forward. "You said I could go." I wiggled until he almost dropped me. Esmeralda tumbled to the pavement and I stretched out my arms to try to reach her. "My doll! You made her fall."

Daddy shifted me sideways to carry me over his hip, then he whirled around and bent to pick up Esmeralda.

"She's barefoot. We have to get her shoes." I kicked and begged, but he didn't listen and slung me over his shoulder like a sack of potatoes.

He gestured with his thumb to Danny to get going. As Daddy returned to the manager's office, I bounced along upside down, hanging over his shoulder, crying all the way.

Clyde waited for us and his face looked pale, like he'd seen a ghost. "Do you know when she climbed on?"

Daddy shook his head and let me slide to the floor. He sat down suddenly, as if he'd lost his balance.

They both took a few deep breaths and then Clyde said, "Come on, Sally. How 'bout I buy you an ice cream cone on the way home?"

I wiped my eyes with the edge of my sleeve. "I don't want ice cream. I want Esmeralda's shoes."

Clyde and my daddy traded looks, like there was something they were not going to say.

I stamped my feet. "Danny can bring them the next time he visits our house."

But he didn't. Danny and the shoes and my excitement about maybe learning to fly when I grow up all disappeared the next day when I heard that his motorcycle crashed soon after he left the airfield.

When Daddy told Mother the news of Danny's death, she threw two china figurines at him, one after the other smashing against the wall, and then flopped on her bed, burying her sobs in her pillow. He didn't hold her hand or pat her shoulder or even offer her an ice cream. He just walked out of her dressing room, leaving me to wait until her crying stopped.

I was worried she had smothered herself in the pillow. I asked her if she wanted a glass of water, but she screamed at me to get out of her room. I raced out into the hallway and burst into tears, until Mrs. Gussmann came and hugged them away. She explained that when Mother got upset, it was like she didn't recognize anyone, even me, and I should ignore her nasty tone of voice. But I couldn't forget how mean she sounded.

The next morning, Daddy left on a business trip, and I was glad he'd gone. Mother didn't come down for meals until three days later, and there was nothing I could do to make either of us feel better. By the time she returned to the hospital the next day, I was starting to forget what Danny looked like, but Mother couldn't even remember who he was.

CHAPTER SEVENTEEN

The whimpering of an aborted siren summons me to my front porch. After the captain assures me someone will be in touch, he climbs aboard the last of the three red engines as it chugs its way through my circular driveway and stops at the far end. With the show over, the neighbors disappear inside their homes, and the street remains all but deserted.

Parked across from my house sits the long, gray limo I had seen at the art gallery on Saturday. I turn toward Angelique, who drifts across the trampled lawn to stand next to me. "What's he doing here?"

"Waiting." Angelique waves at him.

I scowl. "For what?"

"He's concerned." She coughs twice, from deep in her lungs. "And he'd like to be of any assistance, if you'd let him."

My father gets out of the limo and crosses the street. Once he reaches the edge of my driveway, the fire captain hops off the truck to greet him. Of course they are previously acquainted, since Nate's connections extend beyond ordinary boundaries. They exchange a few words, and the captain nods several times.

Nate pulls a small white card from his inside suit pocket and hands it to the captain. They shake hands again, and my father walks toward us as the fire truck drives away.

"What was that all about?" I ask. His concern can wait forever, for all I care.

"I gather they suspect arson." He glances at the ashes and debris in what is left of my garage. "I offered a reward for information, plus a bonus if it leads to an arrest."

My heart thuds several beats as I stare at him. He can't predict the outcome of his own actions, and yet there he stands, manipulating my life again with his fortune.

"Nate, that's very generous of you." Angelique weaves her arm through his and smiles at me. "But there are some other details you might want to hear." She jerks her head toward my house several times, but I refuse to acknowledge her signal. She clears her throat. "Can we all go inside? Hard to believe, but the smoke out here bothers me."

Before I can object or stall for an excuse, she ushers us up the sidewalk and through the front door. Consumed by a spell of coughing, Angelique heads for the kitchen in search of a glass of water.

My father stands in the entry under the chandelier and looks around my house as if estimating how much money he can make from its sale. "Nice job, finishing the inside like this."

"Mother would have liked it."

He jingles the coins in his pocket.

"In here, you two," Angelique calls from the living room.

What the hell is she thinking?

My father waits for me to pass, then follows me through the

doorway. Angelique has set a tray with three glasses and a pitcher of iced tea on the coffee table. Any other time, I wouldn't mind if she assumed the job of hostess, but it is hard to see my father sitting calmly in the house I inherited from my mother.

"By this hour, Sally, you must be exhausted." Angelique hands us each a glass of tea. "How do you need us to help?" She drops to a chair and lays her wrist on her forehead for a moment before she sits erect and holds her head high, signaling the queen's court is in session again. "I can have three dinners sent over from Raúl's restaurant."

Us? Three? Has the smoke gotten to her brain? My gaze bounces from her face to my father's and back. "Do you mean one extra for Colton?"

"Of course, that'll make four if Mike finds him before dinner time." She smiles. "Five, if we can get Mike to stay for supper."

That charming Angelique. In addition to flirting and wheedling, I can now add maneuvering to her playbook. Damned if I will share a meal in my own house with Nate.

"There's nothing anyone can do right now," I say. "The fire captain will finish his report, Mike will take the investigation from there, and meanwhile I'll call the insurance company to file a claim. Then I'll have to find someone who can demolish the garage. Shouldn't take long to rebuild. Carriage houses aren't complicated, but my greenhouse came by special order." I take a sip of tea. "I don't know about the coverage on it."

"I regret to tell you," my father says as he sets his glass on a coaster, "the insurance company won't pay until the inquiry is settled. If the investigator determines the cause is arson, the settlement will have to wait until he rules the policy holder is not at fault."

My knees feel weak, and I plop on the couch next to Angelique.

"Ridiculous bureaucrats." Angelique suppresses a sneer. "No one in his right mind is going to believe Sally set fire to her own house."

I jerk so abruptly that my glass tumps over. Does she think the evidence won't convince an insurance investigator my son resorted to arson? Every citizen in Mason's Crossing has probably come to the same conclusion by now. Why wouldn't they? I am starting to believe it myself.

Angelique dabs at the spreading liquid with paper napkins from the tray, but I end up going to the kitchen for a towel to finish the job. After she clears away the mess, she yawns and announces her intention to take a nap. "Unless you need me to keep vigil with you two until Colton shows up."

"Go ahead and get some rest. I don't know when Mike will be back."

"Don't worry. Mike knows all the hiding places around here. Let's only hope Colton didn't hitch a ride with someone." She turns toward the doorway and the stairs beyond. "He could be halfway to Louisiana by now, well outside Mike's jurisdiction." She yawns again and stretches her arms out in front of her, twisting her shoulders from side to side as if she hears samba music, before she pads out of the room.

Her words drop a bomb. Who would be authorized to locate or detain Colton if he flees Mason's Crossing, much less the county or the state? Sure, Mike can make some phone calls to his associates, but will they exert themselves to find a possible runaway? They will if they think he could be a fugitive, an arsonist.

There has to be some other way to keep Mike's search for Colton out of the official pipeline, and especially out of the news. I can imagine my son hiding until after sunset, afraid to show his face, starved, shivering, ready to faint. Sirens, voices, flashlights chase him deeper into the woods, beyond my power to rescue him. Who can save him from the darkness gobbling up his life?

"So, when Mike Avery finds him, will he bring your son here?"

I blink. My father's voice breaks through the cloud surrounding me, though I refuse to see him as anything but a threat. Angelique might believe introducing Colton to his grandfather will provide the saving grace for my confused, unhappy son, but I know better. The familiar dislike boils inside me, until I remind myself she always acts from her heart. "*If* he can find him."

Nate frowns, as if the information doesn't add up. "He ran away from home."

My eyes burn as I stare at him. "Will you really pay out a large sum if Mike Avery takes the arsonist into custody?"

"I already offered it to the captain."

"You don't know what you've just done." I want to laugh with an avalanche of derision. "You'll have to hand over the reward money to me if it turns out to be my own son."

How 'bout them rotten apples, Mother?

"I see."

Doesn't anything faze him? "You don't see anything." I stand up. "You never have."

"What do you mean?"

Here is my chance to lay the charges at his feet and watch him struggle, the man I've hated almost all my life. What he did to my mother is inexcusable. How can I ever forgive him for deserting us? There can be no defense for his cowardice. I shake my head.

"If you have something to say after all this time, Sally, I'm willing to hear it."

God, he acts cool. Doesn't he realize my accusations will draw blood? I want him to limp back to his big, fancy-assed limo and slink out of town. It won't make any difference to him or to our broken relationship, but it's the only satisfaction I will ever get.

I stand behind my chair, ready to use it for a battering ram, and then step in front of it. I want him to get the full force of my anger. "You're the one who ran away. Every time Mother needed something, you were gone on a trip. Your business deals meant more to you than your family."

"That's not true."

"Oh, no? You were never there the times she got sick. The servants took better care of her than you did."

"Mrs. Gussmann kept me informed of her condition. I tried to make your mother happy."

"Not you. I was the one who did that."

He rises from his seat and paces toward the double doors leading to the library. "Some women thrive when they have children. I thought motherhood would help her . . . get back what she lost."

"And what was that?"

"Balance in her life." He turns to face the center of the

room. "There were so many highs and lows. She rarely seemed to function at a regular pace."

"So you blame her? That's rich. You caused the ups and downs. Never around, never involved. The biggest mistake she made was to marry you."

He grimaces, as if my verbal knife has struck a nerve. "You didn't know her in the beginning, before her illness. I never imagined such a young beautiful girl would love me so much. She was only seventeen, and I was much older than she." He sighs, a sound I've never heard from him before. "Stability. That's what I thought she needed, after her father died."

Nate stretches open his palm and studies the inside of his hand. "When you came along, I hoped tending a baby would help her settle into a routine, but she grew even more unpredictable. I tried to understand her, but I never knew what I would find at home when I returned." He walks slowly toward the windows overlooking the gardens on the side of the house. "She might be tearing out the ceiling in the dining room or having the pool moved to the other side of the lawn. Other times, she couldn't find the strength to get out of bed."

"Mother felt overwhelmed by sadness and couldn't help herself. She thought you'd deserted her."

His voice softens. "I always came back, didn't I?"

"But once she got to be too much for you to handle, you exiled her to the mental institution."

His tone grows stern as he parts the sheer curtains and rests his hand on the windowsill. "I had to."

"No, you didn't. I was old enough to understand her moods.

I could have kept her happy." I raise my voice. "She missed me. You took us away from each other!"

"You don't understand what happened–"

"I know you paid other people to say she was *crazy*! That's how you justified the horrible thing you did. But she *loved* me."

"I couldn't let her stay at home. I was afraid to leave her with you."

"Why? What were you afraid of?"

He shakes his head and lets his hand drop to his side.

"My mother wanted to stay at home and instead you sent her away," I yell. "I needed her. How could you do that to us?"

My father whirls to face me. "Because she tried to kill you."

The bones in my legs might as well be melting. I grab the back of my chair. The room spins. After a few deep breaths, the nausea passes, replaced by a blast of heat, starting at my waist and gushing up to my scalp. "She would never have . . . ever hurt me."

"Not in her rational moments." He rubs his forehead. "You don't remember what happened the first time." My father looks directly into my eyes. "Weesie knew I had a trip coming up, and she was angry. She pitched one of her fits before I left for Toronto. Two days later, Mrs. Gussmann phoned the embassy and told me your mother threatened to jump over the railing of the third floor balcony with you in her arms."

"I don't recall any of that."

"How could you remember? You were only a toddler, not even two years old yet."

My mind's eye was fuzzy, like it was covered with a veil. The sound of deep water rushed by, below my feet. I looked down through an iron maze where gray mist floated toward the sky. There was no water, only laughter. The clouds drifted close enough to touch, but they shied away from my fingertips. I clung to the tree while its trunk swayed in the wind. Its branches reached for me and held me close as the wind tried to lift me and carry me over the edge of . . . what?

We climbed higher than the treetops. We? When did I become not one, but two? If the mist could not hold us, the music would. The violin's tune tickled the soles of our bare feet, as a chorus of singers called my name. Her name. Come back, they sang.

The wind increased its strength, and she, the one not I, pulled the scarf from around our necks and shoulders and tossed it into the arms of the breeze. At first it rose and fluttered like a young bird, and we laughed again. But it could not fly and it fell. Disappeared from sight, down into the gray mist below our feet.

The violin's strings grew silent one by one, as slow chatter drowned its notes. Someone coaxed us away from the sky and pulled me apart from her. The music turned heavy and sad, from a cello doomed to weep. I was tucked and tied into a different scarf, against some other tree trunk. There was neither breeze nor any laughter.

My throat turns to desert, too dry to spit anything but words. "You're lying. It never happened."

"Mrs. Gussmann said Weesie kept muttering how 'this' would get me to come home immediately and fix it. It worked."

The skin around my head feels too tight. I sink into the chair and stare at my hands. "Fix what?"

"We could never discover what she wanted. It always changed from day to day, week to week. Even your Aunt Mary couldn't make any sense of it. There were other . . . threats, too."

"But she remained at home until I was almost ten. Why did you send her to the institution then? Couldn't she have stayed with us at the villa the way she was?"

"Mrs. Gussmann found knives and scissors in strange places, household things–sometimes your clothes–shredded or burned. Shattered lamps, vases. Someone had smashed them against the wall. Everyone suspected, but I *knew* it had to be no one but Weesie. Clyde was around to protect you, and after he left there was no one else I trusted as much. It's why I insisted your door be locked at night. Do you remember?"

I nod. "I thought it was because you were mad at me."

"No, I was never mad at you. It was because of your mother–"

"But she would never have harmed *me*." Even as the words come out of my mouth, I know I am the liar.

"I couldn't take that chance. I relied on Mary to keep a watchful eye on Weesie. She recognized when the behavior got bad enough to call the doctor to administer a sedative. Even as her own illness got worse, Mary realized your mother was faltering."

"But my mother loved me."

I think I hear my father answer, "So do I." But I can't be sure because his voice is too soft. Or maybe the doorbell drowns it out.

CHAPTER EIGHTEEN

The doorbell rings again, insisting on my attention, but my body might as well be strapped to the living room chair. I stare at Nate, grappling with my childhood memories. How can I make sense of his wild claim that my mother had threatened to do away with herself and take me with her? Not once, but multiple times.

Nate waits by the fireplace until he figures out I can't move. "Would you like me to answer the door?"

I nod, numb from the inside out. Even my hostility freezes, no longer erupting. My thoughts choke any words, like an ice floe in a wintry river.

Nate opens the front door, and once they trade greetings and mumble a few other words, Mike strides toward me into the living room. He stops about five feet from my chair, pulling up short as if he has come to the edge of a dangerous precipice.

I raise my eyes to meet his frown. "Find anything?" I can't bring myself to say my son's name.

"Did Colton have any money with him?" His voice gives off an unfamiliar air of detached authority.

His refusal to answer my question perks up my antenna and

I eye him without moving from my chair. "We have to find out where he is and if he's okay. I don't know about any money."

"Do you mind if I take a look in his room?"

Nate comes forward and stands next to Mike. They look like members of the same team. "Sally, Mike's visit here is official. If you give him permission to search Colton's room, anything he discovers could be used as evidence."

Mike's eyes narrow to slits. "He's right."

I bolt to my feet. "You came here, not to comfort me or help Colton, but to prove he's guilty of arson?"

"Sally, damn it, you know I'm only doing my job." Mike removes his hat, revealing a sweaty stain under the brim.

As if switching sides in a debate, Nate moves next to me and faces Mike. "Can't it wait until after you find Colton? Sally has nothing to hide."

Earth and sky exchange places again. The man supposedly in love with me for over fifteen years can no longer be of any help now, while Nate stands poised to become my ally, if not my defender.

"It doesn't matter to me what you do." I feel like punching Mike, uniform and all. That way at least Colton and I will be in jail together. "You want to search the whole house? I'm leaving to find my son!"

"It's been a difficult day," says Nate. "Let's give some thought to our next move."

Is he trying to smooth things over? I have my temper under control.

Mike holds up both hands, palms toward me. "Okay, okay. But stay put. You should be here if he shows up."

Nate sits down. "Technically, you need a search warrant, but where would you get paperwork this time of day?" Using a simple, undisputable fact, Nate doesn't sound argumentative, and the ground under my feet feels firmer. "Couldn't your time be better spent making inquiries and locating her son?"

Mike pushes his hat toward the back of his head. "Who would guess the county judge would go fishing in the middle of the week?" He glares at Nate, clenching his jaw. "You might think you're helping, but really it's just postponing the inevitable." He starts toward the door, and then spins around. "Don't you want to hear why I asked about the money?"

Electricity crackles and zaps my insides, starting at my ankles.

"Do you know something?" Nate says.

"Nothing concrete yet, but there have been two reports. A boy around Colton's age bought a ticket at the bus station in Austin."

"To where?" I press my fingertips against my lips.

"El Paso." Mike settles his hat on his head with a forward tug of the brim. "It's easy to cross the border into Juarez. The kid paid his money, but never boarded. That's the *good* news."

My mind refuses to picture Colton as an escapee. "He's simply a confused, frightened boy who needs reassurance, not punishment. I know him to be incapable of arson. Whatever he might have done has to be an accident." What will it take for Mike to abandon his pursuit of justice, burned tee shirts or not?

"Sally, I'd really like to accept your explanation and call it a day, but even as your, um, close friend, I have to do my work.

I have no choice. You can't shelter him from the consequences of his actions forever."

His tone doesn't sound contemptuous, but Mike might as well toss ice water in my face. Ever since Jack died, I have failed miserably in parenting my son. "Sorry. It's just that, when it comes to Colton, he's been so lost, and I see almost everyone as the enemy. I realize that's unfair to you, and ungrateful."

"It's probably too much to expect you to be helpful,"–Mike's voice grows softer–"but cut me some slack, will ya?"

I appreciate Mike's attempt at a smile, feeble though it appears. Mine isn't any better.

"And the other report?" Nate's tone points me back toward my fears.

"A truck stop owner in Flora Springs noticed a boy hitch a ride in a semi, headed east toward Louisiana. The boy was carrying a gas can. Told the driver his mama ran out of gas on the highway."

Nate follows Mike toward the foyer. "Which trucking company?"

"It wasn't the local MCW Freight Lines." Mike shoots us a crooked smile. "Now, wouldn't that be a lucky coincidence?"

The front door clicks behind him, and Nate returns to the living room. "May I use your phone?"

I point toward the kitchen and wonder what he can possibly need to tell anyone, until I remember who owns the trucking company Mike mentioned. Great-grandfather Augustus Mason started it with horses and wagons, hauling regional harvests to a local market. Before he died, he brought his son-in-law, a local blacksmith named Amos Cobb, into the business. By the time Cobb's only daughter Louisa married, her new husband had already made both families a fortune in oil field machinery. By expanding the fleet along with the territory and upgrading the equipment, Nate Wallace turned his prolific energies into prodigal wealth again.

Snippets of Nate's conversation waft into the living room. Words such as "CB radio," "pre-teen boy," and "missing his mother" catch my attention. When he provides no description, I suddenly realize Nate has none to give. He doesn't even know how tall Colton has grown, almost to Nate's shoulder.

Breathless, I dash to the kitchen. He stands near the counter, his back to me. Without hesitating, I put my fingertips on his arm. "Tell them he has a bandage on his right wrist."

Nate looks down at my hand as if he doesn't recognize it and, after he blinks several times, lets his gaze wander to my face. I stare at him and our eyes lock.

"Do you know what he was wearing?" he asks, his voice hoarse.

I describe the black tee shirt and jeans Colton had, with my help, put on earlier that morning. It seems like a week ago. Nate passes on all the information I give him.

"One more thing," Nate barks into the receiver. "This boy is my grandson." After he hangs up the phone, Nate turns to me and says, "Sorry, but I need to make this next call in private."

I snatch my hand from his arm as if it has become a stoked ember. What ill-gotten strings will he pull now? I don't want to hear any damning conversation and back out of the kitchen.

The patio offers a cool, comfortable seat in the waning light of early evening. I can stay there as easily as any room in my house. With my head resting against the cushion of the chaise, my eyelids droop to half-mast.

After several minutes, Nate opens the back door and walks outside. In silence he surveys the pile of items rescued from my greenhouse, long enough to make me wonder if it brings back any painful memories for him. When he speaks, his voice grows soft. "I'm sorry this happened to you, and to your house."

"Me, too." Sorry twice. Is that all?

"I have to go now." He reaches into his right coat pocket and pulls out his keys. "There are some things I need to tend to in person."

I shift sideways in an attempt to stand, but he holds up his hand. "Don't get up. I'll see myself out."

He hesitates, but I can't think of any reply. Is he expecting me to thank him? The words form slowly on the tip of my tongue, like frozen sludge, but the habit won't surrender. Not yet.

"Colton will turn up soon, you'll see," he says. "Tell Angelique–"

"Tell me what, sugar?" Her voice drifts across from the other side of the patio.

I can't see her face in the dusky shadows, but when she takes a drag of her ubiquitous cigarette, the tip glows like a tiny comet. She must have let herself out the library door for a smoke.

The white of his teeth flashes and I realize Nate, like the rest of us, responds to her warmth and encouragement. Maybe he hungers for it.

Angelique inches a step forward. "Aren't you staying for supper? I ordered a meal for you."

"Give it to Mike. Or Colton."

Neither Angelique nor I move as he disappears into the house. I wait in silence to determine if I can hear the front door close. He slips away as quietly as he came, and suddenly I wonder if I will ever see him again.

I pat the chair next to me, and Angelique floats over to sit down. She stubs out the remains of her cigarette on the cement floor and tosses it into the trash pile.

"How well did you know my mother?' I ask.

"Well enough to see the problems. We traveled in the same social circles. Plus Mrs. Gussmann's cousin worked for me when I was married to my first husband, therefore I heard all the rough and stormy tales."

"Did you hear the story about her threat to jump off the third floor balcony?"

Angelique gives a low whistle. "So Nate finally told you."

I nod. "You think it's true?"

Angelique sighs. "Your mother had every reason under the sun to be happy. A husband who adored her, a supportive family, physical beauty, friends who cared about her, wealth beyond imagination. Then along came the perfect baby." She strokes my cheek with her fingertip.

I pull my knees up and rest my wrists on them. "But . . ."

"Unhappiness wasn't the problem. Nothing could keep her *sane*. Not Nate, not you, not the doctors." Angelique flicks her lighter and fires up another cigarette. "I have no firsthand knowledge of that episode, but I overheard enough reliable kitchen chatter about it later to believe without any doubt Louisa was insane enough to commit such a terrible act."

She exhales, grinds out her smoke, and stands up. "We should go inside right now."

"Are you cold?"

"I don't want lightning to strike me."

"There's no thunderstorm in the forecast. And besides, you're sheltered under the eave."

"Nothing will protect me if someone, your mother, perhaps, decides to zap me with a bolt. I shouldn't have spoken about the dead that way."

"That's the gypsy in you talking." I peek at the sky anyway.

"Nevertheless." She drifts toward the door to the kitchen and opens it. "Someone is knocking. Must be our dinner delivery."

We return to the foyer and open the door, tip money ready in my hand. Still in uniform, Mike twirls his hat. He isn't smiling, but he looks happier than the last time I saw him. Relieved, maybe.

My eyebrows shoot up in anticipation. Behind me, Angelique reaches for my hand and clutches it.

"Some trucker got Nate's relayed message on his CB radio and pulled into a Valu-Mart just outside Houston, in Katy. The store's security guard is holding Colton."

"Sally, you must go get him." Angelique squeezes my hand.

Mike waves his arm toward his squad car. "I'll drive."

It isn't that I don't want to retrieve my wayward son. I am ready to do my duty as a mother. Even if he spits in my face, I'll walk across hot coals to snatch him from the jaws of hell. Colton's monsters, whatever haunts him, don't scare me. What does frighten me is the thought that I have become one of those monsters.

Eyes pleading, I turn to Angelique. "Come with me."

"Of course, darling girl. I wouldn't let you do this by yourself."

Once we collect our purses, Mike clasps Angelique and me by the arms and steers us to his cruiser. Departing Mason's Crossing for the highway to the east, he speeds up and we take off like a bullet into the gathering darkness.

CHAPTER NINETEEN

With the sunset behind us, we ride in silence. Angelique extends her long legs sideways across the back seat of Mike's blue Marauder, and I squirm in the front on the passenger side.

Grimacing, Mike clicks his seatbelt across his lap. "Oh, crud, I almost forgot." He nods at me to do the same. "It isn't law yet, but it's coming sooner or later."

Obediently I draw the strap across my hips. Too bad it won't keep my life from careening out of control.

The events of the last two days cartwheel through my thoughts like crazed circus clowns. Emergency stitches, shattered glass, and heart or lung ailments dance circles around stories of premeditated death. The clowns won't squeeze back into their tiny trick car. Bright tongues of flame lick the sky above my greenhouse. A devil's nightmare.

The questions begin tumbling. What has Colton endured to reach the distant community of Katy? How much farther would he travel to escape? Maybe agreeing to sell my house will make him want to come home. Does Mike have evidence enough to detain Colton for questioning about the fire?

What cunning scheme has my father set in secret motion? I can't help shivering.

"Do you want me to crank up the heater?" Mike asks. "How 'bout back there, Angelique? You cold?"

Before she can answer, I gasp and look over my shoulder. "We have to turn back. I forgot to bring Colton's medicine."

"Not to worry, sweetie." Angelique reaches forward to pat my shoulder. "I grabbed it off the kitchen counter on my way out."

"Oh, thank God. You think of everything."

Mike estimates the trip should take an hour and forty-five minutes, plus time to stop for gas. Since his car doesn't need refueling after less than an hour, I figure he pulls into a convenience store on the other side of Columbus so Angelique can stretch her legs and enjoy a smoke. He shoos her away from the gas tanks, and her heels click all the way across the pavement until she reaches the store's entrance.

With the door ajar, she pivots and calls, "Sally, are you coming, honey?"

I nod and trail behind her like a kite that won't go airborne. The dark-skinned clerk at the counter returns her cheery smile as he points us toward the restroom. Holding the door open, Angelique stands back, and I choose the stall on the right.

Her voice carries under the beige metal partition. "Have you considered what you're going to say to Colton?"

How should I start? Questions or assurances? Hold him accountable or wait for him to explain? I flush and stare at the water until the swirling ends. The thoughts stop spinning and my mind goes numb. "Won't Mike do most of the talking?" I step to the sink and wash my hands, not daring to glance in the mirror.

"I'm sure he'll have plenty to bring up at some point, but . . ." She flushes and waits for the noise to subside. "Now's your chance to help Colton face some difficult circumstances. He'll need your support."

"He doesn't want to hear anything from me." I wipe a paper towel across my hands and toss it into the trash.

"He may act that way, but you're nevertheless very important to him." She exits the stall and checks her lipstick in the mirror before she turns on the faucet. "What you say and do is critical. Let Mike be the bad guy for now. Your job is to help Colton feel loved and affirmed, even if he's done something terrible."

"Like burn down the garage and the greenhouse?" In the mirror's reflection, our eyes meet.

She takes her time drying her hands, as if absorbing every last drop between her fingers matters. "You can't make your love conditional on his proper behavior. Why, what would families be good for if only the well-behaved members receive all the love? It's the thirsty ones like Colton who need the water."

Shaking my head, I regard her reflected image as if I need to explain the solution to a long bothersome puzzle. "Sometimes not even the well-behaved ones get the love they need." It had never turned out that way for me.

"Very true, my dear." She puts her hand on my arm. "Someday I'll remind you of what you just said."

I return to wait in the car while Angelique sashays up and down the aisles, filling a shopping bag with packaged treats and drinks. Colton will find his favorites among the snacks, sweet and gooey, salty and crunchy, and otherwise tempting. If I can't make him feel loved, will a Snickers bar do? Angelique doesn't deserve my sarcasm, so I keep my mouth shut for the rest of the ride.

WHEN WE PULL INTO a parking space at ten minutes past eight, the lot at the Valu-Mart sits three-fourths empty with the lights along the perimeter already extinguished. We trudge toward the entrance under a ghostly aura of a single globe that shines on us like a spotlight. Mike presents his photo ID to the uniformed door attendant, who points us to the manager's office.

I feel like a prisoner marching toward the firing squad. Will I know what to say or how to act? I stare up at the high ceilings in the warehouse-style store, awed by the tall rows of merchandise on pallets, and wish I could disappear among the cartons.

Angelique mutters a few "tsk-tsk" noises, appalled at the wave of future retail. We turn left by the middle cash register, one of at least eighteen lined up like boats in an invisible dock.

My stomach contracts as we approach the door to the manager's office and I concentrate on the scuffmarks along the wall. Mike raps on the door, then pushes it open, wide enough for me to pass through. Angelique follows and stands between Mike and me.

Cradling his right wrist, Colton sprawls on a black metal chair. The overhead fluorescent lighting robs his skin of color, and I can't tell if sweat or tears caused the dirty streaks running down his face.

Although I call upon her, my mother's voice in my head

fails to issue orders or even drop hints. My mouth goes dry and any words I might conjure up on my own stick in my throat. Feeling the warmth of Angelique's hand on my shoulder, I take a step forward. "Colton?"

He looks up, his eyes shifting back and forth like windshield wipers, but can't meet my gaze. His breath comes in shallow panting, almost heaving.

Is he on something?

From behind his desk in the corner, the store manager stacks some papers. "I'll need to see some identification, please."

Before I can express my annoyance for the interruption, Mike inches forward. "Of course." He sidesteps around Angelique and me and pulls out his wallet again. He jerks his thumb toward me. "She's his mother."

With very little cash in my purse, I wonder if the manager will ask for reimbursement for whatever misdeeds Colton might have committed. Perhaps he will accept a postdated check.

The instant the path to the door clears, Colton jumps up and bolts through it. His howl echoes down the hallway before the outer door slams behind him.

Mike whirls around and yells, "Hey, come back here!" He takes off after him. In his haste, he knocks Angelique's purse off her shoulder.

I dart after Mike and Colton, leaving Angelique to thank the store director and pay for any repairs or shoplifted items. It's all I can manage to chase the sound of the screaming and shouting.

By the time I reach the front door, Mike has caught Colton in a headlock halfway across the parking lot and is preparing to push him face down. He won't hesitate to use handcuffs. Colton cries and shoves backward with all his weight, but Mike is too strong for him.

"Stop! Stop!" I cry, crashing through the door.

"Give it up, Colton!" Mike shouts in his ear.

"Let him go!"

"Back off, Sally!" Mike growls. "I'll handle this."

I grab at Mike's left arm. "You're hurting him."

"You all think you're so smart, but . . . none of you . . ." My son cackles with such derision, I can't help shuddering.

With a sharp gasp, I make myself reach to touch my son's shoulder. "Colton, whatever you've done is–"

"Shut up!" he snarls.

I draw my hand back as if he tried to bite it. His voice doesn't even sound human.

As Colton struggles to twist violently up and down, Mike locks Colton's arms behind him. "Ready to quit, son?"

Colton collapses like a marionette with the strings cut. "Don't call me 'son'," he sobs. "You're not my father. An asshole like you could never be my father."

"No one but Jack was your daddy, my sweet boy," Angelique says from behind me. She grasps my hand. "Mike only wants to help you get home again. We all do."

"I'm not going back to that house ever again!" His sobbing turns to squeaks and hiccoughs and grows louder, pushing his spiteful words into the shadows. With the heels of his hands dug into his eye sockets, he tries to cover his face.

After he stops sputtering, I swallow hard. "I know you miss your father." I let my purse drop to the pavement. "Dad loved you very much. There's nothing we can do to bring him back, but at least we can try to accept his death as unintentional." I glance at Mike, who spins his head sideways as if I have slapped him. "Even if the official ruling says otherwise."

"Dad's death wasn't an accident." Colton's voice loses its youthful pitch and assumes an air of cool maturity.

"What do you mean?" My hand flutters to my chest.

"All this time, you thought he shut the garage door and left the motor running because he was too drunk to know the difference."

"That's exactly what—"

"You weren't there. Dad didn't close the garage door." He peers up and his eyes might as well be distant moons. As his gaze settles on me, his voice cracks. "I'm the one who shut the door. I did it. I killed my father."

"What are you saying?" Frowning, I kneel on the asphalt in front of him. "No, you were in bed asleep when he came home. We both were. It was very late."

"That night I got up to go to the bathroom and heard his truck in the driveway." He picks at his bandage. "Remember the time my bike got stolen last year? You got so mad because I didn't put it away in the garage and close the door."

Nodding, I gulp the night air, like ice in my lungs.

"I noticed Dad's brake lights from my bedroom window. I waited, but he didn't close the garage, so I went downstairs. He was still in the truck, leaning forward on the steering wheel. I thought he had fallen asleep, like he does on the couch sometimes, and he'd come into the house later."

"You must have been dream—"

Angelique's hand on my shoulder silences me. With a pang, I mash my lips together. How many times has my stubbornness stifled Colton's urge to talk? I wish I could call the words back. Maybe our hard year of anguish could have been softened.

"Then I pressed the button to close the door and went back upstairs." Large drops, like iridescent crystals, shimmer down Colton's bright red cheeks. "I didn't know he had left the motor running." He looks up at Mike. "I swear I didn't know."

His words dissolve into sobs again. I reach for him and pull him into my arms, cradling him like a baby. Racked from exhaustion, his body gives way and he loses all resistance. At last he throws his arms around my neck and nestles his wet face into my shoulder, and our tears mingle. As I rock him back and forth, he keeps repeating, "I didn't know. I didn't know."

As my arms tighten around him and I brush the hair from his forehead, I wish for us to become a young mother and child again. A fresh start. A better growing up together. How could I not see what I was doing to my own son?

My mother, Saint Trixie, even Jack and all the other angels must be gazing down from heaven and crying out with great pity for us. Pity for the mistakes, the blindness, the fears, the stupidity, the hurts we inflict on each other and on ourselves, the love we withhold. Maybe their combined weeping possesses the power to wash all that away. Surely, in that sanctified moment, our tears do.

CHAPTER TWENTY

Angelique sits in the front passenger's seat of Mike's patrol car, while Colton and I climb in the back. Strange how it reassures me when he clings to me, as if he won't be able to breathe without holding on. I cradle his shoulders across my lap, rest his head in the crook of my arm, and let him sleep. Before he dozes off from sheer exhaustion or the pain medication, he wraps his bandaged arm around my neck like a vine.

I have no reason to talk on the return trip to Mason's Crossing and feel grateful the others choose silence, too. All the words that make a difference have been said. Tomorrow there will be other words, and we will deal with them then. Somewhere, God knows how, I will find strength again.

Soon the monotonous hum of the tires and the warm air from the car's heater make me drowsy, too, and my head bobs against the padded headrest. I can't tell if I dream or not.

Clyde and my father stood talking together in the garden. The expressions on their faces looked serious and I was worried something was wrong. I left Esmeralda, still barefooted after all these months since she lost her shoes at the airfield, in the breakfast room. As I walked to the back veranda, I still couldn't hear them.

I crept down the steps and followed the garden path. As I came around the corner to join them, a little boy jumped from behind a bush about ten feet in front of me. We didn't get many visitors to our house, but other children have never been allowed. I stopped. "Hey, where did you come from?"

He looked at me with large dark eyes. We were about the same height, but he was skinny. His legs were too long for his pants and he wore sneakers without any socks. I was glad I left Esmeralda in the house. He probably wouldn't want to play dolls with me.

The boy didn't answer my question. Instead, he came up to me and squeezed my curls like they were a sponge.

I pushed his hand away. "What do you think you're doing?"

"Just checking to see if they're real." He smirked. "Your hair's so bouncy."

I laughed. "Want to race?" I pointed to the other end of the path.

"How far?" he asked.

"All the way to the wall."

"And back?"

I swallowed. "Sure."

He lined up beside me. "One, two three, go!"

I should have changed into sneakers before I came outside. My Mary Janes were no match for his Keds, broken shoelaces and all.

We thundered past Clyde and my father, who called our names. We ignored them until the return leg. The boy kept running but I stopped because there was a third grown-up standing with the men. A lady who also looked very serious.

"I win! I win!" the boy yelled from our starting point.

I waved at him to come back to where I stood. He walked very slowly, like he was marching in a parade wearing heavy boots.

"Sally, come here," said Daddy.

I went to stand next to my father.

"This is Mrs. Avery," he said. "A friend of Clyde's. She and her son have moved to Mason's Crossing."

No one mentioned a Mr. Avery. The last time I had asked someone a personal question, I got in trouble with Aunt Mary, so I shook her hand, the way Mother had taught me. "Pleased to meet you."

Clyde beamed as the boy approached. "And this here's Mike. He'll be in your grade at school."

I looked at the boy and hoped he ran better than he spelled. I didn't want to give up my first place in the school spelling bee for sixth graders.

Clyde put his hand on the boy's shoulder. "And Mike, this

is Sally. Y'all should become good friends."

The boy bowed from the waist, like he was asking me to dance, the way I'd seen in the movies. I hoped he wasn't going to be this stiff and silly all the time.

"Would you like to see my playhouse?" I asked.

He nodded. I took him to the other side of the garden, away from the adults, and showed him what Daddy had ordered for me a few years ago, built maybe as soon as I learned to walk. My playhouse had a gate, a drawbridge over a painted moat, and towers in each corner. Mother said they're called 'turrets.'

"Are you a princess?" Mike asked.

"I don't think so."

"You must be."

Bright lights wake me up, as Mike slows the car to turn into an all-night gas station. "Fifty miles to go," he whispers over his shoulder. "Are you all right?'

I nod and smile, shifting my body slightly, trying not to disturb Colton. He moans softly, but doesn't awaken. The medication holds steady.

Angelique turns around in her seat. "Need anything?"

I'm okay, I assure her. My joints have gone rigid, but if Colton and I turn petrified before we reach Mason's Crossing, it won't matter. I wouldn't mind being set in stone with my sleeping son, like a modern *Pietá*.

Once we get under way again, Mike's firm hand on the wheel somehow comforts me. The drowsiness returns and I drift in and out of awareness of the miles we cover.

It was not my birthday, but Clyde brought me a gift, something he'd never done before. He said it was to thank me for being so nice to Mike and helping him get settled at school. I told him Mike was good at sports and right smart enough, plus he was polite to everyone. The principal had already let him be captain of the safety patrol.

I couldn't imagine what was in the unwrapped package Clyde held. We sat in the swing on the front porch, the same place we had sat together when we first met.

I was too excited to keep seated, so I stood in front of Clyde as he balanced the box on his lap. He watched while I pried off the lid. Tissue paper hid the contents and I poked my fingers down in it until they touched something solid. I pulled the object out and held it up. A pair of red leather shoes dangled from a cord, but they were no bigger than my thumb. "New shoes for my doll?"

"Miz Cromwell helped me buy these. I thought Esther would like 'em, since she lost the last pair."

"Esmeralda will be quite happy to wear them." I didn't care that he never got her name right, as I leaned up to kiss his rough cheek. "Thank you very much."

Clyde stood up with effort. He put his arms around my shoulders and gave me a hug. Maybe I loved Clyde because he cared about children, or at least he thought I was special. He smelled like Ivory soap and pine trees. After a moment, he let go, and then rested his hands on my arms. "Take care of your daddy, will ya?" His eyes turned wet in the corners as he blinked very fast, like he had gotten something stuck in his eye.

"What's wrong?" I asked. "You look sad."

"Nothing." He picked up his jacket from the bench. "I got to be going. Tell Mike I'm proud of him."

"Why don't you drop in at our school? You can see for yourself on Parents' Day how good, um, how well he's doing."

But Clyde was already halfway across our lawn, walking toward the street where he had parked his truck. I wondered why he didn't pull up in the driveway like always. "Bye, Clyde. See you tomorrow," I hollered.

When he didn't turn around and answer, or even wave at me, I dropped the little shoes on the swing and jumped down the front steps. The truck's engine roared and I ran faster to the edge of the lawn. He never heard me call his name.

As I strolled back to the porch, I hoped he would come to visit our school. Mike would like that okay, I guessed, but *I* would've been proud to hold Clyde's hand and take him around the classrooms and the hallways. I would've introduced him to all the teachers and the principal and the cafeteria ladies.

He could have sat in the empty seat reserved for Mother or Daddy. And I could have pretended to be like all the other kids.

After he turns on my street, Mike slows the cruiser to a crawl until he parks in my circle drive. He switches off the engine and looks over his shoulder at Colton and me. While Angelique waits, Mike comes around the back of the car. As he slowly opens the rear passenger door, he holds out his arms while I stroke Colton's hair, trying to wake him up enough to move.

His sleepy weight proves too heavy for me, and Mike crouches next to me, balancing half on the back seat and half on the night air. As I scoot toward the center, Mike lifts Colton's upper body and pulls him partway out of the car. Angelique leans across the back of the front seat to help push. Colton's lungs let out a long 'hmmm,' but his eyelids don't even flutter.

For a moment, I fear the two of them will topple over backwards, but Mike tightens his grip and stands up, catching Colton's legs before they hit the doorframe. Mike nestles him against his chest as easily as if Colton were an infant in his father's arms. I hold my breath and wait.

Mike whispers, "Let's get him in the house." He turns toward the front door. Our breaths come out in little puffs from the chilly air, as Angelique and I trail up the sidewalk to the porch. She picks up the plastic bags of dinners left by the delivery boy from Raúl's restaurant.

Before I can get the key out of my purse and unlock the door, the grandfather clock in the foyer chimes midnight. I wish we could all turn into pumpkins, at least until tomorrow.

Once the door stands open, I gesture for Mike to follow me. The stairs creak louder than usual from the double weight. With only the hallway light for illumination, I paw the bedcovers in Colton's darkened room and shove them back. Careful of his bandaged wrist, Mike lays Colton down gently on his side, and I pull the comforter over his shoulder. Once more I brush the hair from my son's forehead and watch him inhale and exhale.

It takes several moments to realize the mother in me has been starving for lack of touch. Some internal artery had gotten clogged or shut off, but now it is unbound, allowing all my affection and tenderness to gush like water from a busted pipe. With my arm draped across his back, I sit on the edge of Colton's bed until Angelique's hand comes to rest on my shoulder.

"He'll be all right now," she says.

I lean around her and glance into the hallway. "Where did Mike go?"

"Can you come downstairs for a moment?"

I have to pry my arm from Colton's sleeping body. After a few seconds, I nod and follow her to the living room. Leaning against the far wall, Mike stares into the crown of his hat as he waits for us.

Angelique doesn't sit down, so I remain standing, too.

Her eyes sweep the room, like she's trying to remember where she dropped something. "I'm leaving with Mike, so you and Colton can be home together in the morning. You two have quite a bit to talk about, all by yourselves."

I sniffle. "I have a lot of *listening* to do, for a change."

"Darling girl, I know you'll do a good job of it." She hugs me for a long while, tight enough that I feel warmth from her hands through the padded back of my jacket. Her skin brushes soft and silky against my cheek. "Remember, there's plenty of love inside you, enough for everything. You'll see." She picks up the strap of her overnight bag and drags it behind her, as if it's the only thing anchoring her to the ground. "Mike, I'll wait for you in the car." Her jangly earrings flash like stars as she floats out of the room.

I stride toward Mike until we stand no more than two feet apart. "I can't thank you enough. You've been so very kind, and I haven't appreciated you properly. I don't see how, even with Angelique's help, I could have–"

"It wasn't just kindness." He fidgets with his hatband. "Look, I'll speak to the judge and the county coroner tomorrow. They'll definitely want an official statement about that night, but it can wait until Colton feels better. I'll find out what else it'll take to get this all straightened out."

"If it's possible."

"There you go, with those doubts again," he teases. "Can you just put them on hold until we get some more information?"

I nod, and my gesture feels inadequate. Without another word, I rush right up to him and throw my arms around his neck. His hat falls to the floor as his arms wrap around me and we press against each other. At first, I can't form whole sentences without feeling a flood of tears ready to burst, so I laugh and keep repeating, "Thank you, thank you."

After a few moments, he runs his hands over my arms and I release him, glad I had succumbed to the urge to nuzzle his neck. Once I step aside, I can't tell if my wantonness has embarrassed him or his face turned red from bending forward to pick up his hat.

I link my arm through his as we walk toward the front door. "Get some rest. You deserve it after that long drive." Something warm and magnetic stirs inside me, telling me I don't want him to leave. Before we reach the threshold, I stop us both and hold onto him, weaving my fingers through his.

"Angelique is waiting," he says.

"Of course, you still have to take her home." I let go of his hand.

"She's not–" He frowns. "We all need a good night's sleep."

The door closes behind him, but I feel a sudden twinge, as if I should run outside and make them both come back.

I sigh and look around the room. There is plenty of mess to put away, but exhaustion overtakes me and I head straight for bed. During the night, I dream about Clyde and my mother. Or at least, it seems my mother appears in certain scenes. Maybe I simply hear her voice.

Across rolling hills, I traveled down a long, unpaved road while the wind stirred up dust devils. Toward the foot of distant mountains stood a small cabin, but as I got closer, it transformed itself into a large Victorian house. Lacy curtains billowed from the open windows as if they were trying to escape.

Clyde waited in the shadows on the wide porch. "I'm glad you've come." His boots clunked on the floorboards as he crossed to the front stoop and held out his hand. "Welcome."

Before I could get out of the car and climb the steps, he turned to go inside. He removed his hat as he passed the threshold.

"Wait for me," I called, but he didn't turn around. I followed him into the entryway, a narrow room crowded with books and saddles and easels. The central staircase rose to a darkened ceiling, while shafts of light and women's voices came from the back of the house.

I stepped over the clutter and headed down the hallway, tempted by the laughter and noise. Party sounds of glasses clinking and china plates stacking together reached my ears. I identified Mother's voice among several others. When I arrived at the kitchen door, the only person I found was Angelique, who stood wiping dishes at the sink.

She didn't look at me. "They're all gone, dear."

"You should leave those for Mrs. Gussmann."

"She's gone, too." She turned around to set a dry porcelain platter on the table. "Why did you come?"

"I thought I was supposed to."

"Do you know the reason?"

My eyes searched the room, as if I'd lost something. Where had the people gone? I was sure I had recognized Saint Trixie's voice along with my mother's. "Does someone need my help?"

"No one *here* does." She smiled as she folded the dishtowel. "But–"

The purr of a truck engine interrupted her, and I stretched up on tiptoes to look out the window over the sink.

"Here he comes now," she said.

"Who?"

The window was too high for me, and I pulled a chair from the table. I bent my knee to stand on the seat, but the seat wouldn't hold me, and the chair disappeared. I kept stretching my leg, until . . .

With a shiver, I wake up from the repeated motions of kicking and stepping. During the night, I had pushed the bedcovers off the foot of the bed. I sit up and crawl to the end of the mattress and pull them back over me, snuggling under until I feel warm again. Angelique would say the people in my dream, the ones in heaven, miss me. Maybe my dream is trying to tell me something, like remember what I've lost, or look forward to the future. I can't make any deeper sense of it.

My thoughts return to Mike, and I tingle at the memory of putting my head on his shoulder as we danced. I now believe his extreme helpfulness is due to special feelings for me, and not because my father made some clandestine arrangement with him. Can I return his affection in any reliable measure? The idea strikes me as something to reach for, after years of lukewarm emotions. In fact, kissing him felt downright exciting, all the way to my toes. With a grin, I pull the sheet over my face and wonder if we stand a chance as a couple.

Oh, but what will tomorrow bring?

Anxiety chases the romantic tingle away, and I spend the rest of the night flopping from front to back, speculating how I can convince the authorities of his innocence if Colton decides to clam up again.

CHAPTER TWENTY-ONE

No sooner do I close my eyes than it feels like I open them again. The misty light at dawn hangs like a gray shroud over the house and I shiver. I forgot to turn up the heat last night.

In my bathroom, I flick on the light and head for the shower. No amount of water can wash away my sense of helplessness. With the appointment book lost in the fire, I cannot produce even a hint of doubt to defend Colton. Mike's growing affection for me won't stop him from presenting evidence to prove my son's probable arson. Those three burned tee shirts dance before my mind's eye.

What if a grand jury orders the D.A. to prosecute Colton for his father's death? People might think they can get away with anything in a small town like Mason's Crossing, but the law's the law.

For everything to return to normal, I'd give my soul. Colton is my primary concern from now on. Overprotective or not, I fear that any pursuit of truth might be enough to nudge him back into the darkness again. Though I wish the warm spray could drown my unhappiness, I settle for a tired body scrubbed clean.

My emotions yo-yo between fear and gratitude. Mike will execute his job according to his oath of office, and he has already demonstrated how forcefully he can handle Colton. Thank God Mike possesses more patience than I do, despite getting knocked to the ground and called an asshole.

How will Colton react to questions from the court? For months, I willed myself to endure his sarcasm and anger. If his temper explodes in front of the judge, or if he refuses to answer the D.A., what will become of him? They won't allow him to go unpunished.

After hanging up my towel, I shake out lingerie from the chest in the closet, followed by comfortable jeans and a warm sweater. I pull on thick socks and snuggle my feet into fleece-lined slippers. As I brush my hair, I study my face in the mirror. The last year has painted dark circles under my eyes, which no amount of cream concealer can disguise. My cheek muscles sag. I resolve to smile more often.

In spite of Colton's tearful confession last night, he is still a time bomb, and I worry that any little thing might set him off. How to diffuse him? I look out the window at the burned shell of my greenhouse and sigh. Maybe I can talk Angelique into coming back over.

Dear, beloved Angelique. In all of yesterday's chaos, I forgot to ask about her doctor's visit. How typical of her to put my problems ahead of her own. Even if she were dying from some strange disease, her first priority would still be to focus all her attention on me.

Didn't I pledge to listen to Colton? All right, that's a start. I can almost feel Angelique's encouragement surging through my veins. What else did she tell me? Something about remembering love.

For everything? How much was enough? Heaven only knows, but I swear to find out, even if it produces new scars.

I go downstairs to start the coffee. And to wait. Once I settle on the chintz sofa in the living room, I stare at Grandmother Mason's English walnut secretary on the opposite wall. My china coffee cup matches the ones displayed in the glass-front cabinet. The family heirlooms soothe me, somehow, perhaps because they remind me that I am connected to people other than my crazy, distant, inadequate parents.

After my first few sips of coffee, the door to Colton's room opens and the stairs creak. On impulse, I rehearse an opening line. He needs reassurance or prodding, or maybe more pain meds.

Oh, hell, woman! Can't you just keep your mouth shut?

Colton shuffles into the room, and I point to a mug of hot chocolate on the tray I carried from the kitchen. With a nod, he picks it up and dips the end of his nose into the steam rising inside the brim.

"Hot enough?" My question sounds tolerably innocent, at least to me.

"It's fine." He wraps his palm and fingers around the mug. His dirty blond hair spikes upward and sideways, and the pillowcase has left a crease across his cheek, like the slash I remember on Clyde's face.

I wait, churning on the inside. "Hungry?"

"Not yet."

I try not to monitor his every gesture. It isn't like he'll

disappear if I look away, but my eyes feast on him. We have not sat together except in uncomfortable silence or argument for over a year.

"Mom?"

I hold my breath.

"Um, last night, what did I tell you?"

I pat the cushion next to me, but he sits down at the opposite end of the sofa. Too far away for the warmth of his body to reach me. I wonder, if he felt mine in return, would he object?

Using many of his same words, I repeat the chain of events the night his father died. I pray my voice relays no emotion or judgment. Every now and then, I pause to give him time to absorb the story or ask if he remembers sharing a particular sequence. Our conversation trades back and forth as if we are discussing the purchase of a new stereo.

I keep expecting him to implode. I don't see how he stands it, to hear that he caused his father's death. Maybe God or the angels can shield his broken heart and mind from too much self-blame, yet I know he will have to face what he did. It's the only way he can heal.

When I stop speaking, he sets the empty mug on the tray and rests his elbows on his knees. "I have to talk to Sheriff Avery about this, don't I?"

One wrong word and he'll retreat. I keep my tone soft. "He'll need something like an official statement, but he said he'd wait until you feel up to it." I lean forward and place my cup and saucer on the tray next to his mug.

"What's going to happen to me?"

"I can't say for sure, but I'll be there to help you whether you'd like me to or not." I want to pat his shoulder. "You didn't mean to harm your father."

Sitting up straight, he blinks and looks down at his bare feet. "Is . . . is Dad mad at me?"

For a few seconds, I don't know how to answer him. It has never occurred to me that Colton might worry about Jack's reaction to his mistake. My lip quivers as I imagine the burden my son has carried and how I added to it. Tucking my leg under me, I shift toward him and try to strike a relaxed pose. "Dad loved you with all his heart, more than *anything*, and that wipes out all the other stuff."

"It does?"

"Completely." I wish he sat close enough for me to stroke his cheek. "I want you to remember that, always."

Colton crosses his arms. "What about you?"

Was this the "everything" Angelique referred to? I all but rush at the chance to show my son how much he means to me. "Colton, I hope *you* will forgive *me*."

He jerks his head toward me and frowns. "What for?"

"For not listening to you. For insisting I was right." Tears spill down my cheeks. "For ignoring the signals that you needed help. For not–"

"Mom, stop."

Will I *never* learn? Colton gives me what looks like half a smile. He glances down again and swallows.

I sense the curtain pulling shut across his mind and figure he needs a break. I wipe my wet cheeks. "Are you hungry yet?"

He rolls his head back and from side-to-side, as if his

neck aches. His smile disappears, and I dread that fear has overwhelmed him. Fear and self-loathing. If I wait for his answer, we'll both starve to death.

As I stroll to the kitchen to fix scrambled eggs, I wonder if angels carry grudges against people on earth. Saint Trixie would be justified, considering all the stormy arguments between Big Jack and her. So would Jack. I hope by now he has forgiven me for marrying him in the first place. Maybe he considers Colton a good trade for a less-than-enthusiastic wife.

Is my mother satisfied that her marriage brought me into her brief, unhappy life? My father told me she loved him, but has she also pardoned him? Someday he'll find out.

Meanwhile, Colton needs to see how much my love will support him in the difficult days ahead, no matter what he's done. Tenderness should be matched with strength.

After I set the tray on the counter, I grab a tissue and blow my nose. Another one to dab my eyes, now ringed in red, according to the mirror in the mudroom. I stare at my cheerless reflection. An idea begins to grow in my mind, and I suspect my mother planted it.

Before we finish breakfast, the phone rings. I expect to hear Judith's voice wheedling a favor, but it's Big Jack. He urgently wants me to do something for him. "I'll explain when you get here."

Does he think I can just drop everything and run down to the hospital? "Can it wait until this afternoon? I need to stay home with Colton this morning."

"Bring him along. It concerns him, too. It's important."

Will this be an apology from my father-in-law? Too late for

his son, but maybe his grandson can appreciate it. I resolve to play a little dumb so Big Jack can explain himself. The ruthless son of a bitch doesn't deserve an easy way out.

On the other hand, I have to consider whether to tell him the whole story, given the new details that have come to light. I don't care if he wonders about Jack's death or feels guilty forever, though Colton might have a reason to want his grandfather to know.

Before we hang up, I agree to come as soon as I can get Colton cleaned up. I can't remember if I have told Big Jack about Colton's injury.

When I approach Colton with the idea of dropping by the hospital, he doesn't consent immediately. "You aren't going to start a fight with him, are you?"

Has he read my mind? "What makes you say that?"

"You're always fussing about something he did or said. Can't you just leave the guy alone?"

"Believe me, I'd rather do that, but he's asked both of us to come see him. Don't you think we should go?"

"Okay, but don't say anything that will set him off." Colton holds his fork in front of his mouth and frowns. "Big Jack's stuck at the hospital all by himself," he says, shaking his head. "Who else would go visit him if we didn't?"

Who indeed? Harlene and Skipper. Together they make a miserable little threesome. I look at Colton and wince. He can still manage to express compassion for someone who dished out pain by the truckload to Jack and others, while I can only respond with dislike and bitterness. Angelique will be proud of him.

The phone rings again. Judith wants to know when I last heard from Brett. "He asked Charlie yesterday if we'd spoken to you since Tuesday. Didn't you leave him hanging at the big pow-wow?"

Before I can answer, she introduces another topic and I am grateful she doesn't wait for my response. I forgot about Brett and his kindness during the meeting.

Pots and pans clatter as Judith smooches Charlie and each of her children, one by one, when they appear for breakfast. I sigh and try not to feel envious.

Judith's attention circles back to Brett. "He requested your phone number. I hope you don't mind I gave it to him. Someone has to keep your suitors on their toes." She giggles. "How's the race shaping up? Any favorites yet?"

"Too early to tell."

"Well, I'd say Brett's scorecard looks very positive. He asked what kind of blooms you prefer. Should I have said lilies or roses?"

"Neither." Silence. "Why would Brett send me flowers? We only had one date, and you'll recall it ended on a sour note."

"Aw, c'mon, Sally. How can you pass up those slick manners and that humungous fortune? Even if he's not the handsomest guy in the world, the least you could do is return a little enthusiasm in his direction."

The more we banter, the clearer my feelings become. Brett will never be more than a slightly dull gentleman. Besides, I can't take time for someone else I barely know to fall in love with me, Mike or no Mike. The sooner I discourage Brett, the better. Maybe he will just chalk it up to influences from my erratic family.

As soon as I finish loading the dishwasher, I go back upstairs to change shoes. The door to Colton's room stands half-open and I peek in. With his one good arm, he has been digging through his T-shirt drawer and has scattered several across the foot of his bed.

I clear my throat. "Do you want to shower before we leave?"

He spins around as if I had cracked a whip. "Where's my Jefferson Airplane T-shirt?"

"I don't know." Fear grips my stomach. We'll find out eventually if its burned remains are stashed somewhere in a bag in Mike's office. "What color is it?"

"Dark blue."

"Probably in the laundry. I haven't had time to run the washer lately." I pick up a pair of dirty socks off the floor and dangle them in front of his face. I try to smile. "These would get washed once in a while if you'd put them where they belong."

He didn't notice my expression and teasing voice, because his eyes shoot daggers at me while he chooses a shirt and some fresh jeans. After I drop the socks, I help him cover his wrist with the plastic sack, and he heads for his bathroom.

Once we meet back downstairs ready to go, I redirect us from the kitchen to leave by the front entrance. My Jeep sits parked in the driveway, coated in a thin layer of black ash.

We open the doors of my car, but before we climb in, Colton stands up straight and looks at the burned hull of the garage. He squints, as if he doesn't recognize it, and then his face muscles lose their strength as his eyes bulge and his mouth sags open. How will I answer if he asks what else he has done? Kids are supposed to be resilient, but he shows nothing except fragility.

I vow to pay close attention to any danger signs.

ON THE WAY to the hospital, we listen to Tony Orlando and Dawn sing "He Don't Love You Like I Love You." At least *I* follow the tune and lyrics. Colton sits in silence, inserting between us the physical and emotional distance I have come to expect. How I long for the closeness, the intertwining, of last night to return.

Outside Big Jack's hospital room, I steel myself for an intense confrontation and open the door. Colton follows me inside.

Through the east window, the sun shines on Big Jack's hair, slicked back and still wet from his morning bath. He sits in the chair next to his bed. His aluminum walker stands between the chair and the bed, facing toward him like an open gate. "Hey, Sally-Girl."

If he is ready to act pleasant, I can't be sure I'll go along. It all depends on what he has to say and what he needs me to do. I nod and say nothing.

Big Jack gestures toward Colton. "What'd you do to your hand?"

"Just a cut."

"Be careful. You don't want to end up like me."

How true.

Big Jack motions at me to sit in the other chair near him. Across the room, Colton leans against the wall.

I humor my father-in-law through some meaningless chitchat. "You're sitting up today. That's progress."

"I can't do it by myself. I have to have help."

"You must hate admitting that weakness." A little salt in the wound for starters. "Now what is it you want to tell Colton and me? We came all this way to—"

"I've decided to retire."

If he'd said he planned to get married again, I couldn't be more surprised. "Did I hear you right?"

"There's nothing I can do for the business while I'm like this." He sneers at his legs as if they are lazy employees. "The other day, after you and Mike Avery left, Nate told me he would pay the difference, my percentage. I can cash out completely. That's what I'm going to do." He looks out the window. "It's not what I want, but I have no choice now."

"In all the years I've known you, you've never taken a day off except during hunting season. And the time Trixie made you take her to New York City." She enjoyed the Empire State Building and the Rockettes immensely, but he wouldn't ever consider another trip. "You came back complaining of high-priced food and people who talk funny."

"Nate'll even include the eighteen grand Jack took."

A clean slate for Big Jack, thanks to my father. Must be nice.

Big Jack folds his hands in his lap. "The doctor says I have to go to rehab. I thought that was for alcoholics."

"For how long?" I tick off a calendar in my mind and wonder if I'll be lucky enough to find paid help by the time he feels ready to go home. Whoever agrees to it will be worth twice the going rate. Is there another woman anywhere on earth who can match my mother-in-law's saintliness? Too bad his selfish daughters live so far away.

"Until I can walk without falling." He jerks his head toward the window. "Goddamn head injury is causing a few problems."

You have a lot worse problems than a head injury.

What will I say this time if he asks me to get Jack to drop by for a visit? If he ends up all alone, he can't blame anyone but himself. I try but I can't muster any sympathy, only the desire to punish him. "Wouldn't it be nice if Jack were here to help you?"

Colton gasps and then bolts from the room.

What have I done? I clap my hand to my mouth, trying to shove the words back in. Without waiting for a response from Big Jack, I jump up and follow Colton.

He stands about ten feet down the corridor, leaning against the wall with his head in the crook of his left arm. His shoulders shake as he sobs in silence.

My stomach contracts. If Colton thinks I have turned into a monster, no one will argue. I approach him and stop within two feet. All I can manage is to stare at him.

After a minute, a nurse comes up and puts her hand on his shoulder. "Are you okay, young man?"

He twists toward me and snarls, "How could you talk about him dying?"

"Now, now," says the nurse. "Your grandpa isn't going to die. He'll be–"

Colton points at me. "You hate him." He glares at the nurse and speaks through clenched teeth. "She can't stand to be around her own father either. She's always hated both of them." He sobs and chokes out his next words. "She hates me, too."

He might as well spit nails. Each accusation strikes me until I back up two paces.

The nurse looks at me with a sad smile. She mouths, "Why don't you go back in there. I'll speak to him."

Forcing myself to turn around, I feel like the village pariah. By the time I return to Big Jack's room, he has shuffled to the edge of his bed. He sits gazing at the floor, with his hands resting on the grips of the walker. He can't hold them steady, and I wonder if his balance has waned.

"Sorry," I say. "He . . . we've had a rough couple of days."

"He hates his arm being in a sling, too, doesn't he?" He frowns. "Can you go by my office today?"

"I guess so. Which papers do I need to sign this time?"

"Nothing. Harlene is there."

Just the person I would choose to chat with over coffee. Right after I poison hers.

"Tell Harlene I want her to stay. She doesn't need to make other plans after I close my part of the business."

"Won't Harlene simply go to work for Nate?"

"Not here in Mason's Crossing. He offered her a job in Montana. She talked about taking Skipper with her, so he can start over fresh."

One mother's prayer answered. Two, if I count my wish to have Skipper out of our lives.

Big Jack leans back against his pillow. "But I want her to stay here so she can take care of me at home. Besides you, she's the only one I trust, and truthfully I don't know who else would do it."

Neither do I. Harlene doesn't fit my image of a saint, but maybe I have underestimated her.

In a whoosh of air like a tire deflating, Big Jack sighs. "Will you talk her into staying? Explain my situation better than I can."

Now I am caught between the devil and the deep blue skies of Montana. "I'll see what I can do." I pick up my purse and head for the door.

"You know . . ."

I spin around and wonder if Big Jack might be talking to himself. He stares out the window.

"I always thought I'd eventually bring Colton into the business with Jack and me." His voice fades to a whisper. "My father and grandfather worked together, just the two of them, until I was a teenager and joined the family operation. That's what I wanted to tell him."

My mind floods with regret for the broken old man he has become and with relief for what Colton can avoid. How will any of us ever get what we want?

He seems to retreat into his memories, so I leave the room without saying good-bye. In the hallway, I search for the nurse who tended to Colton. She tells me he has gone downstairs to wait.

On the way down, the elevator stops on every floor, as if eating a human meal, two or three bodies at a time. The leisurely pace gives me time to plan my words. I should apologize, of course, and say how proud of Colton I am for trying to process his mistake. Whatever the hell that means.

Will he accept my praise? His short fuse racks my nerves until I lose any confidence I can find a way to relate to him at all.

The hallway outside the elevator bustles with visitors and employees. Not the place to display an emotional apology or risk an outburst.

I can save myself the edginess. No Colton in sight. Not in

the lobby either. What if he has run away again? My heart races.

By the time I find him outside sitting on the wooden bench in the circle drive, I have lathered up a sweat from my toes to my forehead. He doesn't look up when I come to stand in front of him. I jangle my car keys. "We can go now." My voice sounds small, like I'm a child again.

He rises to walk toward the parking lot. Shivering, I follow and wonder what colossal error I will make next.

CHAPTER TWENTY-TWO

Colton reaches the car first and leans against the passenger door. I head toward him but reverse course when I recall my Jeep came with a new gadget that allows me to unlock his door from the driver's side. Now it is my turn to put a little distance between us until I see how he'll react.

We climb into our seats and he pulls his seatbelt across his lap and clicks it. When I don't start the engine right away, he unbuckles the belt and slouches in his seat.

"Colton, I'm really sorry."

Silence.

"No matter how angry I felt, I shouldn't have said that to your grandfather. And it was terribly insensitive to you."

He shifts in his seat and tugs at the sleeve of his jacket. "Why are you so mad at Big Jack all the time?"

I dust the steering wheel, even though it doesn't need it. "When I got engaged to your father, people said Jack would be 'marrying up.' Do you know what that means?"

He shakes his head. "Is this going to be another one of your long stories?"

"Just listen. Everybody around here considers the Mason

family the upper echelon of local society. My grandparents and great-grandparents always owned more land, oil, and cattle than anyone else." I turn toward him and tuck my ankle under my other leg. "Dad's family was climbing the social ladder, and the Mason connection was a real plus."

"What's your point?"

"His parents, even his older sisters, put a lot of pressure on your dad to achieve, to measure up to their standards, and what they perceived might have been the Mason ones."

"Didn't he?"

"Jack's personality was too laid back for them. You know how he liked to joke around and not take anything too seriously?"

Colton nods.

"Big Jack believed Dad didn't have what it took to grow into a businessman experienced enough to manage the operation." It won't help Colton to hear that I agreed with my father-in-law. "He thought Jack would be better off working as a sales clerk in the sporting goods store for the rest of his life."

"Dad always had such a good time at the store. Who pushed him to do something else?"

"No one. He had his own ambitions. He wanted to achieve something by himself, away from Big Jack."

"*You* made him do it. Because you have such a shitty relationship with your own father. You wanted Dad to be a success, so it would make you look good."

I gasp. How can Colton assign me the role of villain? "It was Big Jack who never saw him as an adult, fully capable of running his own show. And when he tried to break away, Big Jack squelched it." I shake my head. "You don't know what difficult problems they had as father and son."

"So you *do* hate Big Jack, for what he did to Dad?"

"I fault him for the damage he did to Dad's self-esteem. Big Jack'll never admit it, but he played a part in why Dad gave up." I want to put my hand on Colton's shoulder. "By the time he got home that night, he was already defeated."

Colton heaves a sigh, laced with disgust.

I drape my wrists over the steering wheel. "That's why I've been so angry with Big Jack. There was nothing Jack could do about the disrespectful way his father treated him. He just hammered away at Jack's self-esteem."

"He wasn't the only one." Colton pulls the collar of his jacket up around his ears, and his head submerges inside it like a turtle. He puts on his seatbelt again and stares straight out the windshield until I start the engine.

This time, I don't bother to turn on the radio during the ride to Big Jack's office. Perhaps it's better for us both to let our thoughts wander separately. Does Colton think I am also to blame, maybe not for his father's actual death, but for what went wrong in Jack's life?

Ever since I read the note Jack left on the front seat of his truck, I have tried to figure out how he could accuse me of ruining his life. He never threatened me or expressed such hostility while he was alive, and now it's plain he meant the words for his father instead. I'll never know how much punishment my husband endured from such a harsh, domineering parent, one for whom Saint Trixie could never compensate. If I'd written the note to Big Jack, I would have used stronger language.

By now, I can't bear the thought of listening to Big Jack

fuss. He will want someone to wait on him hand and foot, but she can't be black or Hispanic. After Saint Trixie died, he went through housekeepers like a goat through a trash pile. None of them stayed longer than a week, and later he insisted each one had stolen, broken, or lost something valuable.

I avoid passing the Hot Crossed Buns Diner in case the sight of it might send Colton into emotional orbit. He doesn't ask why we drive along side streets instead of Mason Boulevard.

Harlene's baby blue Skylark sits parked in front of the office, all by itself. I hope Skipper stayed at home to pack his scant belongings. I pull into the neighboring space.

How can I do what Big Jack wants? Asking Harlene to stay feels like such a betrayal to Jack. Merely talking to her is distasteful. I'd rather see Harlene's taillights as she and Skipper depart Mason's Crossing forever, especially since she received a generous nudge from the maneuvering hand of my father.

I get out of the car and square my shoulders, ready to strap on armor for a battle I don't want to fight. Perhaps my height will intimidate her. Why didn't I wear higher heels?

Maybe I can talk her into postponing her move until Big Jack improves enough to get around under his own steam. The more time Harlene spends with him, the less I'll have to. At this point, I'd rather confront my own father and demand all his pocket change.

As I open the front door of the office, the suffocating odor of 'Jungle Gardenia' greets me. Behind me, Colton sneezes.

Harlene looks up from her desk and raises her overdrawn, tinted eyebrows. "You've been to see Big Jack, haven't you?" Her words came out with no emotion, like club soda gone flat.

"Anytime I want. I'm family." Maybe she recognizes my animosity, as I do hers. Her son went to prison because my husband testified against him, but she got her revenge on Jack under cover of loyalty to his father. How could our dislike not be mutual?

She sits ensconced behind her citadel of a desk, piled high with file folders. I approach, close enough she has to tilt her head back to meet my gaze, and wait until our eyes lock. "Big Jack's going to rehab."

"I already know." Harlene opens the middle drawer and takes out a staple remover. She clicks it several times like a castanet, but doesn't pick up any papers. What is she going to do? Bite me with it? Maybe she dipped the sharp points in the witch's brew in her coffee cup.

Standing my ground, I hope I make her nervous or at least irritate her by tapping my fingers on the edge of her desk. "His balance isn't what it used to be."

She stands up, but only reaches the height of my chin. "All this never would have happened if you hadn't made him so mad about that damned appointment book."

I am tempted to tell her to get on her broomstick and fly to Montana, but the sound of Colton's collapse in the chair behind me changes my mind. I whirl around. He sits with his hand over his eyes. I turn back to Harlene and glare at her. "How dare you fault me for that! His own ugly temper is to blame. Besides, you had a big part in what went wrong between Big Jack and his son. I hope you regret it for the rest of your life."

"The only thing I'll regret is not leaving this stinking town sooner. I've put up with your hoity-toity attitude far too long. You're the one who talked Jack into lying at the trial. Lamont never sold drugs from the loading dock."

"Your son has smoked pot ever since he first learned to strike a match. You're just mad he got caught dealing it."

"At least he never stole money from the office safe!"

After suppressing a gasp, all I can do is continue glaring at her.

"You and your school clique acted so mean to him. He couldn't help his stutter, and when he outgrew it, all you rich kids still teased him and called him Skipper."

"Even Big Jack calls him Skipper. Don't try to change the subject." I try to soften my voice, against all the harshness I feel. "Big Jack wants you to help him at home. You'd be doing it for him, not me."

"Lamont and I can get settled elsewhere, and he can live a decent life from now on, no thanks to people like you."

I switch my tone. "You've been dependent on members of my family the whole time you've lived here. You could be out of work again, except for the generosity of my father. Is he aware your son is a convicted felon?" I feel almost silly asking the question. Nate somehow knows everyone's business.

Harlene's face turns three shades of pale. "You wouldn't! Mr. Wallace already offered me a job there and I've accepted it."

"Look, I have no interest in whether you stay or go. But Big Jack needs your help for a short while and wants you to stay."

"Not a chance. I'm putting my son first for a change."

We stare across the desk at each other like two rattlesnakes ready to strike. "The sooner, the better for both of you," I mutter and turn to leave.

She made the right choice. Can I?

No sooner did I reach the front door than I realize Colton has gone. A panicky feeling shoots up from my gut and spreads heat across my face. Will I ever stop worrying that he has run away again?

I yank open the door and bolt outside. My Jeep and Harlene's Skylark sit near each other in the parking lot. I turn left and run to the end of the sidewalk just as he strolls around the corner.

"Where–"

"I wanted to see where Skipper sold the pot." He ambles toward the car, pulls on the door handle, and waits.

"How do you know about marijuana?" I crinkle my eyes to narrow slits. "You haven't tried any, have you?"

He rolls his eyes. "Not yet."

"My God, Colton!" I almost yell. "You want to end up in prison like Skipper?"

For the second time that morning, I could slap my own face. Why do I bring up the possibility of his punishment? Will my son and I never have a normal conversation again?

"Relax, Mom." He tries the door handle again. "I only heard about some high school kids who smoked it."

"Well, promise me you'll stay away from them."

"Okay, okay." He shivers. "Can we get in the car now?"

ONCE WE LEAVE the office parking lot, I decide to take Colton to visit Angelique for the calming effect she always has on both of us.

Taking the long way around to avoid downtown again, we reach Angelique's house about twenty minutes later. Her car sits parked in the driveway. Side by side, Colton and I wait on the front porch, but no one answers the door. After ringing the doorbell a second time, I remember she told me Raúl would be gone for several days.

Colton and I return to the driveway. "I guess she's gone to lunch with some of her friends." I frown and glance at her front door one more, as if I can conjure Angelique's arrival. It won't help Colton to share my worries that Angelique has more than one friend who likes to pop a cork or two by noon. The doctor probably recommended she stop smoking and skip the nightly cocktails. "She hasn't been home in a while either, so she needs groceries."

"And cigarettes." He crosses the pavement to retrieve her newspaper from the bushes and flings it onto the front porch before he climbs in the car.

On the way home, I wonder how long it will take me to get used to the silence Colton inflicts. Maybe I should try to see him as emotionally shut down, instead of taking it as personal punishment. His thoughts probably render him speechless. Mine would, if I had done what he did.

We turn onto our street and Colton sucks in his breath. "What's he doing here?"

I follow his stare. Mike leans against the trunk of his patrol car, parked in our driveway.

"I don't know." I pull up behind him and shove the gearshift into park. "He told me last night he didn't need a statement from you yet." Part of me wants to jump out of the car and dash directly to Mike's arms. My mouth twitches as I remember our kiss at the fairground. The motherly half of me feels like stepping on the gas pedal and screeching the tires through a u-turn to escape with Colton.

Mike watches me as if he can read my mind. He looks concerned, but not angry. Can it be too much to hope that nothing is wrong this time?

Our eyes meet. After I turn off the engine, I get out of the car quickly. Colton takes his time. I don't run to Mike's arms, but I smile and step close to him. "Hungry? You're in time for lunch."

"Let's go inside." He takes my arm and turns toward the front door, ignoring Colton completely. "I have something to tell you."

As Mike steers me to the front porch, I look over my shoulder to be sure Colton follows. Someone has deposited a large arrangement of lilies and roses next to the door. Mike picks it up and I snatch the card from the plastic holder, staked like a pitchfork amid the greenery. While Mike searches for a place on the entry hall table, I tear open the envelope.

In neat block letters, the card reads, "Please accept my deepest apologies. Brett."

Mike follows me into the kitchen and stands, twirling his hat. I have begun to recognize that signal.

Moments later, the phone rings. Brett's voice proves Judith right. He inquires after Angelique's health, the length of my father's visit, how Big Jack is getting along, and whether I am looking forward to school starting again next week.

After I thank Brett for the bouquet, I am about to end the

conversation without suggesting we shouldn't see each other again, when he tells me he has big news. "I've accepted a visiting professorship at Princeton. I'll be leaving in May."

"History, right? That's wonderful." I hope he hears sincerity in my voice. "How long will you be gone?" The instant the words leave my mouth, I wish I could cut the phone line. Instead I jab my index finger upward to indicate one more minute.

Mike holds his hat still for a moment and then leaves the kitchen. I wave him back, but he has already stepped into the dining room. I watch until he reaches the living room across the hall.

"Maybe a year or more, and I feel like I should tie up a few loose ends. That's why I'm calling."

No one has ever referred to me as a loose end.

He clears his throat. "First, let me apologize for taking part in a scheme that caused so much pain for you and your family. That's why I sent you the flowers."

"You didn't really know how it would turn out." Except for his ten percent profit. "Thank you again. They're lovely." I lean around the doorframe, my eyes searching for Mike.

Brett's voice jerks my attention back to the receiver. "Your family is very singular. I've got to admit, I've never met anyone like Big Jack or Nate before."

Lucky him.

"What I'm trying to say is, this situation has become too complicated for me and so I hope we can part as friends."

After one date, which ended abruptly and badly, does he believe he will leave me broken-hearted? I want to set him straight, when I catch a glimpse of Colton. He stands within earshot.

"Brett, it's very kind of you to be so concerned, but please understand my number one focus is my son. That will keep me pretty busy around here for quite some time." I assure him he will settle in nicely at Princeton, aren't they lucky to get him, and the folks here at the University and in Mason's Crossing will just have to struggle along without him. I try to keep the sarcasm out of my voice.

After we hang up, I want to shriek with relief. My feathers aren't ruffled in the least, but Judith will be so disappointed. Not just on my behalf, but also because she can't stand being wrong about people.

Colton trails me into the living room. Resting his elbow on the mantel, Mike appears lost in thought.

I smile at him with as much warmth as I can muster and hope I look sexy at the same time, even in my jeans and pullover. "What's up?"

"Angelique wants to see you."

Colton jerks his head toward Mike.

Mike shakes his head. "Just Sally."

Colton turns and edges toward the sofa.

"That's funny." I glance at Colton. "We just left her house. She wasn't at home."

"I didn't take her home last night."

"Not back to court?" I giggle. "I thought you dropped the trespassing charges last week."

"She's been admitted into the hospital."

Oh, great. "That's just where we went earlier to see Big Jack. I wish I'd known she was there. Is she getting more tests?"

"Not our little medical center. The big hospital in Austin. Didn't she tell you?"

"Tell me what?"

Colton flops on the sofa and puts his head in his hands. I crab-walk around the edge of the end table to be near him, but not close enough to touch his shoulder, even though I want to.

Mike sighs and doesn't look at me. "I guess not."

I inhale, but the air comes in shaky. "What's wrong with her?" I stride toward Mike and grab his arm. He tilts his face down to mine, but no electricity throws off sparks this time.

We both startle at the sound of a loud thud behind me. Colton lies on the floor between the sofa and the coffee table.

I dash toward him. As I clutch his shoulder, he turns aside, away from me, and curls up in a ball, halfway under the table.

"Don't touch me!" he snarls.

It is foolish to expect him to let me cradle him in my arms again, like last night. I stand up and try to take a deep breath, but the air feels too thick, and I sputter. I might faint, too, but Mike comes toward me and puts his arm around my waist.

Gently he guides me back to the kitchen as if I am blind. "I'll stay here with Colton," he says. "You go see Angelique right now. Listen to what she has to say."

How did she sound the last time I heard her voice? Not too tired to speak, but she walked with effort. Or maybe too effortlessly, as if she has already let go. I struggle to remember what she said.

Something about love. Without her, where will I find it? What exact words did she use?

"When is she coming home?"

"She's not."

Fear rushes up like a giant wave and takes away the sun and the earth, and everything in between. Wherever I discover it, I need love strong enough, not only to bring it all back, but also to change the course of the stars.

CHAPTER TWENTY-THREE

I might as well be a leaf tossed on a storm cloud all the way to the hospital in Austin. A dark mood seizes me, so much I can't distinguish the road from other cars, but only feel the rise and fall of the terrain. Once inside the building, the ding of the elevator chimes like a distant bell, while the long hallway seems like an endless drainpipe.

The door to Angelique's room is closed. I gasp as I read a 'No Visitors' sign on the wall. Is she quarantined?

My breath shakes in irregular rhythm. I sniffle and run my hands up my face, trying to push my cheeks into a smile. If Angelique has taken care to hide her condition, the least I can do is disguise my fear. I wish I had thought to bring her Brett's flowers.

I pull up on the handle and push the door open a few inches. "Angelique?"

No answer.

I put my shoulder against the edge and nudge again. It moves enough for me to crane my neck and look into the room.

For what I see, nothing in my life has prepared me.

Almost nothing.

Mrs. Gussmann said I must wear all black, and on my bed she has laid out a long wool skirt with a matching jacket. I balked at the idea of putting on a black silk blouse underneath. No one would see it anyway, except for the tie, as the early spring was still cold in Mason's Crossing, but she rejected my preference for a white one.

She stood in the doorway of my closet searching for black shoes. "You better wear boots, dear, since the ground at the cemetery is still muddy today." She returned to my bedroom with a large box, and then dumped the contents on the bed. One black leather boot slid to the floor with a loud clunk.

"Where's Daddy?"

"Downstairs, meeting with Reverend Atherton." She clucked like a hen. "Hurry up, Sally. The service starts at eleven."

"You can get on with your other duties, if you like." I tried to smile. "I don't need any help getting dressed."

"Of course, dear. Since you've been away at boarding school, I have trouble remembering you're fourteen now." She turned toward the door.

"Oh, wait." I pulled on her arm. "Would you please bring me something?"

As she looked at me, tears glistened at the edge of her eyes.

"Go get one of Mother's diamond brooches from her dressing room. I want to pin it on my jacket."

She cocked her head to one side, as if she didn't hear me correctly. After a moment, a little smile played across her mouth. "Which one, sweetie?"

"The chrysanthemum, the one with the giant pearl in the center." Daddy brought it to her from Japan last year, but Mother never wore it. He showed it to her during one of our visits to the hospital, but he took it home again.

By the time Mrs. Gussmann came back, I had put on the skirt and blouse. She tied the bow while I finished buttoning. She pulled the brooch out of her pocket. "Left or right side?"

"Does it matter?"

"Not today."

We chose the jacket's left side, and I slipped my arms into the sleeves and stood back to admire the sparkly pin in the mirror. I was sure Mother would have liked it.

In the reflection, I noticed Mrs. Gussmann wiping her cheek. I let my arms fall to my side and turned around. "Why are you crying?"

"Your poor father," she sniffled. "He's endured so much. And now this, on top of everything else."

Why did she feel such sympathy for him? He wasn't the one who suffered.

Downstairs, I waited in the entry hall for Daddy and Reverend Atherton to come out of his office. The minister planned to accompany us to the funeral home for the final viewing. Daddy insisted on a closed casket during the service at church, but I didn't know why.

When our driver knocked at the front door, I let him inside. He tipped his cap and stood at attention until my father and the minister appeared. Without speaking, we walked to the limo and climbed in. I preferred to sit facing backwards, so I let Reverend Atherton have the seat next to my father. The minister made small talk all the way to the funeral home, but I didn't pay attention unless he asked me a direct question.

Nothing he said could calm the beehive in my stomach. I'd seen a dead person before. I remembered Aunt Mary looked about the same, dead or alive, like she had gotten dressed up and then lain down for a nap.

But this time was different.

The funeral home was decorated in soft greens and browns, nothing too bright or exciting. The piped-in organ music dragged through the stilted air and made me drowsy. When the manager came up to shake my father's hand, he spoke in low tones, as if his normal voice might frighten people.

It was a scary place. There should have been people coming and going, but instead it was deserted. A place where I didn't know exactly what to expect. A place where reality hit me: I couldn't change what had already happened.

I stood and waited until the manager led us into a back reception room, which was filled with huge bouquets in vases and elaborate potted plants, some on the floor and some on wire stands or on pedestals. Against the far wall, the upper lid to my mother's casket stood open. Her profile was barely visible above the creamy silk lining. A spray of deep yellow roses with frilly white orchids in the center covered the bottom half of the coffin. Maybe Daddy or Mrs. Gussmann ordered it. I would have chosen purple ones, since they were Mother's favorite.

I didn't want to remember her this way. My other memories weren't easy ones either, because she was sick for so many years, but I'd rather have imagined her smiling as she peeked out from under her white broad-brimmed straw hat. Her face would be rosy pink, not bluish-purple.

The doctor said the color was due to the hanging. My father didn't know I overheard them talking. Mother had ripped her hospital bed sheet into strips and tied them together. When it reached long enough, she threw it over the water pipe near the bathroom ceiling, slipped a noose around her neck, and jumped off the edge of the bathtub.

It achieved her purpose. An attendant found her later.

Angelique said I have to find a way to say good-bye. Not to blame my mother for her illness or her choice, but to wish her well on the next part of her journey. Angelique told me my mother's struggle was now over, and I prayed that was true.

I couldn't make myself move closer to her coffin, so I sent a mental note to my mother from a distance.

I know you had no intention to harm anyone else, only yourself. I hope you find peace soon.

My father wouldn't let the funeral home manager close the lid yet, not until it was time to transfer her coffin to church for the service. He stood by its side, staring at her face. Every now and then, he put his fingertip to his mouth or rubbed his forehead. His lips moved, but no sound came out.

After a few moments, I left the room. As if I had called her to meet me, Angelique waited in the foyer, seated on a long divan against the wall. I flopped next to her and she took my hand. With a sigh, I leaned my head against her shoulder, and she reached up and laid her other hand against my cheek.

"Why did Mother have to die?"

"Oh, my dear child. Your mother was a very sick woman. Not her body, but her mind. The doctors tried and tried, but there was no medicine or cure for her." Angelique shifted to snuggle her arm around me.

"Why did she do it? I just don't understand."

"I believe it must be that she could think of nothing except ending her pain. Real or only imagined, it was very real to her. It took over her thoughts, and therefore her actions, and she wasn't even aware that she was a wife and a mother."

"She was sick for a long time."

Angelique nodded.

"She would have died sooner or later, wouldn't she?"

Another nod.

"What's it like to die?"

"When people get sick and are about to die, it's like moving out of an old house. They stroll through the empty rooms one at a time, turning off the lights. Finally, they walk out the front door and close it behind them. Then they are free to go on to the next place."

"Where's that?"

She hugged me tighter. "It's called heaven."

"What do you call it when the sick person jumps off the roof of the house instead? Where do they go then?"

"It would still be heaven."

I wasn't so sure.

Fifteen minutes later, Reverend Atherton led my father out, holding him by the upper arm. My father shuffled his feet like a stiff robot. His face showed no emotion.

We got back in the limo and rode to church. It seemed like everyone in Mason's Crossing had come to offer their sympathies. I didn't pay attention during much of the service, except when Reverend Atherton referred to my mother as a lost lamb. Nice and soft and playful. She'd have liked that.

Angelique's dark hair is splayed across the white pillowcase like spilled ink. A breathing tube snakes from a bedside machine across the mattress, around the back of her head, over her ears, and into her nostrils. Another drip line connects her wrist to an IV bag suspended from a pole. I should have asked Mike about the doctor's diagnosis, but I don't really want to know. Angelique won't say it out loud either, because the words might make it come true. She is still a gypsy.

Her eyes are closed, and I watch her chest go up and down in an irregular rhythm. When I touch her arm, her eyelids flutter and she smiles.

She shifts her legs. "I'm glad you've come."

"Mike told me–"

"I'm okay." Her legs twitch and move as if she's pedaling. "How's Colton?"

"Mike's with him now."

"What a fine man. Don't let him slip away."

I fluff her pillow and stroke her hair, realizing a subtle shift has occurred. I am now the caretaker. "I won't."

"Colton needs–" Her face turns deep crimson as she coughs and shudders.

"Don't try to talk." I lean over her and tuck the sheet up around her shoulders.

Pale once more, she shakes her head and pushes the sheet down to take hold of my hand. "Colton needs to know you're capable of forgiveness. He's afraid you'll shut him out for killing Jack."

I stand up straight. "I've told him already."

"He'll never believe your words. You must *live* your forgiveness."

"How can I do that?"

"I've showed you all along. Now go and *do* it."

The room feels very small and close, as if we have entered a capsule, disconnected from the rest of the world. I caress her forehead. "Get some rest."

Angelique smiles at me, the way she did when we first met, as if she was interested in me, and me alone. She tells me what I need to do because she knows I can't figure it out by myself. She makes me promise. It is the only way, she assures me.

I feel small and unable to reach what floats away from me on a vast and empty sea. "I'll see you tomorrow."

She shakes her head. "Take Colton with you. I'll see you both when you get back."

I kiss her cheek.

She grips my hand tighter while her eyes drill holes into mine, as if she can't surrender touch and sight.

"What else?" I ask.

"Tell Mike to go by my house."

I wait until her coughing stops. "What do you need?"

"My pink coral lipstick."

"I'll get it for you."

She frowns. "You'll be busy, remember?" Her chest heaves and her breathing stops for a moment. "He'll find it in the top drawer . . . of my dressing table." She relaxes and lets go of my hand, then grips it again.

"What?" I lean over her. "Is there something I can get you?"

"My mouth is dry."

I search the room for a pitcher or a glass. "Be right back."

By the time I return, Angelique lies still, too still, while a nurse checks her pulse. Even her legs have stopped jerking.

"Is she–?"

"Just resting." The nurse squeezes the bag connected to the IV, then looks at her watch. "She's comfortable now."

I stare at Angelique. Did she grow paler while I was out of the room? She told me she'd be fine, but now I realize she lied. She is moving through the house of her body, the way she described it to me when my mother died. Which room has she reached?

The nurse turns to leave and hesitates. "I'm very sorry. Are you her daughter?"

Everything inside me wants to scream YES. As tears prick the edges of my eyes, I shake my head. "But she is my other mother."

How will I endure the loss of my comforter and my compass? Tears slide down my cheeks and drip onto my sweater. I back out of the room with the sense that Angelique is shrinking, growing smaller until soon I won't be able to see her at all.

ONCE I REACH MY HOUSE, I can't remember having driven there. All my motions seem mechanical, as if I have no reason for them except to follow routine. Unlock the front door, drop my purse and keys on the table, pick up the mail, plod to the kitchen for something to drink. I drain my glass before I realize I wanted apple juice instead of water.

From the patio, Mike's voice drifts into the kitchen through the open back door. I lean against the doorframe and watch him spread his arms wide as he tells Colton a story about fishing.

When Colton jerks his head toward me, Mike turns around and jumps up. "How is–?"

"Resting comfortably for now." I hope the expression in my eyes fills in the blanks for him.

Colton heaves a sigh. "Can I go see her?"

I shake my head. "Not today. They put a 'No Visitors' sign on her door. I got in only because they thought I am her daughter."

Mike pats the cushion next to his chair, and I sit down.

I try to smile. "What have you two been talking about?"

Frowning, Colton looks at his feet, but when he looks up again, his expression has relaxed. His eyes meet Mike's and a slight grin ripples across his mouth.

Mike shifts his gaze from Colton's face to mine and back again. "Colton asked me about his grandfather."

I cross my arms. "Have you been to visit Big Jack today, too?"

"Not that grandfather."

My reflexes rev up and I start to tell Mike to mind his own business, but I hear Angelique's voice and the promise I made. I sit up straight and turn to Colton. "How'd you like to take a little trip?"

Mike cocks his head toward me. "Where to?"

Colton slouches in his chair. "School starts Monday."

Mike puts his hand on my arm. "The judge says he can't leave Mason's Crossing until we settle a few things."

"You talked to the judge already?" I pull my arm away.

"I had to get some answers. He handed down certain conditions, without much leeway." Mike stands up. "You can't take Colton anywhere."

"Colton, go pack your bag." I point at his feet. "You'll need your boots."

My son raises his eyebrows and looks at me as if he doesn't recognize me. "We should stay here and take care of Angelique."

"She made me promise to take you with me now to this particular destination. We'll leave right away. She'll be disappointed if we don't, well, it's the best way to honor her wishes."

Without moving his head, Colton glances at Mike from the corner of his eye. After a moment, he stands up and ambles toward the kitchen door.

Once he goes inside, I rise and move close enough to Mike that the tips of our shoes touch.

He rubs the back of his neck. "Sally, you can't disobey the judge."

"You'll have to arrest me."

Mike puts his hands on my shoulders and peers into my face. "You want me to drive you?"

How did he know that is exactly what I would like, but it would be breaking my promise to Angelique. "I have to do this on my own." I stretch on tiptoes to kiss him, more friendly than passionate. "Will you be here when we get back?"

"Count on it."

BY NIGHTFALL, Colton and I reach the outskirts of Kerrville, where we stay in a Holiday Inn. He doesn't ask questions, and I wonder if he has any idea about my planned destination. After a late breakfast the next morning, we head west on Interstate 10, and I enjoy the change from flat terrain around Mason's Crossing to the rolling hills, which grow higher as the day wears on.

Shortly after one o'clock, we exit the highway for lunch in Ozona at a little café in the center of town. It reminds me of the Hot Crossed Buns Diner in Mason's Crossing, but I don't mention it to Colton. The memory of our last meal there with Angelique is almost more than I can bear.

After I pay the bill, I am tempted to turn the car around and head home, but there is nothing I can do to help Angelique now. I shove my sunglasses back on my face and go outside.

During the afternoon, we talk intermittently, mostly one-sided. I tell Colton about my childhood, what I remember of my parents. He had already heard from local busybodies that my mother was considered the most beautiful woman in five counties. And my father the smartest man.

"We get our blond hair from her and our height from him."

Sometimes I think he isn't listening, so I let my voice trail off. After a few minutes of silence, he asks how Jack and I met, and he snickers at the stories about Jack's pranks at his college fraternity, especially the one involving purple underwear. Colton shares a few hazy memories of Saint Trixie, and I fill in the gaps so he will regard her as a generous hostess who treated everyone with kindness.

We stop at a Dairy Queen for an ice cream about four o'clock. As I lick the chocolate swirl, I begin to relax until he asks about Nate and my mother. From habit, I want to say nothing, but choose my words carefully instead. Colton might be mature enough to understand loss, but it won't help him to hear that insanity circles like a shark in the deep end of our gene pool. The grisly details could send him into a tailspin.

"My mother seemed like a frail butterfly. And Nate was stronger and much older."

"How much older?"

"Not quite fifteen years."

"Why did she marry him?"

Good question. If she had known he would abandon her, would she have chosen another? She was a young bride, like me, and crystal balls were still in short supply when I became engaged. Maybe no one else would have married her, once word of her mental state circulated, but there's no point in raising that specter with Colton. "She loved him, I guess."

"How did they meet?"

"He worked for my mother's father, Amos Cobb, in the oil field machinery business."

"Nate's rich, isn't he?"

"Very."

"Are we rich?"

A stack of bills awaits my return. "No."

"Why not?"

"I wanted us to be independent of our parents." How can it harm anything to include Jack in my philosophy? "We never asked them for help or money because we knew the importance of standing on our own two feet."

"But Dad took money from Big Jack all the time. I used to overhear them arguing about it." He chews on the tip of his straw. "Nate never gave you money, did he?"

"No." Not directly. I frown, hesitant to take the next step. "Have you ever wondered why you've never met your grandfather?"

"You hate his guts."

"I don't hate him, I just–" The ugly truth is, I do hate him for what he did, but it feels wrong to admit it, even to Colton. Especially now that I'm trying to see Nate in a different light.

"What happened to make you hate him?"

I sigh. "When my mother got very sick, he sent her far away to a private hospital. He could have afforded to build a hospital in Mason's Crossing and hire the right specialists to care for her. I needed a mother, not a sickly aunt or a hired nanny." I swallow hard. "And she needed me, too, but he ignored us. She might still be alive today if he had–" I choke out the words, "–taken better care of her." After a moment, our eyes meet and I watch for his reaction.

Colton shifts in his seat and fingers the sugar dispenser. "At least it wasn't his fault she did what she–" He bites his lip.

Will he and I ever speak about the untimely deaths of my mother and Jack without the dam breaking? How will I find the words to help Colton see the change I feel compelled to make? I pray he will believe me.

I push my coffee cup aside. "For the longest time, I blamed my father for causing my mother's death. My only consolation, if you can call it that, was to cut him out of our lives and refuse to have anything to do with him. In my youth and inexperience, I believed I was the only one who suffered from her loss. For whatever reason, he never shared his feelings with me, about her or anything else. I never understood what he went through."

"Was he embarrassed that she was crazy?"

Colton must have also heard that from the local gossips. "Probably."

"So what difference does it make now?"

"I've finally realized I have to try to understand things from his perspective, for all our sakes."

"What does this have to do with me? It's ancient family history."

I can't let him wiggle away. "Well, family relationships are complicated, even when things are going well. People often do or say things without realizing how much they wound others. I can't undo the hurts I've caused your father, but–"

304 ❖ *Cynthia J. Stone*

Colton winces.

I hesitate a moment, waiting for any sign of meltdown. "Taking responsibility for what I've done or failed to do is appropriate." Too adult for him? I lace my fingers together, as if ready for prayer, and rest my hands on the edge of the table. "Colton, you're worried I'll blame you for Jack's death forever. You've seen me as uncompromising and unforgiving, and rightly so, but I've been wrong about some things. Especially concerning Nate. I can try to do better."

Silence.

I venture a weak smile. "A little forgiveness will do us all some good."

"Maybe Nate just did the best he could, under such difficult circumstances."

"Angelique told you that, didn't she?" I squint at him. "Did she explain anything else about Nate?"

"She said it about both of you."

I sit up straight and glance over the back of the booth, as if Angelique might come through the door any second.

Colton remains silent for a few moments, and I wonder if his thoughts return to his own troubles. He turns his head to stare out the window. "Angelique said he sent your mother away to protect you."

"There's some truth to that."

"But didn't your mother love you?"

"I always believed she did, but when she became a danger to herself, and to me, Nate had to make a hard decision."

"Do you think it was the wrong one?"

"For many years, I believed so, but I also didn't know that about her. Lately I've seen that it was his only choice."

"If he loved you, he had to do it. He couldn't let anything bad happen to you."

"I never thought of it that way until right now." How had I failed to realize Nate loved me? In a strange and distant manner, detached and silent, but protecting me was his way of loving me. The only way he knew.

"You're his daughter, his only child. He must have been scared every time he left town. What would he find when he got back?"

"Recently he told me he never knew what to expect other than upheaval, chaos, and conflict. I guess he tried to love her anyway."

Colton sighs. "Maybe it hurt him too much to see her like that."

My father loving, but also heartbroken? How can Colton already understand him better than I ever did?

I reach across the table to pat his shoulder, and for once he doesn't shake off my touch. "Sometimes you amaze me."

Our eyes lock, and something dark and heavy melts away, and the air feels lighter.

As we leave the Dairy Queen, a tiny Mexican woman squatting against the wall in the sliver of shade on the side of the building beckons us. She has spread a red-and-black striped blanket on the sidewalk facing the highway to display silver jewelry and leather belts with fancy buckles. Colton continues toward the car, but I stop to look at her wares. The infant bound to her chest in a serape sleeps gape-mouthed like he's drunk on breast milk. When I pick up the largest dangly earrings in her collection and step back, the silver shimmers in the sunlight. A light breeze makes them flutter like a wind chime. I can almost see Angelique's head turning to make them sway.

"*Para usted, señorita?*" she asks.

I shake my head.

"Maybe *un regalo?*"

"Yes, a gift." I hand her the earring. "*Cuánto?*" I feel the moisture, by now familiar, build up in the corners of my eyes.

She writes a number on a brown paper bag, wraps the earrings in crumpled tissue, and hands them to me as I pay her. She lays her bronzed hand on my arm and holds it for a moment before she speaks. "You are a good daughter."

We stare at each other and I try to smile. Finally I nod. "*Gracias.*"

As I walk to the car, I glance at the sky, clear and endlessly blue, and wonder if Mother has greeted Angelique yet. Surely the two of them sent the little Mexican angel to encourage me on this last leg of the hardest journey of my life.

We ride the final two hours with the sun glaring in our faces. In Fort Stockton, I consult the map Mike drew and turn off the main highway onto a county road. Just before sunset, we cross the cattle guard and enter the Rocking W Ranch.

The wooden two-story house rises against a backdrop of mountains still white-capped from a late spring snow. I steer my Jeep into the circle drive and park near the front steps. My hands grip the steering wheel. From the corner of my eye, I search for movement, a word of support, any hint that Colton understands why we have come.

For a moment, I am frozen by dread. Is anyone home, busy inside the house? What will I possibly say? I have traveled all this way for nothing, because I am too weak and cowardly to get out of the car and climb the steps to the front porch. But then I would break my promise to Angelique, and I'd fail to show my son how far I am willing to go. If I stay in my seat, nothing will change.

"Here we are." I pull on the handle and push. Without waiting for Colton, I stand up, straighten my pants legs, and close the door behind me.

Colton slides out of his seat and hesitates. He waits on the driveway, draping his wrists over the doorframe. Does he think he needs a shield? We look at each other until the front door handle of the house clicks.

As an electric wave shoots through my torso, I catch my breath. First one step along the gravel sidewalk, then another and another until I reach the bottom of the stoop. When I look up, he already stands there, smiling, as if he expected me all along.

"Hello, Daddy."

ACKNOWLEDGMENTS

This book never would have been started if my dear friend, Kathleen Niendorff, hadn't said, "Go and write that novel." It took longer than I imagined, and therefore I'm grateful to the many close friends who encouraged me and believed in me: Pan Adams-McCaslin, Ann Arnett, Paula Damore, John Fincher, Beth Fowler, Dr. Wylie Jones-Jordan, Gloria Moore, Dr. Suzanne Novak-Nemeth, Sylvia Simpson, and Betty Trimble, among others. Lucky me.

Every writer should belong to a critique group, for strength and help, and to keep you from falling into blind traps and using cheap tricks to get out. My El Gee pals—Rick Bolner, Ray Fuentez, Tosh McIntosh, Muriel Perkins, Laura Resnick-Chavez, and Brad Whittington—deserve medals for the innumerable battles they've fought on my behalf.

If you have a friend who can take your ideas, some of which are conveyed by waving your hands in the air, and give you a dazzling design for a book cover, you are doubly blessed. Kim Greyer has vision beyond the written words, with talent and artistry to match. She always says we're a good team. Lucky me.

Who can succeed at this crazy endeavor without the loving support of family? Writers are notoriously solitary and cranky, even when we aren't drinking, so our spouses and children deserve all that heaven allows (who first wrote that?). Here's to Gerald, the man of my dreams and my heart, a husband and soul mate who never expressed doubts or impatience. And here's to my son Jordan, actor and writer, who shares his own creative streak with so much enthusiasm. Clink, clink.

Readers Guide for

MASON'S DAUGHTER

By Cynthia J. Stone

READERS GUIDE
DISCUSSION QUESTIONS

1. Who is your favorite character and why?

2. Why does Sally have such a hard time hearing Colton? The more she tries to fix it, the worse it gets. Do you feel sympathy for her? Why or why not?

3. How does Angelique help Sally learn the hard lessons? Angelique has her own problems, but she unselfishly focuses her attention on Sally. Have you known anyone like Angelique? What did she mean to you?

4. Why does Sally blame Nate for her mother's death? Her view of family events as a child is incomplete, but she insists Nate never cared about her or her mother. What does it take for Sally to change her opinion? Have you ever changed your mind about a family member or close friend? What caused you to change?

5. Is Nate a mystery to you? Sally doesn't understand him and criticizes his actions, until Colton opens her eyes. What drove Nate to those drastic choices? Could you forgive him?

6. Did it surprise you that Mike has been in love with Sally? At times, she's not very loveable, but he persists. What draws him to Sally?

7. Did you feel sorry for Jack, Sally's late husband? He seemed to get the short end of every stick, but remained optimistic.

How could such a nice guy have someone like Big Jack for a father?

8. Does Sally envy Judith and Charlie's relationships with each other and with their children? They represent the opposite of her and her family situation. How hard is it to be friends with someone who has everything you don't?

9. Why does Sally talk to her dead mother and mother-in-law? This story has no ghosts or supernatural events, but in some way, Sally feels connected to them. Have you ever felt a presence, asked for help from, or dreamed about a person you have lost?

10. How does suicide reverberate through the generations? It's a topic seldom discussed openly, yet it can pervade every relationship and every major decision. What are the difficulties in bringing such an intense subject to light?

11. Would Sally have turned out very differently if Nate had been a demonstrative father? Fathers and their influence on daughters is a subject for the ages, and Sally missed out almost entirely. Who filled that void for her and how?

12. Do the losses Sally suffered reflect Nate's life as well? Compassion is a quality that is, by necessity, painful to acquire. What keeps us from showing it? How would our lives be better if we did?

ABOUT THE AUTHOR

Cynthia Stone believes she and Sting were twins separated at birth, because they share the same birthday and original last name. Since she's a native Austinite, some complications in proving their kinship are sure to arise. All of which provides creative fodder for the family sagas she loves to write. Cynthia wrote her first story at age five and has continued to indulge that Muse ever since. Her checkered career includes magazine publishing, copywriting, professional fundraising for the fine arts, antiques importing, and interior decorating. She still lives in Austin with her ever-patient husband, Gerald, a restaurateur.

Connect with Cynthia online: www.CynthiaJStone.com